The *Kaleidoscope* *Sisters*

A NOVEL BY **RONNIE K. STEPHENS**

ODDITIES KJB

This is a work of fiction. All names, characters, places, and incidents are a product of the author's imagination. Any resemblance to real events or persons, living or dead, is entirely coincidental.

Published by Akashic Books
©2018 Ronnie K. Stephens

Paperback ISBN: 978-1-61775-702-0
Hardcover ISBN: 978-1-61775-703-7
eISBN: 978-1-61775-704-4
Library of Congress Control Number: 2018936330

Kaylie Jones Books Oddities
www.kayliejonesbooks.com

Akashic Books
Brooklyn, New York, USA
Ballydehob, Co. Cork, Ireland
Twitter: @AkashicBooks
Facebook: AkashicBooks
E-mail: info@akashicbooks.com
Website: www.akashicbooks.com

CHAPTER ONE

Quinn was happy to see that the neighborhood park was empty. She was several years older than most of the kids who frequented the playground after school, but her younger sister, Riley, loved to climb all over the structures and play make-believe. Quinn's mother was busy making dinner, so taking Riley to the park had become a sort of ritual for the sisters.

"Hurry, Riley! The trolls are coming. Get up here!" Quinn shouted, peering through the miniature teleidoscope she wore around her neck.

"I'm too small," Riley hollered back.

Quinn reached down and took Riley by the hand, pulling her up the gray plastic boulder. Together they scurried up a set of stairs and into the turret at the far end of the playground. Quinn peered through the yellow side rails, then grinned at Riley and said, "That was close. So what do you think, should we charge them?"

"I just . . . need . . . a . . . minute," Riley wheezed. She had more energy than the doctors had expected, but even brief exercise drained the strength from her six-year-old body.

"No sweat. Come here, boo."

Quinn shifted her weight and set Riley in her lap. She was used to these pauses, to Riley's icy hands and flush-red cheeks. Though only fifteen herself, Quinn had spent almost seven years in hospital waiting rooms while doctors checked Riley's heart.

"I . . . don't . . . think . . . I can . . . go after those . . . trolls today." Riley's voice sounded far away, barely moving like the way the leaves shift in the wind before a storm.

Quinn studied her sister's face, which had gone as white as her hands. Riley's chest shuddered up and down like a weary piston.

"Yeah. You don't look so good. We better get back home. Mom'll have dinner ready soon, anyway."

Quinn spoke with a maturity that startled most adults, but life has a different way of moving when your baby sister is born already fighting death. Lately Quinn had noticed that their time at the park was getting shorter and shorter—ever since Riley's last birthday. She thought over all their trips to the hospital, searching for a number that seemed just a little out of reach.

Quinn was just eight years old when Riley was born, too young then to understand the soft way adults said her sister's name. Three times that first year, Quinn had folded herself into waiting room chairs, their cushioned laps already worn and tearing with the weight of worry. She had watched her mother turn the crochet hooks over and over until every room in the house was a blanket fort.

Doctors had noticed Riley's condition almost immediately; they heard odd sounds when listening to her heart, and her oxygenation levels were noticeably lower than they should be. That's when a nurse told Riley's mom that they would be moving Riley to the neonatal intensive care unit. Quinn was obviously too young to go with Riley, so she stayed with her mother while a doctor moved her new sister. Of course, her mother pushed hard and got herself released later that day.

The two of them followed brass signs from one hall to another until the hospital felt like an endless labyrinth. Quinn had lost all sense of direction, so she trailed after her mother, peering into hospital rooms when they passed an open door.

Most of the patients were much older than her parents, connected to more machines than Quinn could count. Some of them had family in the room with them. Others looked off into space, blankets pulled up to their chins, hands shaking. Quinn knew then that the only real meaning of hollow was a woman lying in bed dying, entirely alone. When they finally reached the NICU, Quinn and her mother were held up at the desk by a young woman in pink scrubs.

"I'm sorry, ma'am. We tried to reach you in your room, but you had already been discharged. Riley was taken to see Dr. Howe in pediatric cardiology a few minutes ago."

"Excuse me? Shouldn't I be consulted before my daughter is taken to a doctor I've never even met?"

"I'm very sorry, ma'am. We tried to contact the father—"

"There is no father."

"The nurses noticed some anomalies that couldn't wait," the nurse continued, ignoring Jane's interjection.

"What kind of anomalies? Is Riley okay?"

"You should really speak with Dr. Howe. I've paged someone to take you to him."

Quinn held her mother's hand, which had gone cold as they stood waiting to be escorted to Dr. Howe. She didn't understand what the nurse meant by anomalies, but she could tell that her mother was scared. Quinn squeezed her hand and leaned into the crook of her mother's arm. She felt her mother relax her muscles and pull Quinn closer, then kiss the top of her head.

"Hello, ma'am. I'm Beth," said another nurse approaching them.

"Are you the one who's going to take me to my daughter?"

"Yes, ma'am," she answered. "Follow me."

Quinn and her mother walked a few paces behind the nurse, who led them back the way they had come. She turned abruptly to the right down a drab hallway with beige walls. Aside from black plaques with the names of doctors and their specialties, the walls were bare. Quinn tried to read the names, but the nurse quickened her pace, and Quinn's mother dragged her along almost at a jog.

"Here we are," Beth said, opening a door to their left.

Once inside, the nurse approached a glass window and spoke with an assistant on the other side. After a few moments, she returned to Quinn and her mother.

"Someone will take you to your daughter in a few minutes."

"Thank you," her mother said, but Beth was already out the door.

When they were finally shown into a room, Quinn was dumbstruck by the surreal scene. Her baby sister, barely two days old, was sleeping in the center of a long hospital bed. She was naked except for a diaper. A man with silver hair and fat fingers was moving something across Riley's chest; he appeared to be studying an image on a computer monitor. Quinn tried to make sense of the picture, but all she saw was a fuzzy black-and-white blob. The man hit a few keys, and parts of the screen turned red and blue. Quinn saw a large black spot in the middle of the screen, with a long white strip on one side that opened and closed like a mouth.

"I'm Jane, Riley's mother."

"Quiet, please," the man said.

"Excuse me? That's my daughter. What are you doing to her? Where's Dr. Howe?"

The man laid the device next to the monitor.

"I'm sorry, ma'am. I don't mean to be rude. This is an ultrasound, and getting a clear picture of your daughter's heart is extremely difficult. I should be finished in a few minutes. Dr. Howe will review the ultrasound and then come to speak with you."

"Her heart? What's wrong with her heart?"

"Really, ma'am. I'm not able to discuss what I see on the screen. If you'll allow me to finish up, Dr. Howe will be able to explain everything for you."

Quinn and her mother sat in silence, watching the man move the device across Riley's chest again. Each time he used the keyboard, an image froze briefly on the screen. Quinn assumed that he was taking pictures, but the man didn't speak again. When he was satisfied with what he'd found, the man left the room, informing Quinn's mother yet again that the elusive Dr. Howe would be with her soon.

When Dr. Howe did enter the room, he carried a folder with Riley's name and several pictures showing the outline of a heart. He drew on the pictures as he talked with Quinn's mother.

"Your daughter has a form of stenosis. The purple you see here," he said, motioning to a purple smudge on the paper, "indicates oxygenated blood moving back into the heart and mixing with unoxygenated blood. Imagine a river flowing into the ocean: on a normal day, the water from the river simply pours into the ocean; after a storm, however, the tides are disrupted and water from the ocean pushes against water from the river. The result is murky water where the two intersect. That's what we'll be working to prevent in Riley's heart. Hopefully a simple valvuloplasty will do the trick."

Quinn tried to follow the conversation, but the words were long and unfamiliar. The longer Dr. Howe spoke, the more upset her mother seemed to become. She pressed Riley to her chest, tears falling onto the blanket she had wrapped Riley in while they waited. Quinn would never forget that conversation—the day she learned to listen less to the words people said and more to the way they said them.

* * *

"Mom, what does that word mean?" Quinn asked later that night. She didn't understand why Dr. Howe had taken Riley, or why when they saw Riley again she had tiny tubes coming out of her chest and legs.

"What word, Quinn?"

Quinn fidgeted with one of her kaleidoscopes, studying the way the stained flecks of glass moved around each other without ever really touching. The thin black borders between each color reminded her of family reunions, the way all her cousins used to stand together like a patchwork quilt, coming as close as they could to becoming something whole before the camera flash scattered them back to their respective corners.

"*Stenasiasis.*"

"You mean *stenosis?*"

"Yeah. The doctor used that word earlier when he was talking about Riley. What does *stenosis* mean?"

"Well, your baby sister has a hole in her heart. She has a hard time using the air she breathes."

"And Dr. Howe—he's going to fix the hole?"

"Yes, Quinn. For a little while."

"How?"

"Well, sweetie, he puts a very small balloon into her heart that expands to make space for more of the good blood to get through."

"So she can breathe?"

"Sort of. Like this." She took Quinn's hand, so that Quinn's fist fit inside hers. "Now, open your hand."

Quinn spread her fingers, pushing her mother's hand open.

"You see how my hand opened when you made yours bigger?"

Quinn nodded.

"That's what Dr. Howe does for Riley. The balloon makes the broken part of her heart bigger so Riley has more air in her body."

Quinn thought about this for a long time. "Mom?"

"Yes, baby?"

"Is she going to die?"

"What makes you think that?"

"My teacher says that's what happens to fish when they're not in water, and to people when a house is on fire. They don't have air to breathe, so they die."

"I suppose that's true. But your sister is going to be okay."

"How do you know?"

"Because she has you for a big sister, silly. You'll protect her."

CHAPTER TWO

Riley took her sister's hand as they stepped from the curb and crossed the street. Their house was right on the corner across from the park, so their mother could watch them from the kitchen window while they played.

"Quinn?" Riley ventured, scarcely audible.

"Yeah?"

"Is mom sad at me?"

"What do you mean?"

"She always looks at me and cries. Is she sad at me? I don't want her to be sad at me."

"No, Riley. Mom isn't sad at you."

"Then why does she cry?"

"Well . . ." Quinn didn't really know how to have this conversation with her sister. Riley knew she was sick, but people had a difficult time telling her exactly how serious her condition was. Her mom tried to explain of course, but she'd start sobbing and would have to go to her room for a while. Riley had come to rely on Quinn for the sort of honesty that adults didn't offer her.

"She's not sad *at* you. She's sad *for* you."

"But why? What did I do?"

"Nothing, kiddo. You didn't do a thing."

They stopped and sat in the porch swing that the old man next door had hung for them.

"Your birthday is almost here."

Riley extended her fingers and raised them above her head, her wide smile nearly overtaking her pale cheeks.

"Seven," she said. "I'm gonna be seven this time."

"That's right. Seven."

The doctors had told Quinn's mother that Riley probably wouldn't see her seventh birthday. Quinn shook the thoughts from her head.

"Hey, smell that? Mom made spaghetti!"

Both jumped down from the swing and raced inside.

"Last one in has to set the table!" Quinn shouted, throwing the screen door open.

Riley ducked under Quinn's arm and dodged Butterfly, their brindle boxer. "Better get the soap, then!" she said without looking over her shoulder. They both knew Quinn let Riley win every time, but they made a game of the chase anyway.

"Hey, no running in the house!"

"Gotta beat her, Mom!" Riley giggled. Butterfly was on her heels by the time she slid into the kitchen. Officially he was Quinn's dog, but he took to Riley almost immediately and never left her side. He'd long since worn down the carpet beside her bed, and a patch near the door reminded them all how he kept watch when Riley went in for overnight procedures. He looked enormous next to Riley, but he had the same soft touch with her that Quinn had. Butterfly seemed to know even before she did when Riley was going to have a rough day.

"You beat me again!" Quinn lamented.

Riley smiled at her through jagged breaths. "Helps to be tiny."

Quinn stuck out her tongue. "At least I can reach the plates!"

"Good. Now if you wouldn't mind getting a few down," their mother interjected, "dinner is nearly finished. I made your favorite, Quinn."

"With the olives?"

"Yep."

"And the spicy sausage?"

"Of course."

Quinn beamed. Her mother rarely took the time to make spaghetti anymore. She didn't like the store-bought sauces, so she made her own. The whole process took hours, but the effort paid off. Quinn could eat her mother's sauce with a spoon, which she had done on more than one occasion.

"Yum!"

Quinn dipped a finger into the pot of sauce, then licked her fingertip clean. She went for another taste, but her mother swatted at her with a wooden spoon.

"Get out of that," her mother chided.

The next morning, Jane eased open the bedroom door and peeked in on Quinn and Riley. She leaned against the jamb for a several minutes. Riley was curled up at Quinn's feet, and Butterfly was snoring near the foot of the bed. Everyone was in their place, guarding Riley as she slept.

She decided to make pumpkin pancakes with chocolate chips, Quinn's favorite. Quinn spent more time with Riley than anyone, after all. She had a knack for talking about the things Jane couldn't put into words. Some days Jane thought Quinn was the only thing holding them all together.

Riley was having trouble catching her breath during breakfast, which was unusual even for her. Quinn and Riley still had a few days off from school for spring break, so Jane decided to take advantage of the free time and bring Riley in for a quick checkup—at least that had been the plan.

"Ms. Willow?" A nurse in carnation-pink scrubs had entered the hospital room where Riley, Quinn, and Jane had spent most of the morning.

Quinn stood next to Riley, holding her hand.

On the other side of the hospital bed, Jane traced butterflies on Riley's arm almost without thinking. Riley loved butterflies. There was a butterfly garden a few blocks from their house, and Riley asked to visit almost every weekend. She would spend all afternoon walking the paths if Jane let her. Once, Riley had found a red-spotted purple in the far corner of the garden and watched the butterfly flit around for over an hour. When Jane came to collect her, Riley was completely still. "Look at the blues, mama. The colors are like the daytime and the nighttime are holding hands." Riley was right. The deep blue at the top of the wings faded into a cyan so brilliant the insect almost seemed to glow. Riley spent that evening drawing red-spotted purples over and over until the corkboard in the girls' room was covered with them.

"Ms. Willow," the nurse said, this time with more urgency.

"I'm sorry. Yes?"

"The doctor would like to speak with you outside. I can stay with the kids."

Jane hesitated.

"Really, Ms. Willow, he'd prefer to talk to you alone."

Jane walked to the door, her back stiff and her hands clenched so tightly she could feel the acrylic nails digging into her palms.

"The nurse said you wanted to speak to me," she said to Dr. Howe as she stepped into the hall, leaving the sliding-glass door cracked behind her.

"Jane," Dr. Howe's lips tightened into a thin line. "I'm sorry. We've done everything we can do. Without a new heart—"

"What about the balloon?"

"The valvuloplasty was always a temporary fix. You

know that. Between the scar tissue and Riley's condition . . ."
He trailed off.

"I just . . . I didn't think . . ." Jane leaned against the wall.
"So she needs transplant, then. How do we go about that?"
She pressed her palm against the cold tile and tried to steady
the sadness already swelling in her eyes.

"Well, that's where things get tricky. Riley doesn't qualify
for a transplant."

"What? Why?"

"You have to understand, Jane. Riley's condition is de-
generative. Even with a new heart, Riley would have to continue the valvuloplasty procedures, and we'd be right back
here in a few years. The board won't approve a transplant in
a case like this."

"So you're telling me my baby girl is going to, what, die,
because the board doesn't think she deserves a new heart?"

Jane's whole body shook with grief and fury.

A few minutes later, Jane returned to the hospital room
alone. Quinn could see Dr. Howe standing motionless, peering through the doorway until the metal latch clicked back
into place. She turned to her mother, who sank into the blue
recliner, her shoulders limp and defeated.

"Mom . . ."

"Yeah, baby?" her mom whispered, careful to keep her
eyes shut tight. The conversation with Dr. Howe weighed on
her like a pressing stone. Jane wondered if Quinn, like her,
ever held her breath in the hopes that Riley might keep a little more air for herself.

"You want me to give Riley a bath tonight?"

Quinn's mother gave her a pained smile. "That would be
great, baby. Thank you."

Jane hated to have Quinn take care of Riley, but some

days the inevitability of having to bury Riley was all she had room for in her chest.

"Mom—I love you." Quinn pushed her hand into the bend of her mother's arm, squeezed, then went to get Riley ready for bed. Quinn was used to picking up the slack when her mother buckled. She didn't mind, of course. That's what being a big sister is about, or at least that's what people told Quinn.

"Riley, let's go! Time for a bath!"

Quinn shouted down the hall. She gathered a towel and the robe Riley had left in a pile on the floor. The robe was still damp from the night before.

"Riley, I told you, you need to hang up your robe or the inside won't dry!"

"Sorry. I forget!"

Quinn suspected that Riley never actually forgot. She thought Riley just liked the way Quinn would run the robe through the dryer during Riley's bath so the fabric was warm when she got out.

"Uh huh," she chided, poking Riley in the ribs. "Hurry up, or we won't have time for a story before bed."

That got Riley moving. She often begged to hear Quinn's stories, and Quinn never seemed to run out of them. Once, Riley had wondered aloud if Quinn had other whole lives inside her from the way she could invent a world and know everything about it by the time Riley pulled her pajama top over her head.

After the bath, Quinn folded Riley's robe around her, fresh from the dryer, then brushed the tangles from her hair.

"Quinn?"

"Yeah?"

"What do you think happens to them?"

"Who?"

"The people in your stories."

"What do you mean?"

"When you're not talking about them. What do they do up there?"

"Up where?" Quinn asked, creasing her brow.

"In your head. Isn't that where they live?"

Quinn laughed. "Yeah, I suppose so."

She thought for a long time, running the brush down Riley's hair until was smooth.

"I don't know. Live their lives, I guess. What does anybody do when no one's looking?"

"Wonder," Riley answered so softly that the word was almost swallowed by the humidifier humming beside Riley's bed.

"Wonder what?"

"That's what people do when no one's looking. They wonder."

"Okay, Mom, Riley's clean and tucked in," Quinn said, climbing into her mother's lap. She was too big, she knew, but her mother smiled and made room for her all the same.

"What did the doctor say?"

"Don't worry about that right now, baby."

Jane couldn't hide the telltale way her tongue trembled when she got bad news at the hospital. Quinn knew that her mom would eventually tell her what Dr. Howe had said—what choice did she have? Jane's parents had died the year she graduated high school, and Quinn couldn't remember ever meeting her father's parents. Any extended family they still had lived hours away, and most had drifted into memories. One more side effect of Riley's condition—people don't know what to say to the mothers of dying children, so they don't say anything. Silence becomes a sort of exit.

"She's almost seven," Quinn whispered.

Tears were beginning to swarm just behind her eyes.

"Yeah. What do you suppose she wants for her birthday?"

"I don't know. A real butterfly, maybe."

"Is that what you want to get her?"

"No."

Quinn was silent for a long time.

"I'm going to get her a new heart."

Quinn felt her mother's arms tighten around her as tears made a home on her cheek. Her mother didn't know, but Quinn had already started a campaign the only way she knew how: when she'd written a letter to Santa earlier that year, she'd asked for a new heart for Riley; when they went to church with grandpa, she prayed for new heart; the wishing well at the zoo, the note in the balloon she sent up into the sky with Riley one Saturday afternoon, the book under her bed where she wrote her stories. She had even slipped a note into a kaleidoscope she had built from an old kit she found in a box of discarded toys and clothes they were taking to the women's shelter. Always, the wish was the same: *find Riley a new heart.*

"Quinn—"

"Mom, I'm serious," Quinn interrupted. "Riley needs a new heart, and I'm going to get her one. You just have to believe. There's all sorts of magic if you believe."

CHAPTER THREE

The next morning, Quinn was up before the sun. She had fallen asleep in her mother's lap, so she eased down from the loveseat and walked to her and Riley's bedroom, lingering outside the door for a moment. Riley didn't snore, exactly; the sound was more like a coo, a soft contented sigh every few minutes. The cooing was so loud some nights that Quinn had trouble sleeping, but this morning she couldn't imagine a more peaceful sound. She checked her watch. Her mother and Riley would be awake soon. Quinn wanted to be back before they noticed. She pulled her jacket from the hall closet and slipped out the door, pushing her arms through her sleeves as she walked.

She couldn't believe she hadn't thought of the butterfly garden—the only place that made Riley happy—sooner. Of course she should leave one of her notes with the butterflies. What better place for a miracle? Quinn had gathered a handmade card and her favorite purple pen. She'd have to move quickly if she wanted to get back before her mother and Riley woke up.

Quinn loved being awake before everyone else. The streets were so quiet that Quinn could feel the world around her buzzing. The morning air was cold, and Quinn could see her breath as she hurried along the sidewalk. She felt the teleidoscope bouncing beneath her coat and pressed a hand to her chest. She had become enthralled with her first kaleidoscope when she was just a toddler, shrieking each time her father tried to free the toy from her grasp for a nap or a meal.

Her collection grew over the following years, until Quinn's bedroom shelf resembled a futuristic skyline. The skyline, like the circle of friends she had built in her first two years at school, stalled abruptly on the day Riley was born. The week Riley first came home from the hospital, Quinn got a package from her father with a note. Inside the package, she found an odd contraption, something called a kaleidoscope.

This is just like your teleidoscopes, Quinn, the note read, *except that this one reflects everything you see instead of trapping everything inside. Our world is going to be very different now. Whenever you get sad, just put this to your eye and you'll be able to see all the beauty in front of you, all the wonderful things we sometimes forget.*

Quinn tried to remember where her father had been, what had been important enough for him to miss Riley's birth, but the memories were like ghosts she couldn't hold onto. The harder she fought, the more the images transformed into muddled wisps. She could remember the words in that note exactly, and the way the paper smelled of marshmallows and dust, yet her father's face eluded her.

The garden would be closed, so she'd have to find a way inside. That wouldn't be easy, as the owners were very careful about housing and protecting the butterflies. Normally, visitors had to stand in a small room with glass doors on either side. One side would open, allowing visitors to step in, then close behind them. The next set of doors wouldn't open until the first set had closed and locked. This was supposed to keep butterflies from hitching a ride out of the garden. The entire space was surrounded by glass panels like a greenhouse. The building was relatively large, with several trees and even a small pond in the middle. Quinn had no idea how she'd get in, but she had to try.

She tiptoed toward the edge of the enclosure and put her hands against the glass. Once, she remembered, Riley had found a small gap between two panels where a hose connected the inside air to the outside. If she could find that spot again, maybe she could fold her card and slip the note through the hole. Quinn followed the perimeter, feeling the space between glass panels for any hint of an opening, kneeling now and then to inspect the seal at the bottom. The owners were careful and meticulous—they had to be to keep so many butterflies contained. Even the smallest gap would be enough for most of the butterflies to squeeze through, and it wouldn't be long before every butterfly in the place found their way out. Living things are funny that way—they hate to be contained. Freedom pulls at them like gravity, or maybe the tide. Quinn didn't really understand the difference if there was one.

She had nearly circled the garden when she felt a faint breeze tickle the back of her hand. To her surprise, Quinn was standing in front of a heavy black door. She had never seen the door from inside the garden. The door didn't have a handle, but Quinn saw a gap at the door jamb just large enough to fit her hands. Quinn gripped the edge of the door, pressed until the tips of her fingers went white, and pulled. The door didn't budge. Neither did Quinn. She pulled again. And again. Finally, the door gave way and squeaked open. The room beyond was dark. Quinn squinted against the sun, which was just beginning to creep over the horizon, and felt her way into the room. She smelled cleaning supplies. Must be a storage closet, she figured. There were shelves on both sides of her. Quinn ran her fingers along their edges to guide her through the dark. She hadn't gone very far into the room when she felt something sharp and metal press against her hip. She moved her hand down to discover a handle, which

she turned and pulled toward her. Nothing. She tried pushing the door open, and suddenly she was surrounded by the
sounds of the garden.

Quinn looked around, getting her bearings. She and Riley
had come here nearly every weekend for two years, but she'd
never seen this corner. The side of the door that faced into the
garden was green so that, from a distance, the paint blended
in with the foliage. Quinn stepped through the bushes, careful not to crush any butterflies underfoot as she searched for
the trail she usually followed. She felt the familiar crunch of
sand and gravel beneath her feet almost immediately. Once
on the trail, Quinn had a better sense of where she was.
She headed toward the pond where Riley liked to sit on her
bad days. Riley had told her once that she liked the way the
butterflies reflected in the water because she could see both
sides of their wings at once. Several large stones had been
placed around the pond, as well as a series of thick bushes.
Quinn planned to leave the card in the bushes, where Riley
and others wouldn't notice. Quinn didn't much care for butterflies, but as she approached the pond she was transfixed
by a spectacular purple flash. The color was so bright that
Quinn thought that there must be some sort of light placed
near the water, but then the flash darted between the green
leaves. Quinn followed the trail of purple to the water, where
she saw a butterfly the size of her fist perched on the surface.

Quinn moved forward, and the butterfly dipped beneath
the water. *How strange*, she thought. Quinn couldn't remember ever having seen a butterfly willingly go under water. And
for this long? Quinn was at the edge of the pond, kneeling.
Without thinking, she pushed one hand into the water. She
expected the pond to be shallow; what need would they have
for a deep pond? She was nearly elbow-deep in the water,
though, and still couldn't feel the bottom. She pushed further

until her entire arm was in the water—no bottom. Inexplicably, Quinn ducked her face beneath the surface. She didn't know what she expected to see, but she certainly didn't think she'd find a small, swirling galaxy inches from her face. She held out her palm and extended slowly until she touched what felt like the edge of a thick bubble. She pressed harder, and a semisolid, glistening edge wavered in the water. Quinn pushed her hand through the bulbous layer until her fingers disappeared into the drowning stars. Realizing that her now-drenched arm and face were wetting the card in her hand, Quinn set the card at the foot of a bush, then sank her whole body into the pond.

The water was cold for a moment; then it seemed to close around her almost like a sleeping bag zipped around a body. She checked her jacket, then her pants, but neither felt wet. The sounds and smells of the garden were fading. Her calves and forearms burned as if they were being stretched to their very limits. Quinn opened her mouth to scream, and she found that the air around her tasted like raspberries. She tried to raise her arms above her, but they were pinned down. She had fallen into an enormous cocoon, she thought. But that was nonsense. There was no such thing as a cocoon big enough to hold a person. She was so busy trying to understand why she couldn't move that she hardly noticed her sight returning. The space around her grew. She stretched her arms instinctively, shedding the cocoon-like coating, and looked around. She was surrounded by an opalescent sphere. Her legs were free, but she wasn't standing. Rather, her entire body was being cradled by another layer of the bulbous film she had touched in the pond. The more she moved, the further she sank into the iridescent layer. Without warning, she dropped from the bulb and landed on something solid.

She tried to breathe, but no matter how much she gasped,

her lungs shouted for more air. She remembered a trip to the mountains she took with her parents before Riley was born, and how hard it had been to breathe. Her father had taught her to take slow, shallow breaths so that she wouldn't get light-headed. Quinn concentrated on the rise and fall of her diaphragm until she had slowed her breathing. Her heart, which had been thumping hard, settled.

She tried to move and realized that whatever had been holding her had vanished. She rubbed her eyes and turned to her right, then left. The ground was dry, cracked like her lips during winter, but her hands burned when she went to push herself up. She swallowed hard. The butterfly she had followed into the pond now flitted in front of her. She could see that the wings were electric indigo, and they shimmered in the light—the sun, maybe? Quinn couldn't tell. This place was definitely bright, but the light didn't seem to come from anywhere at all. No yellow spot in the sky. No shadows on the ground either. She heard a scratching sound behind her and turned to see a dark figure rush past on a giant hen.

Quinn rubbed her eyes again and squinted to be sure she had seen what she saw. Sure enough, what looked like a woman was riding back toward her on an enormous, white hen. The thing's legs were impossibly long. Quinn guessed the hen was at least as big as a full-grown horse and just as fast. The pair slowed and turned toward Quinn.

"Sorry about that, kid! You sure came out of nowhere."

Quinn furrowed her brow. "I was just—and I put my hand—"

"Slow down, peach. I'm Meelie," the woman said, climbing down from the hen. She had on long green pants, a bomber jacket, and an old leather pilot helmet with eye goggles.

"Hi," Quinn replied. Her eyebrows were bent into confusion and her voice felt like sand in her throat.

"Have you been here long?"

"I don't—I don't know. Where is here?"

"Oh, this place hasn't got a name that I know of."

"How'd I get here?"

"Same as the rest of us, I figure. Tried to find the bottom of something dark and wound up in the middle of something bright?"

"You could say that, yeah."

"Yep. That's how I got here. One minute my plane is nosediving toward the ocean waves, the next I'm lying on the ground and coughing up dust."

"You're a pilot?"

"Used to be. Haven't figured out how to get this dang chicken in the air, though."

"So that is a chicken? I'm not crazy?"

"No, you aren't crazy. Darnedest thing, huh, a six-foot chicken?"

"There's no such thing as a six-foot chicken. That's ridiculous."

"I'd have said the same thing before I got here. Say, what's your name?"

"Quinn."

"Pleased to meet you, Quinn. So what brought you here?"

"I already told you, I don't know."

"No, not *how* you got here. We all have something that *brings* us here."

"What do you mean?"

"Well, like me. The last thing I remember was praying I wouldn't die when I hit those waves. Then here I was."

"So I'm dead?"

Meelie laughed so hard the goggles fell down onto her face. She touched the hen's wing and slid the goggles back up onto her forehead.

"No, baby. You aren't dead any more than I am. This place has a way of answering when you ask for things, is all."

"Like the genie in *Big*—Zoltar, I think?"

"What's a Zoltar?"

"You know, the machine in the movie that grants wishes."

"Oh, I've never seen a moving picture."

"What? How long have you *been* here?"

"That depends on how you figure time, I guess."

"How do *you* figure time?"

"Well, what is the year back home?"

"Two thousand fifteen."

Meelie let out a whistle.

"I came here in the summer of 1937. What's that, almost eighty years? Mercy, time flies."

"But you don't look old."

"Funny thing: folks spend their whole lives trying to stay young when all you need is a change of scenery."

"So you haven't been home in eighty years?"

"Well, I've been home. I just can't stay long, and nobody knows I'm there, or they don't believe I am, anyway."

"I don't understand."

"I don't either, honey. Just the way things work around here. You learn to manage. So have you been asking for something? I don't mean a present or anything. Something big. Bigger than most folks can imagine."

"Yeah, I guess I have."

"You don't say."

"My sister. She's got a bad heart."

"I'm sorry to hear that, Quinn." Meelie lowered her goggles. "Well, come on, now. Hop on."

"Excuse me? I'm not getting on that thing. And not to be rude, but I don't even know you. Here I am in this weird place with no sun, and giant farm animals, and a lady who flew into the ocean, and—"

"Take a breath, kid. You're right. I'm asking a difficult thing of you. I don't mean to push. Just trying to get out of this desert before dark. Besides, ol' Pidge is as gentle as they come."

"Where are you going?"

"To get something to eat. You must be hungry. Bet you're thirsty too, huh? The air sure isn't easy on the throat." Meelie laughed.

"No, I guess not." Quinn swallowed hard again, then took a small step toward Meelie and the giant hen. Pidge turned and looked down at her. Quinn jumped back.

"Relax. She won't hurt, kid." Meelie held a hand out to Quinn and hoisted her up. "Now hold on. She may be gentle, but she's awful quick-footed!"

Quinn wrapped her arms around Meelie's waist, closing her eyes against the wind as Pidge took off in a sprint.

"We'll have to get you a riding hat," Meelie shouted.

"Do we have to go so fast?" Quinn cried out, her voice rising and falling as she bounced on Pidge's back.

"The desert will be dark soon enough. We need to get to the caves before then, or we'll be out here all night. Don't you worry, peach. I'll show you around."

CHAPTER FOUR

The caves were much cooler and had a soft pink glow like the Himalayan rock salt Quinn's mom used to put in Riley's food, one of the myriad home remedies they'd tried to help Riley grow stronger. Quinn and Riley even had pink salt lamps on their nightstands back home that stayed on all night. The caves smelled like those salt lamps too.

"My family must be so worried," Quinn thought aloud.

"I wouldn't worry about them."

"What do you mean? I've been gone for so long. My mom has to be scared, and no one is there to walk with Riley and—"

"You sure do get worked up in a hurry, honey."

"But—"

"They don't know you're here," Meelie interrupted. Her voice was hushed, and Quinn heard pain in the words. "They don't know you're here."

"That doesn't make any sense, Meelie." Quinn was close to tears.

"Time is a funny thing. Back home, we talk like things move in a straight line, but maybe that's just the direction we all have grown accustomed to. I couldn't tell you the science. All I know is that the ones who come here on purpose say time moves more like a clock on the first visit—you know, around in a circle till you're back where you started."

"What do you mean, the first visit?"

"Well, some folks need something that you can't fix in

one go. They've got to keep coming back. Coming back, now that's the hard part."

"Why?"

"Quinn, when you go home, things will be . . . different."

"Different how?"

"You ought to talk to Aimee."

"Who's Aimee?"

"She's been here longer than anybody. Went sailing and didn't make it back to land again or something like that. You wouldn't know looking at her, but she's been here more than three hundred years."

"How will we find her?"

"There's only one place she could be. Like I said, she never did make land."

"She's been on a boat for hundreds of years?"

"Yep."

"Meelie, that's absurd."

"You know, I suppose she is a bit odd."

"But you think . . . you think she can help me get back to Riley and my mom?"

"I sure do, kid. She's as smart as they come. I'll take you to see her in the morning. Right now, you ought to eat something."

Meelie handed Quinn something that looked like a big piece of fruit, about twice the size of Quinn's hand, and with a waxy skin. The strange object could have been an enormous mango except that the skin was white and much thinner than the mangoes Quinn was used to.

"Take a bite," Meelie urged.

"I don't think I've seen anything like that before."

"We call them moonfruit on account of the skin."

Quinn was suspicious. "What do they taste like?"

"They're good, a little tart. Something like a cross between a grape and a persimmon."

"How do I eat them?"

Meelie smirked and bit into her own moonfruit. "Skin and all, kid. Easy as pie."

Quinn took a small bite, and juice sprang from the skin and trickled down her chin. "Not bad." She continued to nibble, but she didn't have much of an appetite. She put the fruit down and sank onto a smooth rock, making herself as small as she could. The pink stones at her feet grew wet with tears. Quinn sat like that for a long time, her shoulders moving up and down to the rhythm of her sadness. She didn't make a sound—just let the tears slip down and pool in front of her.

"I'm sorry, Meelie."

"No sweat, bunny. Happens to all of us the first night."

"How—how many people live here?"

"Hard to say. Everyone comes and goes. This cave is like a home to us, though. There's always someone here when you need them," Meelie smiled.

Quinn hid her face, wiping her eyes with the sleeve of her jacket. She felt like a child sitting on the ground, crying into the shoulder of a strange woman with a giant hen for a pet.

"Hey, do you want to see something magnificent?"

Quinn nodded again.

Meelie grabbed her hand and led her toward the mouth of the cave. She was smiling. "Oh, you're just going to love this." Meelie led Quinn out of the cave and felt around for a rock.

Quinn sat down beside her and stared into the blackest sky she could imagine. "I don't understand. What am I looking at?"

"Just wait, bunny. Just wait."

They sat and watched without talking. Quinn squinted against the dark. She thought she saw something far off, moving through the sky. Glowing pinpricks of indigo. All at once, the space in front of her was full of these pinpricks. Small, incandescent butterflies like the one she had followed lit up the plain until the horizon was humming with a deep purple haze. They moved toward Meelie and Quinn like a fantastic fog.

"Riley would love this place," Quinn whispered.

"Maybe you can show her someday." Meelie's face was stunning in the light of the butterflies. Quinn noticed that Meelie's hair was silver, the only thing that gave away her age. The haze turned the strands into a faint violet that shimmered when Meelie moved her head. The two peered out at the colorful migration for a long while. Meelie sat close to Quinn, who laid her head against Meelie's shoulder and succumbed to sleep.

CHAPTER FIVE

Quinn woke to find herself on a makeshift pallet of blankets and bits of fabric deep inside the cave. Next to her, a brilliant red-bulb protruded from a waxy, green shoot. Quinn raised a finger to the bulb. The outer layer felt warm against her skin, and she could hear the softest beat coming from inside.

She rose and looked around for Meelie, but Meelie and Pidge were gone. Quinn cupped the base of the bulb, which slipped off the shoot into her palms, then shifted her grip so that the glowing orb sat in her right hand. She felt a pulse each time she heard the sound coming from inside. A butterfly landed beside her. There, in the glow of the butterfly wings, she saw a message etched into the rock:

You will find what you seek at the heart of the flower.
This one bends best when held close to the chest.
You will know when the time comes.

"Bend?" Quinn asked the empty space. The words didn't make any sense. She thought hard about the message, what she was holding in her hand, what would happen when the time came. Then she recalled something a teacher had said during science class: astronauts' hearts change shape in space.

"Hey, you're up!" Meelie called from across the cavern.

"Meelie, do you know what this is?" Quinn raised the bulb toward Meelie.

"I can't say that I do. I haven't seen one of those here or anywhere."

"I found writing on the ground," Quinn said, relaying the words that had appeared in the rock.

Meelie furrowed her brow and stayed silent for a long time. "Strange, indeed. You ought to share this with Aimee later."

"So we are going to see her today?"

"That's the plan, bunny. But first, we need to get some breakfast. Lord knows how long we'll be out there looking for her."

"I thought you said she stayed in the same place."

"Well sure, but the ocean is awfully big, and Aimee's awfully small."

Quinn sat beside the small fire Meelie had built, studying the note and the strange flower that pulsed in her hand. Meelie ground something brown into a fine powder with a makeshift mortar. Meelie sprinkled water into the bowl and squished the mixture with her hands until she had made a paste. She pulled the paste apart and rolled the pieces into balls, then she smashed them flat like pancakes. When she set the first one on a hot stone over the fire, the mixture cracked and smelled like marshmallows.

"What is that, Meelie?"

"We called them corn cakes back home. Just some smashed grain and water. They're a little lighter and sweeter than you might expect, but they sure stick to the bones. We'll have a few and take the rest with us to be safe." Meelie handed one to Quinn, who studied the cake like a math formula.

"What's that smell?"

"Just take a bite," Meelie chided. "They're good."

Quinn hesitated, then bit into the edge of the cake. Meelie was right. The cake was delicious. The outside was crispy with a hint of caramel, and the inside reminded her of short bread. "I could get used to these."

Quinn took another bite. Then, for the first time since she'd arrived, she smiled. Really smiled. Her stomach felt warm and her shoulders lifted. She took a deep breath. Then she thought of Riley. Riley hadn't been able to take a deep breath in months. Her lungs were working fine, but her heart couldn't keep up anymore. The stenosis was like a small leak in a bike tire. You could add air for a while, but eventually the tire just gave out, and you had to get a new one. Only no one had a heart for Riley.

Quinn looked at Meelie. Her eyes burned, and she told herself the smoke was just aggravating them. "Do you think Aimee can help me get home?"

"I'm positive, bunny." Meelie put an arm around Quinn. "Let me wrap up these last few cakes and we'll set out. Don't you worry. Like I said, time doesn't go in a straight line here. Aimee will explain things better, but I promise you, you'll see Riley and your mother soon enough."

They raced across the desert, bobbing in rhythm with the giant hen's head. The animal was remarkably tame, shifting direction and speed with the slightest movement of the reins in Meelie's hand. Quinn tried to study her surroundings, but the wind kicked sand into her eyes. She gave up and buried her face between Meelie's shoulder blades. The bomber jacket was cool against Quinn's cheek. She felt Meelie's back tense and Pidge began to slow down. Quinn lifted her head and looked around.

The desert had given way to a lush landscape filled with every shade of purple Quinn could imagine. Tall trees with peeling bark that smelled of lavender stretched on as far as Quinn could see. There were bushes with large leaves the color of ripe plums. Some of the flowers were bright and shimmered like glitter, while others were a rich purple that reminded her of eggplants. Beyond the plants, Quinn saw a fast pool that seemed to flow like the butterflies they'd watched the night before, only this time the motion was more fluid. Quinn could hear the tide rush in, then pull back. The rush of water sounded like a secret each time the tide pulled back. *Shh, shh, shh.* Quinn shielded her eyes and trained them on the horizon, but she saw no sign of Aimee. No boats at all.

"How will we find her?"

"We've just got to be patient. I figure if we walk the coast long enough, either Aimee will see us, or we'll see her."

"Patience isn't my strong suit," Quinn sighed.

"Well then, consider this a learning opportunity," Meelie laughed, poking an elbow into Quinn's ribs.

Pidge walked along the beach, sinking her claws into the sand. Occasionally Pidge dipped her head and pecked at the ground. Quinn assumed she was checking for worms or other food, though Quinn saw neither.

Meelie scanned the water. "The last boat I saw Aimee use was a white dinghy. Of course, I can't be sure if Aimee has moved on to some other vessel, or if she's finally come ashore."

Quinn tried to focus on the horizon, but something about the way the sky and water came together made her dizzy, so she studied the beach instead. The sand was white and sparkled like crushed pearls. Quinn remembered a picture in one of her mother's photo albums. Her mother had visited a place in New Mexico where the sand looked just like snow. *The most wonderful thing I've ever seen,* Quinn remembered her mother saying. Her mother hated the cold, but she loved the electricity in the air that came with winter. She'd said that the desert in New Mexico had the same song in the silence before sunrise. Quinn had wanted to go there one summer, but Riley had a hard time being far from home. The strange plants and temperature changes made breathing even harder for Riley.

"Do you see that?" Meelie shouted. Her voice made Quinn jump, and Quinn lost her balance and slipped from Pidge's back. The sand may have looked like snow, but the white powder wasn't nearly as soft. Quinn could already feel a bruise forming on her right hip.

"See what, Meelie? I don't see anything." Quinn stared at the water, but the purple waves seemed to roll on forever.

"Right there." Meelie held her arm straight out.

Quinn followed her hand and saw a tiny dot bobbing up and down. The speck could just as easily have been froth from the waves except that the object didn't disappear into the water the way the other white caps did. Meelie dug her heel into Pidge's side, and Pidge let out a loud squawk.

"Do you think that's Aimee?" Quinn was tense with excitement and fear.

"I can't be sure, but I figure we ought to check just in case." Meelie dug her heels in again. This time the squawk was long and hung in the air.

Quinn could see the small white spot stretch higher into the sky. As they moved closer, she could just make out two oars spinning around like the hands on a clock. Whoever was steering the boat had heard Pidge.

"Meelie, you said Aimee doesn't come to shore."

"That's right."

"How am I supposed to get to her? You said yourself that this chicken doesn't fly."

"There's a sandbar not far from here. We can walk out on that until you're close enough to swim to her."

"Swim?"

Quinn hadn't planned on getting wet. She was wearing the only clothes she had, and stripping down in front of two strangers wasn't on the agenda.

"You'll be all right. We've got some old clothes back at the cave. We can dry yours out when we get back tonight."

The dinghy was nearer now, and Quinn could see a woman leaning against the back with one hand in the water. Meelie waved her arms above her head, then motioned to her right. The woman on the boat nodded. Both she and Meelie headed toward what Quinn assumed was the sandbar. Meelie guided Pidge to a path where the water was just a few inches deep, washing over Pidge's claws as they walked. The boat stopped a few hundred yards from shore.

"Glad I found you," Meelie said as they neared the boat. "This is Quinn. She arrived yesterday, and she's got some questions I can't answer. I was hoping you could tell her a little more about this place. You know, how coming and going works and all that."

"That would be my pleasure." The woman's voice was quiet but calm—*not unlike water,* Quinn thought.

"I'm Aimee. Pleased to meet you."

"Hey."

"Come aboard." Aimee had a disarming smile and gray eyes that seemed to see all of a person. Quinn tried to look away, but couldn't. For a moment, she forgot all about the butterfly garden, and the pond, and the impossibly-large hen beside her. The water, much colder than Quinn expected, was a sharp reminder that Quinn was not wading into an ocean, at least not as she knew oceans. For starters, the ripples that broke against her thighs and torso impacted with a noticeable thump, then dissipated almost instantly into a shock of glitter. Though she felt cold, the part of her body beneath the surface didn't drag or resist the current. Even the spray, which coated her exposed skin, defied everything Quinn knew about both solids and liquids. The shining mist tasted sweet on her lips.

"Oh!" Quinn shouted, putting a hand to her mouth worriedly. "The water . . . I drank the water . . ."

"You're okay," Aimee said. "Everyone here drinks the ocean. You're a long way from home, Quinn."

Quinn relaxed her arm and made her way to Aimee, who reached over and pulled her onto the boat. Quinn was shivering. Aimee produced a woven blanket made from a thick, warm material that reminded Quinn of cotton, though the blanket was light as air to the touch.

"What is this made of?"

Aimee smirked. "I've learned a few tricks about this place." She motioned to the water, then submerged her hand.

Quinn watched in disbelief as a net poured from Aimee's fingertips.

"Some folks like the land. But with me, well, let's just say the sea and I have an understanding."

"Meet you back here when the moons come through?" Meelie interjected.

"We'll be waiting," Aimee answered.

"Thank you, Meelie. For everything." Quinn waved as Meelie climbed onto Pidge and sprinted back toward shore. Quinn thought she heard Meelie say something, but she was too far away for Quinn to make out the words.

CHAPTER SIX

"So what brought you here, Quinn?" Aimee asked, turning the dinghy out to sea.

Quinn explained Riley's condition. She was careful with the details, a skill Quinn had learned after seven years of filling in teachers on why she missed more school than her peers. Every August, she would use the same analogies, then put one hand on top of the other to illustrate the procedures, just as her mother had done for her. Aimee seemed to study her as she spoke, her eyes collecting moisture like clouds before a storm.

"That's tough." Aimee put a hand over Quinn's and squeezed. "How did you come through?"

"Well, I went to this butterfly garden that my sister likes—I went to leave a note—there's a pond Riley sits beside for hours—" Quinn stopped to gather her thoughts. "I know the whole thing sounds silly. I don't actually expect anyone to find my notes and give Riley a heart. Putting all the sadness into . . . prayers, I guess. I hadn't really thought of the cards that way, but they are like prayers. So I sneaked into the garden and I was going to hide one next to the pond, but then I saw this glowing purple flash—"

"—and you tried to catch the light?"

"Yes! And then I was here, dodging Meelie and her enormous chicken."

Aimee smiled. "She sure likes that wind in her face."

"Yeah," Quinn laughed. "She said she's been here for eighty years, but she doesn't look that old. And you—you look like you're in college. How can that be?"

"Well, I'm sure Meelie mentioned that time is a bit different here. See, the days and nights are a lot like what you're used to. There's no sun that comes up, at least not one I've seen, but the sky gets lighter, and the temperature rises during the day. The night can get quite cold, and much darker than home since there aren't any stars."

"But why doesn't anyone get old?"

"That's a bit harder to explain."

Aimee put her index finger on Quinn's palm. "If I start here—" She drew a circle with her finger, "and end up here, where I started, has any time passed?"

"Of course. Time doesn't have anything to do with where you are." Quinn paused. "Right?"

"Actually, no. When people first come here, they tend to move in a circle, all the way around to where they started. The place you call home."

"So when I go back—"

"—then you haven't gone anywhere at all. And while you're here, this time anyway, your stay is like an interlude. The space between."

"How do you know all this?"

"I've been here for a very long time."

"How did you get here?"

"Much the same way you did. I was a young girl, about seventeen, and my parents sent me to a school in Paris. They were born in France, but they lived on a small island off the coast of South America. That's where I was born. Anyway, there wasn't much in the way of schooling on the island, and my family was well-off, so each year I'd cross the Atlantic in a large clipper ship. One summer, as I was returning home for break, the ship caught fire. I've heard that many folks these days believe we were attacked by pirates. The legends really are more magnificent. You ought to look them up when you return. The simple truth, though, is that the water was quite choppy that day, and a lantern fell in the cargo hold. The hold was filled with clothes, so the fire spread quickly. The crew couldn't get the flames under control, and the boat split in half. As I fell into the water, I saw something move beneath the waves."

"Like a shark?"

"Goodness no, nothing like that. More like a precious stone, only glowing. I tried to reach for the object, which kept sinking farther and farther. I don't know why, but I dove under the water. When all my air was gone, I rushed back to the surface, but the ocean was very different. The water wasn't as heavy and had turned deep purple. Almost like wine."

"So, you didn't ask for anything? You just ended up here by accident?"

"I wouldn't say that, exactly, but I didn't find this place by searching. And unlike most others, I've never left."

"You mean, you never went back home? Not even once?"

"No." Aimee stared past Quinn. "I didn't have anything left to go home to. Besides, I prefer water. The melody here is much simpler." She let her left hand sink back into the waves. "Doesn't sound like you have much choice, though. Your sister needs you."

"Wait . . . if you never went home, does that mean everything and everyone you know is just stuck in time?"

"No. I don't know how long before things begin to move again, but a few people have taken weeks or even months to decide that they want to return home. We don't see many of them come back, but the few who have were in shock. The home they had left was not the home they found at the other end of the portal. Life had gone on without them."

Quinn watched the rope-like strands stream from Aimee's

fingertips. Aimee moved the fingers up and down like she was playing a piano. Beneath the surface, the strands knotted themselves into a net. Before long, small starfish collected near each knot until Aimee had an underwater constellation trailing behind her like some goddess from the stories Quinn read in elementary school.

"Quinn, have you found anything . . . strange here?" Aimee asked after a long while.

"Oh, yes!" Quinn cried out, remembering the bulb she had hidden away in the knapsack Meelie had given her. She retrieved the pulsing object, handing the bulb to Aimee.

"Do you know what this is?" Quinn asked.

"Not exactly, no. Everyone finds what they need here, so I suspect this is what you need to help your sister."

"You mean—this is a heart?"

"Possibly, yes, or at least something that will help heal her. That's what you prayed for." Aimee looked perplexed. "Did you happen to find a message nearby?"

Quinn nodded and repeated the words she had seen next to the butterfly that morning. "Sounds about right," Aimee said after a short pause.

"So I just take this to Riley, and she'll get better?"

"For a little while, yes, but magic doesn't last forever, Quinn. This is only a temporary fix. Riley will continue to get sick, just like she always has. You're going to have to make a decision. Do you want to help her for a little while, or do you want her to live a long and healthy life?"

"Obviously I want her to have a long life."

"Your decision is not that simple. When you go home, things will be different. And every time you visit this place, returning to your family will get harder."

"I don't care. I'll do anything to help Riley."

"I'm not sure you understand. What I mean is, for each

thing you take from this place, you leave a piece of yourself here. The world craves balance that way."

"So, what—I can leave this magic heart flower here and nothing will change, but Riley will die, or I can heal her and deal with some weird changes?"

"That's right. But you need to understand, these aren't innocuous changes that you'll hardly notice. Your entire history is going to be affected."

"How much history can I have? I'm fifteen."

Aimee tightened her jaw. "Quinn, you need to trust me. If you take this bulb to your sister, you must come back at once."

"So I'm supposed to sneak into my own house like some sort of burglar, give this thing to Riley, and then just leave when no one is looking?"

"Yes." Aimee's abruptness startled Quinn.

"I can't do that."

"Quinn, listen to me. Don't linger at home. Things will only be harder for you if you stay. You have to trust me. I've seen a lot of people come through here, and one thing I've learned is that there's no such thing as closure. Goodbyes don't make endings any easier."

"I don't want to talk about this anymore." Quinn tucked her knees under her chin.

"Okay." Aimee pulled one of the starfish from her net and slipped the creature into Quinn's hand. "To remember me, in case you don't come back. Such a wonderfully human trait, the need to be remembered." She smiled at Quinn.

"How do I get home?" Quinn's voice was flat, her eyes fixed on something far away.

"There's something special about the water here. The oceans and pools act like gateways between this place and what we used to call home. First-timers need to use a very unique pool deep inside the cave Meelie took you to last night. When you're ready, you'll use that to go home."

They didn't speak for the rest of the afternoon. When the two moons began to peek over the horizon, Aimee steered the boat back toward the sandbar. Meelie was waiting when they arrived. Quinn tried to smile, but her face refused to lie. She climbed onto Pidge's back, wrapped her arms around Meelie's waist, and cried all the way back to the cave.

Quinn sat alone for the rest of the night, shifting the weight of the bulb from one hand to the other. She wondered when the heart would be ready for Riley, how she would feel when she saw her sister again. How could she slip out without saying goodbye to Riley, without holding her or reading her a story? But she had to come back, didn't she? She could stay with Riley and her mom, and Riley would be okay for a while. Wasn't that the point, all of them together for a little while longer? But then, Riley may never get to drive a car. Or go on a date. Or pick a prom dress or go to college or have—

Quinn was exhausted thinking of all the lives Riley could or could not have. Quinn was only fifteen, and she had to decide how many memories her sister could hold, how many of them had space for Quinn at all.

CHAPTER SEVEN

The next morning, Quinn felt something thin brush against her cheek.

"Riley, come on. Go back to sleep."

Riley loved butterfly kisses, and she often climbed on top of Quinn to bat her lashes on Quinn's face when she slept in. Quinn forced her eyes open, swatting in the direction of whatever was touching her, but Riley wasn't there. Instead, she saw a magnificent butterfly with stark-red wings bordered by deep black. The coloring and wing pattern were new to Quinn, even after so many trips to the butterfly garden. As she searched her mind for the name of the insect, she heard someone snoring a few feet away. Quinn realized then that she was still in the cave with Meelie. She pushed herself up to a sitting position, trying to shake the surreal surroundings from her head like a dream, but the floor of the cave cut into her palms. Aimee, Meelie, Pidge—they couldn't be real. This place couldn't be real. What sort of place grows hearts, anyway?

"The bulb!"

Quinn searched the ground around her in a frenzy, waking Meelie in the process.

"What's wrong, kid?" Meelie asked with a yawn.

"The bulb must have slipped from my hand while I was sleeping. I can't find the bulb, Meelie!"

"Relax, honey. Your bulb is right there."

Meelie motioned to a pile of blankets between them.

Quinn pulled the blankets from the top of the pile and

threw them aside. After a few more moments of panic, Quinn discovered the bulb resting in the center of the pile. "Did I do this?"

"You sure did. You said that you were worried that the bulb might break or get too cold, so you asked me for extra blankets and built a makeshift nest. You don't remember?"

"No, not at all."

"Well, I can't say that's a surprise. This place is hard enough to make sense of for those without someone back home to take care of."

Quinn had managed to coax the red butterfly onto her finger. "Do you know what type of butterfly this is, Meelie?"

Meelie studied the wings for a moment. "You know, I think I have seen something like this before. Years back I flew the fire horse down to Mexico City. I remember all sorts of bright-red butterflies on the hike outside the city. The tour guide called them Cramer something-or-others. You ought to look that up . . . when you go home."

Quinn rolled her eyes. "You give more homework than my teachers. Besides, Aimee said I shouldn't stick around home if I'm going to keep coming back."

"And what do you think?"

"Honestly, I don't know, Meelie. Of course I want Riley to have a good life, to be healthy, to have the chance to experience everything she's ever dreamed of. But what happens if I come back here? If I keep coming back?"

"You and I both know that those questions are yours to answer, peach." Meelie spoke with an ominous calm that reminded Quinn of the wall of clouds and green skies before a tornado. Something about the inevitability of destruction allowed grief to sit in the chest without aching. Meelie put her hand over Quinn's, and the butterfly, which had settled onto Quinn's forearm, lifted into the air. The wings looked even more red as the insect fluttered past Meelie's silvery hair.

"Meelie, have you ever seen one of these butterflies *here*?"

"Can't say that I have."

Quinn chewed the inside of her cheek.

"Do you think maybe he's a sign or something, like maybe this place is telling me that I should go home?"

"Could be, kid. Sounds like you're picking up on the way this place works."

"But I'm not ready. I don't know what I'm going to do."

Meelie pulled Quinn in and wrapped an arm around her shoulders. "I don't know, Quinn. Some folks say life never gives you something you can't handle, but I've seen plenty of people buckle."

Quinn's chest rose and fell like a sleeping child's. Tears slid down her cheek and onto Meelie's jacket.

"I've got to say, bunny. You don't seem the type to buckle. You're stronger than you think."

Quinn didn't respond. They sat together until light streamed into the cave. When Quinn finally straightened her back and looked around, she was stunned by what she saw. They'd left to find Aimee before the day had taken shape, so Quinn was only just noticing the city of people peppering the cave. What had been her private corner in which to grieve was actually filled with blankets, small fires, and even a few children.

"Who are all these people, Meelie?"

"I tried to tell you, there's always someone here when you need them."

"You mean all these people live here?"

"Most of them, yes. Some, like you, are just passing through, wrestling with their own decisions."

"How come nobody back home has ever heard of this

place? I mean, how can this many people go missing and nobody looks? How do people visit and go back without ever talking about what's here?"

"Oh, I imagine lots of folks talk about what's here. Trouble is, those folks are eventually forgotten altogether. Sure, the stories might linger in the minds of those back home, but they have a word for all this that sets people at ease."

"What's that?"

"Fantasy. Magic. The stuff of children's books."

Quinn wrapped the bulb in a threadbare blanket Meelie had given her, grabbed one of the marshmallow cakes for the walk, then lifted her hand to eye level. She spoke directly to the red butterfly, which had not left her all morning.

"All right. If you're meant to take me home, we might as well get going."

The butterfly rose into the air and fluttered deeper into the cave.

Meelie watched as Quinn followed the butterfly into the cave's far recesses. She hadn't been sure where Quinn could find the pool of water that Aimee had mentioned. The cave stretched out beneath the desert for miles. She had told Quinn that she had never had much reason to look for a way home, but that wasn't entirely true. She didn't share her past with many people, and Quinn had enough to worry about anyway. She tried not to feel guilty about keeping the truth from Quinn.

I don't know whether or not the butterfly has anything to do with you returning home, she had told Quinn, *but since that's the only clue you have you might as well follow through and see where the little thing takes you.* She didn't have much faith that an insect would lead Quinn to the water, though perhaps getting lost in the caves for a day would help to clear her head. Quinn had confessed that she still hadn't decided whether or not she would return to this realm. *What makes people remember?* Quinn had asked her. *How long before they forget me entirely?* Quinn was beginning to understand that she couldn't protect her mother. No matter what she decided, her mother would lose a daughter. Which one she would lose, and how, was up to Quinn.

The butterfly never got more than a few feet ahead of Quinn. Like the indigo butterflies she had seen on her first night, this one appeared to glow. The darker the cave got, the brighter the wings became until the path was bathed in red; whatever coated the stalactites and stalagmites shined white in the light of the butterfly. Quinn wasn't afraid of many things, yet she struggled to keep moving. The eerie hue made her feel like she was being swallowed by something enormous and angry.

Quinn had been following the butterfly for what seemed like hours. She had long since eaten the last of her marshmallow cake, her body ached, and the bulb was beginning to wear a hole in the fabric Quinn was using to carry the object. She kept having to shift the bulb from one hand to another to keep her arms from cramping. Now both arms burned. The bulb didn't seem to be getting any larger, yet the weight in Quinn's hand felt heavier and heavier as she walked. She was having trouble lifting her feet, too, which made navigating the uneven terrain ever more difficult. She stumbled every few steps, stiffening her ankles and knees to stay upright.

The awkward movement reminded Quinn of Riley just before her first birthday. Like Quinn, Riley never used a walker or the sides of furniture when she began to walk. One day, she simply stood up and put one foot in front of the other, then again and again. Quinn smiled to herself, thinking of the stubborn way Riley would stare at the ground when she fell. She never cried. Just gritted her teeth and pushed herself up, taking each deliberate step until she was moving across the floor like children twice her age.

Quinn tripped, landing hard on her knee. She felt the skin break.

"This is useless!" she shouted at the butterfly, which now hovered in front of her. "I don't even know where you're taking me, or if I'm supposed to follow you at all!"

The butterfly hovered near her for another moment, then darted farther into the cave.

"Oh, great. Now I'm lost *and* I can't see." Quinn screamed until her throat felt raw, then began to cry again. How would she get home, and what would she do when she got there?

The blood coming from her knee slowed to a trickle. She could feel a bruise forming, making the joint difficult to bend. Still, she had never been the sort to quit, especially when Riley needed her, so she felt around for a rock to use as leverage. Once she had located one small enough to grip comfortably, she pulled herself to a standing position and looked around. She couldn't see anything. The expanse before her was ink black, suffocating like the kind of darkness that makes your eyes throb when you stay under water for too long. Quinn stopped crying, and her frustration turned to despair. She was lost. She remembered what Aimee had said about time and how if she returned home, things would be as though she hadn't been gone at all. Then she wondered how long Riley and her mother would be trapped in unending sleep. This place was supposed to fix problems, yet the people she loved most would remain in their beds forever, because she couldn't find her way back to them.

Suddenly aware of the weight in her hands, Quinn raised the makeshift rucksack to her chest. "Of course!"

Between the fog of her injured knee and panic over failing her family, Quinn had forgotten that the bulb was luminescent. She eased the fabric from the top of the bulb with her left hand, careful to steady the object with her right. The bulb lit up the cavern easily, casting a red glow that pulsed each time Quinn felt a beat in her hand. She walked deeper into the cave, the way the butterfly had gone. Before long, she came to a room with several paths jutting out in different directions like the spokes on a bicycle wheel.

"Now what?" she asked herself.

As if in answer, the butterfly reappeared at the mouth of one tunnel. Quinn didn't know whether to be grateful for the insect's return or annoyed that the stupid thing had abandoned her in the first place.

"You again, huh? Thought you'd gone off and left me," Quinn mumbled under her breath.

As she approached, though, Quinn saw another red flash of light, then another and another until the path was alive with glowing, red butterflies. She was tempted to take one of the glorious creatures home to Riley, but of course that would only encourage the sorts of questions Quinn wouldn't be able to answer. So she settled for following the swarm down yet another path. With any luck, the pool they'd been searching for wouldn't be much farther.

When Quinn finally rounded a bend and came upon the pool, she was unprepared for the majesty of the shimmering water. She stood in awe, watching the perpetual ripple move across the surface like a thousand small tremors. The red glow of the butterflies and the shining white skin of the stalactites and stalagmites took on a silver sheen, and the whole cave seemed to sway in time with the bulb pulsing in Quinn's hand. She sat down on a rock and tried to memorize the space. If she could bring nothing else back, Quinn was determined to describe this room to Riley. She wanted to capture every movement, every color, every flashing, red wing. If Quinn did decide to come back, perhaps her stories would remain somewhere in the recesses of Riley's mind. Perhaps this would be enough to stave the slow collapse of Quinn's own heart, already imploding under the weight of her indecision.

CHAPTER EIGHT

Quinn set the bulb in the center of the fabric she had been using as a rucksack, then folded the corners around the edges until she held a quilted heart in her hands. She noticed again how this heart seemed to grow heavier as she got closer to home, and she wondered if what she felt was her own worry, a physical manifestation of the tightness she felt in her chest. She held this thought in her lungs, shut her eyes, and stepped into the pond. This time, the cocoon-like sensation and raspberry air were familiar. Without the panic she had felt in the garden, Quinn realized that she was able to see and hear and smell after all. Fear must have muted some of her senses, instinctively trying to calm her as she passed between realms.

With the discovery that all her senses were working, Quinn focused on her surroundings. What she saw was beyond anything she had imagined. The sky was blind dark, but white stars streaked across the black in every direction. There were planets too, or at least large balls pinned to the sky, the way planets appeared in her science textbooks. Some were red as the butterflies that had shown her the way home; she saw balls of cyan and marigold and sienna. Every color she could name, and several she couldn't, the entire universe laid out like a painter's palette. Art class rarely held her attention, but she saw in this bridge—if that's what she was looking at—the same wonder that artists throughout time must have seen when they looked out at the world.

The sounds were surreal. Quinn had always heard that

space was completely silent. Perhaps she was not passing through space after all, since the sky around her was anything but quiet. What she heard was unearthly. The stars seemed to hum like the buzz of electricity, but the pitch was higher, and there was harmony in their song. She also heard something like the recordings of tectonic plates shifting at the bottom of the ocean, an almost weary groan, each time she passed one of the enormous balls of color.

She closed her eyes and tried to focus on the raspberry air moving in and out of her body. She felt cold when she inhaled, as though a winter wind was moving right through her. She held her breath until her chest was an empty balloon, then exhaled through her mouth and memorized the taste of the strange atmosphere leaving her. Her arms were pinned to her sides, but Quinn could feel the cocoon expand and collapse with her breathing. She turned all her thoughts to the way the encasing met her skin, soft as the muslin baby blankets her mother used to wrap Riley in before naps.

Quinn remembered asking her mother one afternoon why Riley calmed down when she was wrapped in one of the blankets.

"This is the closest thing to her first home," her mother had explained.

"What do you mean? This *is* her first home."

"No, Quinn. Her first home was here." Quinn's mother put a hand on her belly. "Everyone learns the womb before they learn the rest of the world. When the rest of this," her mother swept a hand through the air, "becomes too much, we instinctively return to the safest place we know."

Quinn must have shown her confusion, because her mother kept explaining.

"Think about the way you sleep, all curled up on your

side, or how you can sit in the bath for hours—those are just some of the ways people imitate being in the womb."

"So Riley thinks she's inside you?"

"Perhaps. Or maybe the blanket just makes her feel connected to something, like she isn't alone. Loneliness is one of the most human conditions. Some of us spend our entire lives trying to fill empty spaces. Whether we're putting a couch in the living room or listening to a song for the hundredth time, the goal is always to feel a little less vacant, a little less hollow."

"Do you feel hollow?"

"No, honey. I have you and Riley."

Even then, Quinn had recognized the way her mother's voice changed when she was lying to them. "You don't miss Dad?"

That was the last thing Quinn remembered saying that day. Her mother had gone silent, as she often did when Quinn asked about her father and, lately, about Riley's heart.

The cocoon peeled down Quinn's body until her limbs were free. She imagined she was an orange, and she felt an invisible pressure wedged between her skin and the cocoon. The parts of her that her clothes didn't cover felt raw, like the skin had been ripped from some other part of her and was suddenly aware of a much larger world. She took a deep breath, pushed against the thin, iridescent edge separating her from the water, and raised her body to the surface. The air stung her face and legs. She checked for the bulb, which she had wrapped and tucked into her jacket pocket with the starfish from Aimee. Quinn looked around and saw that she was back in the butterfly garden. She took another deep breath, then another, basking in the ease with which the air moved down into her lungs.

She was home.

CHAPTER NINE

Her mother and Riley were still asleep when Quinn slipped back into the house. In her room, she checked the clock on her cell phone. She had been in the other realm for at least two days but, according to the screen on the phone, she had been gone for a little less than an hour. Butterfly had burrowed under a blanket at the foot of Riley's bed. Quinn started toward him, but his head rose and he stared at her, holding a low growl in his throat.

"What's wrong, Butterfly?"

Quinn stopped where she was and kneeled, holding her hands out to him.

"Come here, boy."

He didn't budge.

"What's got you spooked?" Quinn pressed, but she stayed as still as she could. She could feel him studying her, deciding whether or not she was a threat to Riley.

After several long minutes, he rose and moved toward her. His steps were cautious, his ears stiff. Quinn could hear him sniffing the air, then her shoes, her pants, her jacket and, finally, her hands.

The moment Butterfly pressed his nose to her cupped palms, Quinn could see his body soften. He nuzzled the crook of her arm, then began licking the knee she had scraped in the cave. Strangely, there was no blood; the skin had closed over the wound and healed completely. Quinn ran her fingers over her knee. Curious, she pressed the tips of her fingers into the skin.

"Ow!"

While the physical signs of her fall had disappeared, the bruise remained, a painful reminder that Quinn was not, in fact, crazy. The other realm had been real.

"What happened?" Riley mumbled, pulling the comforter up to her neck.

"Nothing, kid. Everything's all right. Just knocked my knee into the dresser." Quinn leaned over Riley's bed and kissed her sister on the top of the head. "Go back to sleep," she whispered. She lowered herself onto the ground alongside Riley's bed, watching the blanket rise and fall to the rhythm of her breathing.

When she was convinced Riley had fallen back asleep, Quinn unwrapped the glowing bulb, which she had set on the floor beside her. On the walk home, she had discovered that the bulb was even heavier than she remembered from the cave, and she had decided that the weight must have something to do with the gravity in the other realm. That was the only explanation. The closer she got to home, the heavier the bulb became. She saw that the smooth, rounded edges had also gotten longer, less symmetrical. In fact, Quinn realized, the bulb was now shaped almost exactly like a human heart. She closed her eyes and concentrated on the pulse in her hand, tried to memorize the pattern. What she found filled her with a joy so overwhelming that gooseflesh covered her body. The strange shape was beating in sync with her own heart.

Neither Meelie nor Aimee had known what Quinn was supposed to do once she brought the bulb to Riley, yet Quinn instinctively laid the object down in the space between Riley's chest and arms so that Riley seemed to curl around the glowing orb. As Quinn watched, the red glow grew brighter and brighter until light filled the room. Butterfly whimpered and pushed his head under Quinn's hand, pressing his ribs against her. Riley stirred, but didn't open her eyes. Almost as quickly as the light had come, the glow faded to a pinprick. Quinn moved closer to Riley. She saw that the small wink of red light was coming from Riley's chest, right above her heart. Most would probably mistake the spot for a freckle, but for Quinn the mark was a sudden, impossible point of origin. The beginning of a life without an expiration date. She lingered there, Butterfly tucked under her arm, tracing the sunlight that had started to spill over Riley's face and upper body. In the living room, Quinn could hear her mother reshaping the pillows on the sofa, then the familiar whine of the cedar chest where she stored the throw blankets.

Jane eased down the lid of the cedar chest, so as not to wake the girls. She thought back to the night before, how she and Quinn had huddled on the couch, neither giving voice to the finality of the doctor's words. He had tried to be discreet yesterday when he pulled Jane into the hall, but she had never hidden Riley's condition from Quinn. Sometimes this seemed selfish, leaning on Quinn the way she did, but Jane reminded herself that Quinn had as much right as she did to know how quickly Riley was deteriorating. She knew Quinn well enough to know that, when the time came, she would try to carry Riley's coffin on her own shoulders. She simply wouldn't trust anyone else to bury her sister. Jane was beating back tears again. She tried not to fixate on the inevitable, but the thoughts crept in anytime her mind wandered.

She walked into the kitchen and gathered ingredients for Belgian waffles, naming and renaming each item to push the words *bury* and *coffin* from her head. *Cinnamon. Flour. Sugar. Salt. Baking powder. Eggs. Milk. Vegetable oil. Vanilla. Orange zest.* She knew the recipe by heart. Belgian waffles were Riley's favorite. Jane pulled strawberries and whipped cream from the refrigerator. She mixed the dry ingredients in a bowl until cinnamon tinted the flour a light-rust color, then cracked two eggs and let them drop into the mixture. She used extra vanilla and a spot of maple syrup, but the real secret was the orange peel, which gave the waffles just a hint of French Madeleine. When the iron was hot, she poured batter in and watched the color of the batter change. By the time she heard Quinn and Riley stirring in their room, she had a stack of crisp, golden-brown waffles waiting for them.

"Girls, breakfast!" she shouted down the hall.

"Coming!" Quinn hollered back.

A few moments later, Quinn walked in. She looked exhausted, and Jane wondered again if she depended too much on Quinn to pick up the slack around the house.

"Everything all right, Quinn?"

"Yeah," she yawned. "Just didn't get much sleep."

"Well, dig in. Maybe we'll go for some coffee in a little while." Jane forced a smile. "Then the aquarium?"

"What about Riley?" Quinn asked, dropping one of the waffles onto her plate.

"I guess we'll have to see how she feels this morning. Dr. Howe wants us to stop by again tomorrow, just to check in before you girls go back to school. Today's our last day to do something fun."

"Okay. Are we out of peanut butter *and* syrup?"

"I don't know. Check the pantry."

Quinn went to the pantry and found both on the shelf. She wondered why her mom hadn't pulled them out. Quinn got a butter knife from the utensil drawer and spread a thick layer of peanut butter over her waffle, then drizzled maple syrup on top. She didn't remember when she had first acquired a taste for the odd mixture, but it was one of the few flavors Quinn didn't tire of. She combined the two every chance she got: on toast, bagels, even with celery. She didn't care for most sweets—they were too rich for her—but the peanut butter muted the syrup a bit, and she liked the way the toppings complemented one another.

"You know your father used to do that."

"I know. Who do you think taught me?"

"You were so young. I didn't know you remembered."

"Mom, you've seen me eat waffles a hundred times."

"What's taking Riley so long?" her mother wondered aloud, ignoring Quinn's comment.

"You want me to go get her out of bed?"

"Too late!" Riley said, spinning into the room. She had her robe on, and she twirled in the center of the kitchen, laughing at the way the edges lifted into the air.

"You seem to be feeling better," Jane said.

"Yep! What are we going to do today? Go to the park? See the butterflies?"

"Mom was thinking about the aquarium," Quinn interjected.

"Okay!" Riley grinned.

Quinn watched Riley as she piled sliced strawberries on her waffle, then spooned a small mountain of whipped cream on top.

"Hungry, kid?"

"I guess so. Feels like I haven't eaten all week."

Quinn looked over at her mother, who was studying Riley. The change was too immediate and too drastic to ignore. She could see in her mother's eyes that she didn't trust the sudden burst of energy or Riley's appetite.

"Maybe we should stick close to home. Just in case."

"So the butterfly garden?" Quinn asked.

"That's my favorite!" Riley squealed.

"I know. We all know." Quinn rustled Riley's hair and pinched her cheek.

Jane sat with them at the table, but she didn't eat. She watched Riley. Quinn watched her. As a family, they had learned not to get too comfortable with the good days. Like a roller coaster, Riley's heart could only rise so high before everything bottomed out again.

CHAPTER TEN

On the way to the butterfly garden, Quinn held Riley's hand. Their mother walked a few steps behind, stopping once in a while to admire a neighbor's landscaping or comment on the way a new paint color could make a crumbling home look proud and complete. Riley hadn't stopped chattering since breakfast. Quinn inspected Riley's chest for the glowing red freckle, but she couldn't see anything out of the ordinary in the sunlight. In fact, if Riley hadn't been skipping her way through the morning, Quinn might have forgotten her visit to the other realm. Aimee had been right: life was moving on as though Quinn hadn't been gone at all.

When they arrived at the garden, Riley pulled away and ran down the path toward the pond. Quinn felt a moment of panic, remembering the note she had left in the brush. What would Riley say if she found the envelope, if she learned of Quinn's quiet campaign to keep her alive? Quinn considered trying to retrieve the note before Riley got to the pond, but a small, framed display case in the gift shop window caught her eye. Inside the case, pinned to canvas, was a butterfly with stark-red wings bordered in black. Quinn moved closer to read the handwritten inscription: *Cramer's Mesene, Mexico.*

Quinn entered the gift shop and turned toward the cashier, an older woman with frizzy hair and a steaming cup of Lady Grey tea. Quinn could smell lavender wafting from the woman's cup as she approached.

"Excuse me. Is the display case in the window for sale?"

"Which one are you referring to, hon?"

"The one with the red butterfly. Cramer's something."

"Sure is. You interested?"

"Maybe. Could you tell me more?"

"About the butterfly?"

"Yes."

"Well, the colorings you see are pretty standard. They live down in Central America, I believe."

"I mean, do you know where this one came from? Who caught this one?"

"There may be something on the back of the display. Why?"

"Can you check?" Quinn heard her mother calling for her in the garden. "I'm in a bit of a hurry."

"Sure, hon. No problem." The woman retrieved the case from the window and walked back to the counter. "Says here the butterfly was caught in Mexico City back in the Thirties." She let out a sigh. "Pretty good condition, if you ask me."

"How much?" Quinn asked, fidgeting. Jane called again.

"Just a minute. I'm asking about something I saw in the garden," Quinn shouted from the doorway.

"The tag says $75. Seems a bit steep. I could knock the price down to $60."

"Quinn, come here!" her mother insisted, poking her head into the shop.

She turned back to the garden, the door swinging shut behind her.

"Okay—um, thank you. Sorry. I have to go, I guess," Quinn muttered, shuffling toward the door.

"You sure you don't want me to wrap that case up for you?"

"Another time, maybe. Thanks again," Quinn answered, leaving the gift shop.

She found her mother standing near a fountain, her arms folded across her chest.

"Sorry, mom. Is Riley ready to go already?" she asked, startling her mother, who appeared lost in thought.

"Quinn, does Riley seem—" her mother chewed on her lip.

Quinn could tell that she was searching for the right word, something they both often did when discussing Riley's health. Sometimes one word was the difference between a break down and a celebration.

"Excited?" Quinn suggested.

"I suppose that works. Yes, excited."

"Yeah. She definitely has more energy than she's had in a while."

"Yesterday was a bad one. Do you think she's just bouncing back?"

"I don't know. Could be. But hey, we have to take her in tomorrow anyway, right? Let's just try not to worry today. She deserves a little joy."

Quinn tried to sound hopeful without letting anything about the other realm slip. Her mother would never believe her and, if she were honest with herself, she didn't quite believe Riley's rapid improvement, either. She hadn't expected Riley to heal so quickly or so easily.

"I suppose you're right. Where did Riley run off to?" Her mother stood on her tiptoes and scanned the garden.

"Where she always is, mom. The pond."

Quinn felt a resurgence of panic. What if Riley had found the note while Quinn was fooling around in the gift shop?

"Of course. Would you mind checking on her?"

"Sure." Quinn started to walk away. "Mom?"

"Yes, honey?"

"Riley's going to be okay. All of us are going to be okay."

Her mother offered a forced smile. "Oh, Quinn . . ."

Quinn found Riley as expected, sitting on a rock by the pond. Her eyes darted to Riley's hands, but Riley wasn't holding anything. She exhaled and relaxed her shoulders.

"Think fast," she said, tossing a pebble in Riley's direction.

Riley jerked her head around and snatched the pebble from the air.

"Nice, kid. Your reflexes are getting better!"

Riley threw the pebble back at Quinn. "I feel weird. Remember my breath got short at the park? Today everything is buzzing like when my toothbrush touches my teeth. I can *hear* the butterfly wings. And my chest feels full, sis. My legs won't sit still. I feel like I swallowed a thousand laughs and they're jumping around inside me."

"That's great!"

"I don't know." Riley stared into the water.

"What's wrong, boo?"

"I just—I never really get better. I *feel* better, but I'm *not* better. You know, like how Mom says my body makes that stuff that makes you happy when I get shots or come out of surgery."

"You mean endorphins?"

"Yeah. What if my body is playing a trick on me so I won't know I'm dying?"

Quinn sat down and pulled Riley onto her lap.

"Well, I suppose you'll just die with a smile on your face then, huh?" She dug her fingers into Riley's ribs until they were both buckled over with laughter. They sat together, catching their breath while a colorful array of butterflies flitted around them.

"Ready to go?" Quinn finally asked.

"Yeah. I'm ready, sis."

CHAPTER ELEVEN

The weather was holding, so Jane decided to take the girls for frozen yogurt. They left the butterfly garden, rounded the adjacent museum, and ambled down the grassy expanse on the opposite side. The hill was large and, as usual, filled with an array of tourists and locals all seeking the perfect spot for a few good pictures. Jane could easily spot the tourists, because they rarely had an entourage. Most were couples who had read about the rose garden. They walked hand in hand, pausing every now and then to snap a photograph with their phones. The locals, on the other hand, were usually dressed to the nines. The rose garden had long been a favorite backdrop for senior pictures, family photos, and wedding parties. Halfway down the hill, Jane caught sight of a photographer directing a young couple who appeared to be taking engagement pictures. Each time they posed, the photographer would check the lighting, adjust his camera, inch an elbow up, brush a spiral strand from the woman's face, check the lighting again, then snap a dozen pictures. The couple was wrestling with large, white letters which Jane assumed were their initials. The letters were in stark contrast to the woman's dress, a long, marigold gown with shining gold inlays that matched her skin. When the light hit her just right, the woman disappeared in a shimmering cascade like a sun goddess. The man wore a tuxedo with a gold cummerbund. His nerves got the better of him every time he posed, and Jane couldn't help but laugh along with him and the woman as the photographer tried to loosen his shoulders for the fourth time.

Dread rose from Jane's stomach, pushing the smile from her face. Riley was a child, yet Jane avoided thinking too much about her future. She thought somehow that the inevitable grief would be more manageable if she acknowledged the reality of Riley's short life. Riley would never take engagement pictures, or senior pictures for that matter. The idea settled in her throat and ached. She could feel her eyes begin to water. Maybe the doctors were wrong. Maybe this newfound energy was real. Riley had more color than she'd had in months. She could breathe normally. Who could say whether or not her daughter's heart would heal, anyway? *Anomalies are a part of science*, she told herself. Riley's condition was an anomaly. Somehow the word felt lifeless, an arbitrary label used by scientists and doctors who felt compelled to find reason in the inexplicable. The mothers of dying children were simpler. *Miracle* suited them fine. Miracles didn't need a reason, and, if Riley really was better, Jane wouldn't need one either.

Riley tugged on the sleeve of Jane's jacket. "Mom, can we go to the bakery instead?"

"I suppose we can."

The girls had been asking to try the new bakery for months, one of those artisan shops that's only open for a few hours on weekdays. Normally the girls were in school, and Jane was at work before the bakery opened, and the shop closed before Jane went to lunch.

"Really?" Riley cried out, breaking free of Jane's grasp and hopping up and down. "What do you think they have? Oh my goodness, mom, I'm so hungry. How will I choose? Do you think they have chocolate?" The questions tumbled out of Riley as fast as she could find breath for them.

Jane laughed. "We'll just have to see what they have when we get there."

She looked at Quinn, who had a genuine, bright smile spread across her face. Jane couldn't remember the last time she had seen Quinn *really* smile. Quinn often smirked, or faked smiles for Jane and Riley, but she kept her jaw tight. Jane pretended not to notice, just as Quinn pretended not to notice her own masques. They had become a necessary evil like an old Christmas sweater—something all of them wore to stave another broken holiday.

"Mom?" Quinn whispered, barely audible in the cacophony of the rose garden.

Riley was farther down the hill, and Quinn was trying to get her mother's attention without Riley noticing.

"Yes, honey?"

"About Riley—"

"Quinn, please. Let's not talk about this. Even if her energy is a reason to worry, I want to have this day. I want a memory that doesn't end in tears."

"Okay . . ." Quinn took her mother's hand, grasping it tightly.

Jane pulled her in and Quinn laid her head on her mother's shoulder.

"I love you," Quinn said, but the words were lost to the wind.

They walked the rest of the way in silence. Riley stayed several yards ahead, waving at strangers as they passed, sometimes stopping to pet a dog. When she reached the shop, she turned to her mother and pointed to the door.

"Yes, Riley, you can go in. We're right behind you," her mother called.

"You'd think the kid had never eaten fresh bread," Quinn quipped.

The customer-facing side was remarkably small, with

just enough room for one wrought iron bistro table and two chairs. A planter with two white-and-fuchsia orchids was centered on the table, and a copy of the day's newspaper sat in front of one of the chairs. Most of the walls were periwinkle, but the streetside wall was the color of persimmons.

"What a beautiful contrast," Jane said, running her hand along the accent wall. "Maybe we should do something like this in your room."

"Seriously?" Quinn responded in a tone more pointed than she had intended.

"Why not? Don't you like the colors?"

"The orange one is fine, but you know I hate blue."

"Really? Why?"

"Blues are just . . . depressing."

Quinn was confused. This wasn't anything new. Quinn had hated blue tones since she was old enough to know what the colors were called, especially the darker hues like midnight and cornflower. They were the only colors not included among the kaleidoscopes on her shelf. Quinn's mother had even argued with her father one Christmas after he surprised Quinn with a shiny blue and white tricycle. "She hates the bike," Quinn remembered him saying later that day. "Well what did you expect?" her mother had whispered. "That's her least favorite color. You'd know that if you took the time to talk to her once in a while."

"Didn't you have a blue bike or something? You loved that thing."

What was she talking about? Her mother remembered everything her father had ever done wrong, which Quinn had pointed out to her more than once.

"Welcome to Marie's. Do you have any questions?" the clerk asked as they approached the counter.

"We've never been here before. What do you recommend?" Quinn's mother replied.

"Of course. The fruit galettes are very popular. We have a few peach, one plum, and one cinnamon apple left this morning."

"Oh, the peach sounds nice. How about one of those to share, Quinn?"

"Mom, I'm allergic to peaches. You know that." Quinn's tone was intentionally harsh this time. Forgetting that she hated blue was one thing, but Quinn couldn't even touch the skin of a peach without breaking out in hives. One bite and the whole family would be in the emergency room before lunch.

"Are you?"

"What the hell, mom? Are you on another planet this morning?"

"Check your tone. Now." Her mother's voice was stern.

"I could literally die if I eat peaches!" Quinn shouted, frustrated. "Am I being unreasonable to expect my *mother* to remember the things that could kill me?"

"I want those!" Riley exclaimed, pointing to a pile of teal and baby pink cookie sandwiches.

Quinn turned toward her sister, grateful for the interruption.

"Are you sure, kid? Do you even know what they are?"

"That's our take on whoopee pies. A bit of marshmallow crème between two macaroons," the woman behind the counter answered.

"All right. How about three of those, one of the plum things you mentioned, and—" their mother scanned the glass cases. "—anything else, girls?"

"What's that?" Quinn asked, pointing to a blue-and-purple slice of cake.

"That's our blueberry lavender cake. I have a sample. Would you like to try a bite?"

"Yeah!" Riley interjected.

The woman reached into the case and cut three small squares, placing them on a thin wafer.

"Here you are, one for each of you."

She smiled at Riley, who ate the sample and the wafer in one bite.

"Oh my," their mother gasped.

"We need that. Get that, Mom. Lots of that. Please," Quinn begged.

"Well, I shouldn't. Not with your attitude. But I suppose today is a special day. Let's have three slices of the cake, three of the macaroon sandwiches, and the plum—I'm sorry, what was that one called?"

"A galette."

"Yes. That should do for today."

The woman began bagging the items. "Would you like anything left out of the bag?"

"Can I have my cookie now, Mom?" Riley said, her voice pitched with joy.

"Of course."

The woman handed one of the macaroons to Riley, who plopped down at the bistro table and bit into the cookie. The crisp shell crumbled, forming teal spots at the corners of Riley's mouth.

Quinn laughed, sitting down in the chair next to her. "I think she approves."

Their mother turned to see Riley, now littered with crumbs, licking the marshmallow crème from her fingers. "Geez, Riley. Did you even have time to taste the cookie?"

"Yep!"

Riley ducked Quinn, who was trying to wipe the crumbs from her mouth with a napkin.

"Get over here, kid!" Quinn scolded half-heartedly. "You

look like a rabid pastry fiend." She chased Riley to the door, then out onto the sidewalk. Their mother called after them, probably reminding them to stay out of the street, but neither could hear her over the string of bells still rattling on the bakery door.

The walk home was tranquil. Riley was not so much subdued as enamored by the things they passed. She bent down every fifty yards or so, inspecting a caterpillar on the sidewalk or the yellowed edges of a dying plant. Quinn watched her run her delicate fingers along the underside of a tulip. The careful way Riley's skin met the petal reminded Quinn of how scared she had been when Riley first came home from the hospital. Riley had been so small, just under five pounds, and Quinn was convinced that the slightest touch would break her in two. Her mother had asked time and again if Quinn wanted to hold her, but Quinn was content to lie next to Riley in their mother's bed, stroking her baby sister's head, just as Riley was now stroking the flowers, as if she were convinced that a heavy hand would ruin all the beautiful things in the world.

The sisters played in their room while their mother prepared dinner in the kitchen. Quinn had been back nearly twelve hours, and Riley showed no signs of slowing down. Whatever the glowing bulb had done to Riley's heart, Quinn saw a side of her sister that she hadn't seen since before Riley started school. She tried to catalog all the changes she'd noticed just in case Riley fell off again, in case Quinn had to go back to the other realm. She made mental notes: the lightness of Riley's laugh, the pink tint in her cheeks, the pitch of her voice, the strength of her hugs, the sheer number of hugs, the way she spun in circles to make her dress billow, Quinn's name in her mouth, the new red freckle over her heart.

Scientists will tell you that what make up a human are a series of genes twisted into a ladder, but Quinn knew better. What makes a human is the carousel of memories you leave behind. Life isn't as short as people pretend. The end of a life has nothing to do with coffins and dirt and beating hearts; the end of life is a forgotten face, a voice that no longer has sound. Quinn understood this, and she made a promise to herself that she would never let the most human parts of Riley slip from her. She would keep Riley alive one or way or another.

CHAPTER TWELVE

Friday was the last day to visit Dr. Howe for a brief check-up before the girls went back to school and Jane went back to work. Jane and Quinn watched Riley closely during the weeklong break, hesitant to accept the energetic and carefree person who had manifested over the past couple days. Ironic, Jane thought, that she had spent the last two years wishing Riley would bounce back, only to distrust the recovery when she did. Jane wondered if she would ever be able to look at Riley without seeing a coffin too small to hold all her daughter had become. How was a mother supposed to carry all this?

Jane sighed, then went to her bedroom door and called down the hall. "Quinn, Riley—time to get moving! We've got an appointment with Dr. Howe in an hour!"

Jane folded the robe over her body. Gooseflesh rose on her skin where the water clung. Jane walked to the bathroom where steam still filled the room like an early morning fog. *Funny*, she thought. The brain and the daylight both seemed to wake up in a haze. Of course she had coffee to help her along. She picked up her mug from the counter, laughing at the blue and pink words printed inside, just below the brim: *YOU'RE MY FAVORITE UNICORN.* Quinn had given her the mug for Christmas several years ago, a tradition that had begun almost by accident. Though the mug had a thin crack stretching down one side and a small chip in the handle, the gift remained Jane's favorite.

Jane finished getting ready, then went to the pantry to

gather food for the girls. They wouldn't have time for breakfast, so she pulled two energy bars from a box and set them on the counter. She had picked up a few opal apples from the farmers market. She washed two of them, one for her and one for the girls, then used the apple slicer to split each of them into eight even pieces. Riley would want almond butter with hers, so she spooned a little into a small Tupperware and snapped the lid shut. She placed all the food into a paper bag and hurried the girls along with another shout down the hall.

Jane laughed at the girls, both half asleep, as they stumbled into the kitchen.

"Did you brush your teeth?"

"Yes, mother," Quinn grumbled.

"Riley?"

"Yep."

"All right. I've got some food to eat in the car. Grab a drink if you want one."

Quinn opened the refrigerator and stared into the light as though the shelves were covered in math equations. After a few moments, she reached for a caramel Frappuccino.

"Get me a Yoohoo!" Riley said, her voice startling Quinn.

"Yes, ma'am," Quinn responded, sliding a yellow box from the back of the refrigerator. She started to hand the box to Riley, then thought better of the idea. "Better let me put the straw in for you. I'll give you the drink in the car."

The three of them filed out the door and to the car, where Quinn elected to ride in the backseat with Riley. She would have an easier time helping Riley with her breakfast that way, but the decision was not without sacrifice. Being so far from the radio meant that their mother would get to choose what they listened to during the drive. This usually meant that the girls were subjected to a TED Talk or an audiobook.

Quinn pushed a thin, white straw through the foil covering on Riley's box of Yoohoo.

"Remember not to squeeze the box, kid. You'll get milk all over yourself."

Of course there wasn't any actual milk in the box. Quinn chuckled at the blue lettering that proclaimed Yoohoo a "chocolate drink," a perfectly ambiguous designation that only worked because few kids were discerning enough to question what was in their favorite foods.

Riley took the box and began sipping while Quinn dug through the paper bag. The apples would be hardest to eat in the waiting room, so Quinn pulled them out and set them on the console between her and Riley. She then pulled the Tupperware from the bag, unsnapped the lid and set the almond butter in one of the cupholders on the console. She dipped an apple slice into the almond butter, then bit into the fruit. The sweet crispness of the apple was perfectly complemented by the creamy saltiness of the almond butter.

"Thanks for remembering the almond butter, Mom," Quinn called up to her mother.

"Oh, do you like them with almond butter, too?" their mother replied. "I didn't realize. I hope I packed enough for you both."

"Duh. I'm the one who showed Riley how good almond butter tastes on apples."

Quinn rolled her eyes at her mother, trying to mask her worry. Her mother had been forgetting things ever since Quinn returned from the other realm. At first Quinn had tried to explain away the memory loss, but the lapses were getting harder to ignore. Was this what Aimee meant when she said that things would be different?

The girls finished their apples and started in on the energy bars, each staring out her window, trying to ignore the audiobook their mother had chosen for the ride. The narrator's voice was nasally, though, and Quinn had a hard time blocking out the sound. Their mother preferred smaller streets to the major roadways since the busier roads were constantly under construction. This morning she wove through a side street with a private golf course on one side, sprawling houses with stucco walls and terra-cotta roof tiles on the other. The grass was overgrown, brushing against the side of the car whenever they passed a sharp bend in the road. Quinn thought the way this particular street snaked through the city center, despite the near-perfect grid that the city planners had designed, was wonderfully ironic.

She had begun to notice the patterns that the city used to help people navigate. She saw that streets moving laterally, west to east and vice versa, followed a chronological sequence, decreasing as they approached downtown and increasing as they moved toward the neighboring town. The streets running north to south and vice versa were laid out alphabetically, so Quinn could anticipate the first letter of each street as they approached. This made remembering the street names a little easier. Currently, they were moving east on Sixty-First Street toward Yale Avenue, where the pediatric hospital sat atop a hill overlooking one of the larger parks in the city.

Quinn had virtually memorized the various routes her mother took to get to the hospital, yet she seemed to notice something new each time. *Distraction is a powerful thing*, she thought. Pushing one thing from the mind set her senses on edge until every sound, every color popped like an overexposed photograph.

At the doctor's office, she flipped through *Brown Bear, Brown Bear* for the eighth time. Her mother and Riley had been with Dr. Howe for more than an hour. She tried not to be concerned, but she had been to enough appointments to know that Dr. Howe was seeing something he didn't expect. Riley's checkups rarely took more than fifteen or twenty minutes. Had the bulb healed her? Would their mom know that Quinn had done something? She was usually wary of Riley's good days. Being even more suspicious if Riley showed unexpected improvement just made sense.

"Quinn? Quinn Willow?"

The voice yanked Quinn from her thoughts. She looked up to see a woman in teal scrubs standing in the doorway between the waiting room and the patient rooms.

"Yes, I'm Quinn."

"Your mother is asking for you. I'll show you to her." The woman smiled, and Quinn fixated on the hot-pink smudge across the woman's front teeth.

Quinn rose, walking deliberately slower than usual. Whatever had taken Dr. Howe so long, Quinn was sure that the news would be bad for Riley. She shuffled behind the nurse, who moved swiftly through the corridor and stopped so abruptly that Quinn nearly ran into her.

"Quinn!" she heard her mother shout from inside the room. "I'm so sorry we took so long, honey. Come in!" Jane's voice sounded excited—the bulb must have worked! Quinn tried to hide her joy, pushing her eyebrows low and opening her mouth slightly, the way her theater teacher had taught her. She must have worn her confusion well, because her mother began rambling, the words pouring from her high-pitched and frantic.

"Oh, you just won't believe what Dr. Howe found, Quinn. Wait'll you hear. Riley's heart—he used a stethoscope, but he couldn't hear anything—Riley's heart is . . . *better*—that technician, oh, what's his name—the ultrasound didn't show any stenosis—"

"Mom, slow down," Quinn interjected. "You're not making any sense."

Her mother stopped speaking and took a breath. "Riley's heart shows no signs of stenosis."

"What does that mean?"

"She's better."

Dr. Howe entered the room carrying several papers that resembled the ultrasound Quinn had watched after Riley was born; something was different about them. Quinn studied the black-and-white masses, the bits of red and blue, but she couldn't pinpoint the difference. Dr. Howe began to explain, marking on the printouts as he spoke.

"With Riley's heart, we're used to seeing this narrow area here," Dr. Howe gestured, drawing a black circle around one part of the white mass, "fail to siphon oxygenated blood into the bloodstream, allowing the blood to move back into the heart. Each of the valvuloplasties widened the area so that the blood would flow out into the bloodstream properly. Unfortunately, the walls of the heart thicken as Riley ages, and the last procedure was unsuccessful. That's why you noticed Riley struggling more and more to catch her breath. Now, normally I'm able to listen to the blood flow and identify the severity of the prolapse—that is the amount of oxygenated and unoxygenated blood mixing—but today I wasn't able to hear anything out of the ordinary. We checked Riley's heart with the ultrasound, and that confirmed that the passage has somehow widened enough to filter the blood normally."

"How is that possible?" Jane asked. "I watched the ultrasound and I saw the pictures, but hearts just don't . . . *get better*, do they?"

"What I see on the screen is a healthy heart. That much I know. As far as how the heart healed, I'm as confused as you are."

Quinn had been studying the pictures, trying to discern what was different about them.

"The purple!" she exclaimed. "There's no purple in these pictures!"

"That's right," Dr. Howe said, turning to Quinn. "Just two days ago she was showing major blowback struggling to move into the bloodstream. Now, for whatever reason, everything is simply normal."

Riley had been sitting on her mother's lap, tracing the seams between floor tiles as though she were looking for some escape from the dizzying conversation. When she spoke, her voice was small and full of air.

"Does this mean I'm—I'm not going to die?"

Dr. Howe's jaw tightened. He furrowed his brow, his face suddenly much darker than usual. "That's a difficult question. What I see is a healthy heart. What I know is that conditions like yours don't just correct themselves. There's no way for me to tell you how your heart will grow and if the degeneration will return."

"But—*right now*, I'm okay?" Riley pushed.

"Yes, right now you appear to be perfectly healthy."

Riley turned to her mother. "So, I'm going to turn seven? I get to have another birthday?"

Their mother opened her mouth to respond, but she burst into tears before she could speak. She tightened her embrace around Riley, pulling Quinn to them with her free hand. The three of them cried together, and Quinn realized that, for the first time, she and her mother were letting Riley see their grief. They had spent the better part of her life mourning in private, after Riley had gone to bed. Then she recognized that they weren't crying out of grief at all. After almost seven years, what they shared was pure, unbridled joy.

CHAPTER THIRTEEN

The ride home was quiet. Not the uncomfortable way people paused their conversations in elevators or the haunting silence of a school hallway after a student passes away—more like the way air seems to vibrate after a lightning strike. Quinn kept her eyes closed, focusing all of her energy on the absence of Riley's labored breathing. She had become so accustomed to the ragged gasps that the car felt empty, as though they had left a part of the family in Dr. Howe's office. She rode shotgun and felt safe in the front seat. More importantly, she felt like Riley was safe on her own. Quinn had protected Riley since her sister was old enough to crawl. What would she do now that Riley was better? She hadn't considered what being a big sister meant beyond taking care of Riley and making sure she never felt alone.

Quinn and Riley returned to school the following Monday, and their mother went back to work. The three settled into their routine, with one noticeable difference: Riley had energy in the evenings, so she and Quinn busied themselves by going for walks, visiting the park, and wandering through the butterfly garden until dinner was ready. Riley had become adamant about bathing herself almost overnight, which Quinn appreciated at first, but after a few nights she realized how much she relied on her time with Riley. She suggested that Riley practice reading her chapter books out loud while Quinn followed along, which Riley also refused. Most sisters long for their younger siblings to become more independent; Quinn wasn't most sisters. Riley no longer needed Quinn, and Quinn felt lost without someone to look after. Even her mom, who had leaned on Quinn so heavily the past year, didn't have much time for her; she had taken up reading again, too, something Quinn hadn't seen her do in several years. The house, which had so often felt more like a hospital than a home, was finally at peace. Everything was right in the world. Everything except Quinn.

Between her annual state tests and Riley's drastic improvement over the last month, Quinn had all but forgotten about Aimee and Meelie until her English teacher introduced their last major assignment before summer.

"You will all complete a research project to close out the year. Each student will select a historical figure from the jar on my desk. You'll need to learn enough about your historical figure to impersonate them at an after-school event."

Screw this, Quinn thought. *Why did teachers always have presentations at the end of the year?*

"You will interact with parents and answer their questions as part of your grade—"

Quinn tried to tune out her teacher and focus on the assignment sheet in front of her. Though she loathed presentations, there was a bright spot: research was one of her favorite pastimes. According to her mother, she had been curious since the day she was born. She also preferred working alone since Riley's condition often required spontaneous doctor's visits. Of course, Riley hadn't been to the doctor or had any trouble with strenuous activity in almost two months.

"Quinn!" the girl next to her whispered, forcing the air from her lungs so that the sound exited like a sharp, ethereal slap.

Quinn stared at the girl. Her face was familiar. Emmy,

maybe? They had shared at least one class every year since
first grade, but Quinn had long since accepted that she didn't
have space in her life for friends. Most people spoke to her
with a sympathetic lilt that grated on her anyway.

The girl flicked her thumb toward the teacher's podium
and made her eyes wide.

"Ms. Willow," the teacher said sternly.

Quinn looked up to see her teacher holding out the jar.
She walked to the front and drew a folded slip of paper,
then returned to her seat. She waited until the other students
turned their attention back to the teacher, then read the
words: *Amelia Earhart, pilot.* The name sounded familiar.

She thumbed the teleidoscope around her neck as she
cycled through where she might have heard of Earhart. Instinctively, she raised the tube to her eye and peered into
the lens. She often stared into the vast mulberry expanse to
calm herself. Something about the juxtaposition of a wide,
dust-colored section and the pair of dim circles hanging in
the corners gave her peace.

Quinn's teacher flicked off the lights and began lectur-
ing. Quinn searched for the light from the projector, aim-
ing the teleidoscope toward the bulb until the picture
inside the tube brightened. Then Quinn saw something
she hadn't noticed or, at the very least, didn't remember:
moving through the sandy semicircle at the bottom was
a small, white speck. When Quinn squinted, the mysterious
object took shape. She was staring at Meelie's hen. The
rest of the scene began to manifest into a single, concrete
image: the exact spot where Quinn had entered the other
realm.

"How was school?" Quinn's mother asked when she and Riley returned from their usual walk.

"Fine," Quinn shrugged.

"Well, don't talk my ear off," her mother chided.

Quinn pulled plates and cups from the cabinet. "There's nothing much to say. Classes are winding down. Teachers are tired. Students are tired. We're all just counting the days to summer."

"So no homework?"

"A little. I have to do some research for English."

"What about?"

"Some woman from the Great Depression. A pilot or something."

"I always wondered what flying would be like. I used to pretend to be a pilot when I was Riley's age, running around the backyard with goggles and a bicycle helmet strapped to my head."

"That's pretty lame, Mom." Quinn spooned taco meat into hard shells for herself and Riley. "Riley, come eat!" she called toward their room.

"Okay! Coming!"

Riley entered the room wearing purple fairy wings and wielding a multicolored plastic wand. "Look what I found in the closet!"

Their mother laughed. "I don't think I've seen you wear those since you were maybe two or three. I didn't know we still had them."

"What are you supposed to be?" Quinn asked, tousling Riley's hair and sliding her chair close to the table.

"I'm a butterfly. Duh."

"Then what's the wand for, genius?"

"Magic." Riley stretched the last syllable, rolling her eyes.

"Geez. Someone's feisty tonight," Quinn smirked. She sat down next to Riley. "You eating, mom?"

Their mother usually picked at dinner as she cooked,

but Quinn couldn't remember the last time she had seen her mother eat a full meal.

Her mother shrugged and slid into the empty seat at the head of the table.

During dinner, Quinn explained the assignment, emphasizing the torturous nature of the presentation. Riley thought that meeting all the historical characters sounded like a lot of fun, and Quinn immediately began plotting how she might convince her teacher to let Riley play the part. Maybe Earhart had a sister, too. If so, Quinn could make a case for adding Riley to the presentation. That would at least make for a more entertaining night. Quinn made a mental note to investigate Earhart's family history first thing in the morning.

After Riley had gone to bed, Quinn's mother called her to the living room.

"Riley's birthday is next month. Has she mentioned anything to you about a party or something she wants to do? Any friends at school that she talks about?"

"Not really. I think all of us have tried not to think about Riley turning seven for so long that the possibility just doesn't seem real."

"I suppose that's true."

"Don't you have to invite her whole class anyway?"

"Yes, that's the school's policy. If we invite anyone, we have to invite everyone."

Jane looked past Quinn, absentmindedly tearing at her cuticles. She began to speak, reconsidered, then tried again.

"Do you—what happens if—all those kids—what would we tell them?"

Quinn put her hands over her mothers, then pulled her into an embrace. She didn't need to speak. They had shared this silence too many times. The only thing heavier than grief is hopelessness, and Jane had given up hope a long time ago.

"You know, Quinn, you might be the only real friend she has."

Quinn frowned.

"She could do worse," her mother added.

"What are you getting her?" Quinn asked, trying to change the subject.

Jane bit the inside of her cheek. "I hadn't given a present much thought. I guess I've been scared to."

Quinn sighed. "I suppose you're right." She paused long enough to convince her mother that she, too, was fearful of Riley's recovery, then told her about the framed butterfly at the museum.

". . . some Central American variety with bright red and black wings. The price is a little high, but the clerk said she would work with me."

"What gave you that idea?"

"Oh, nothing," Quinn lied. "I just like the colors."

They sat for a while longer before Quinn excused herself to begin her homework.

"I'll talk to Riley about her birthday tomorrow, see if she wants anything special."

"Be sly," Jane called.

The anguish in her voice hollowed Quinn.

The next morning, Quinn rushed straight to the school library. She sat away from other students and hurriedly typed *Amelia Earhart* into the search engine. Quinn scanned an article describing her disappearance during an attempt to fly around the world, anxious to find a photograph and confirm her suspicions.

Quinn clicked on a link just below the name, which took her to an archived article from July 3, 1937, reporting

Earhart's disappearance. What she saw made her gasp. The newspaper photograph was grainy and small, but the flight cap was unmistakable. There, on the front page of the *Wichita Beacon*, was Quinn's friend from the other realm. Meelie. That's why the name Amelia had sounded so familiar! Amelia Earhart, a woman whose mysterious disappearance spawned everything from conspiracy theories to worldwide searches, and Quinn knew exactly where to find her.

She was just about to close out of the article when something else caught her eye: Earhart had a younger sister, Pidge, and the two had been inseparable as kids. But that didn't make sense; Meelie had told Quinn that she hadn't had any reason to leave the other realm. Why would she lie about having a sister? Maybe they had a fight. *Or maybe she died before Meelie left on her last flight,* Quinn thought. But why name her hen after her baby sister? Just then, the warning bell jarred her from her mind. She stuffed her notebook into her backpack and rushed from the library, already counting the hours until she could sneak back to the other realm.

CHAPTER FOURTEEN

Quinn was distracted for the rest of the day. She had dozens of questions she wanted to ask Meelie, like why she hadn't mentioned Pidge, or why she had told Quinn that she didn't have any reason to go home. Something didn't add up, and Quinn was determined to get to the bottom of Meelie's obfuscation. The best time to disappear was overnight when no one would notice, so she would have to wait for her mother and Riley to go to bed before sneaking off to the butterfly garden. Quinn didn't fully understand yet how time worked in the other realm. Aimee had tried to tell her more about passing between the two realms, but Quinn had interrupted her. Not that anything Aimee could have said would have mattered; Quinn was determined to find Meelie. She had been so evasive about her past, and for good reason if she had chosen to abandon her little sister for a giant chicken that couldn't fly and glowing butterflies.

During dinner, Jane asked how the research project was going.

Quinn prevaricated. "Haven't found much yet. The wireless network at school is so slow."

"I suppose you may have to do some of the research here, then," her mother suggested.

"Maybe. I still have a couple of weeks. I did find that she had a kid sister named Pidge, though."

"Pidge?" Riley laughed. "What kind of a name is Pidge?"

"That wasn't her real name, silly. Pidge was a nickname she used with her family."

"How come I don't have a nickname?" Riley asked.

"You used to, when you were a baby," their mother chimed in. "Didn't stick, though."

"Tell me!"

"Toast," Quinn said, laughing.

"Huh?" Riley looked perplexed.

"Toast. That was your nickname."

"Why?"

"You used to love toasted rye bread with butter. You'd end up covered in butter and crumbs every time. You looked rabid," their mother said, stifling a laugh. "Of course that was just a phase. You forgot all about toast the Easter we let you try a bite of a chocolate bunny."

"What about Quinn? Does she have a nickname, too?"

Jane chewed her lip for a moment, then shook her head. "Nothing comes to mind."

Quinn stared at her mom in disbelief. "Really? You forgot already?" She pushed herself away from the table and sulked to her bedroom, easing the door closed and burying herself in the comforter on her bed. The rules of the other realm had been lingering at the edge of her thoughts since her return, but now they forced themselves to the front of her mind. This must be how people feel when someone they love gets dementia or Alzheimer's, she thought, except for one excruciating difference: Quinn was the ailment, bringing the amnesia that was spreading through her life.

Riley asked Quinn to give her a bath while their mother cleaned up the kitchen. Quinn wasn't in the mood, but the truth was that she missed bathing Riley. Hearing that her sister seemed to miss their time together too made her momentarily forget why she was angry.

"Will you tell me a story before bed? Please?" Riley begged.

"We'll see." Quinn hadn't told her a story in nearly a month. She was excited to hear that Riley wanted to hear one again, but her curiosity about Meelie was growing. She could hardly conceal her urgent desire to revisit the other realm.

Riley clapped her hands together, splashing water onto the bathmat.

"I said maybe! Now be careful—you're getting me all wet!"

Quinn's expression betrayed her tone and Riley splashed again, soaking Quinn's pant leg.

"Oh, you're going to pay for that, kid."

Quinn reached into the bath and pressed her fingertips into Riley's rib. Riley lurched, laughing hysterically. Before long, Quinn was as wet as Riley.

"What's all the commotion, girls?" their mother asked, poking her head into the bathroom.

Both girls pointed to each other and said, "She splashed me first!"

Quinn and Riley laughed again, both turning to attack their mother, who ducked back into the hall to avoid getting drenched.

"Okay, okay. Call a truce and get ready for bed!"

The two girls collapsed in a fit of laughter. Quinn calmed herself and reached for the shampoo. Riley was plenty old enough to wash her own hair, but she enjoyed having Quinn massage her scalp when she was willing. Once Quinn had finished scrubbing Riley's head, she handed her sister a tooth-brush and toothpaste.

"Better hurry up if you want a story, kid," she chided.

While Riley brushed her teeth, Quinn went to retrieve the robe and towel she had tumbled in the dryer. They were still warm, just as Riley liked them.

"Spoiled brat," Quinn muttered, laughing.

Once Riley was in bed, Quinn pulled the covers to her chin. She went around the room, tossing dirty clothes into the hamper and clearing the floor of toys before flicking off the light. Riley pressed the foot on her pillow pet, a multicolored penguin that glowed. Quinn turned on the night-light, and the ceiling lit up with constellations. This was one of the few compromises the girls had made in sharing a room: Riley couldn't sleep when the room was too dark, and Quinn couldn't sleep when the room was too bright. Since Quinn had long been enamored with stars, their mother found a night-light that projected the entire Milky Way galaxy onto the ceiling.

"Story time," Riley demanded. Her voice was shallower than in recent weeks. Quinn started to dismiss the change as a sign of exhaustion, but then she noticed that the red freckle above Riley's heart had begun to fade.

"You feeling okay?" she asked, trying to mask her concern.

"Yep. A little tired, I guess, but I'm okay."

"You're sure?" she pressed.

"I'm fine," Riley insisted.

Quinn told herself that she was just being paranoid and settled onto the foot of Riley's bed, pulling the covers over her feet and calves. She wanted to share the other realm with her sister, but she knew that she couldn't come right out and tell Riley about the bulb or the new heart. Of course, if Riley's breathing really was a sign that her new heart was already failing, Quinn would have to leave her sister for the other realm very soon. Maybe, she hoped, these bedtime stories would stay with Riley even after Quinn had gone away.

"This is the story of two sisters—"

"Like us?"

"Sort of, except that these sisters lived in a place with no sun."

"How did they see?"

"Well, there were two bright moons, and everything in the land glowed."

"You mean the animals?"

"Yes, and even Dot, one of the sisters. Instead of a heart like we have, she had a red spot on her chest that glowed whenever she felt happy. But one day, the other sister, Grit, saw that the red spot wasn't glowing anymore."

"Why?"

"Because Dot was very tired. She slept all day and all night. Grit was worried, so she went to ask a wise woman who lived in a cave what to do, but the wise woman didn't know, and she sent Grit to the ocean."

"Why?"

"There was an even wiser woman who lived there, except she couldn't step foot on land, or she would melt away. Grit had to swim out to her and ask her how to help Dot."

"What did she say?"

"She said that if the spot on Dot's chest disappeared, she would die, and Grit was the only one who could help her. Saving her wouldn't be easy, though. You see, Grit would have to go far, far away to find the medicine for Dot. The healing place was so far away that as soon as she got some medicine back to Dot, she would have to leave to go get more."

"For how long?"

"Forever. For as long as she lived, Grit would have to journey back and forth. If she stayed with her sister for even one night, Dot would die before Grit could get more medicine. Grit didn't want to leave her family, but she loved her sister more than anything, and she knew she was the only one who could save her. So that's what she did."

"Quinn, that's a sad story!"

"I suppose so."

"You should fix the ending so the sisters can be together."

"Not every story has a happy ending. What Grit did is called a sacrifice, and sometimes one person has to make a decision like that so someone they love can be happy."

"Well I don't have to like sacrifice," Riley pouted.

Quinn put her hand over Riley's and drew in a long breath. "Riley, if you—I mean, if you had the choice . . ." Quinn paused, trying to organize the words swirling inside her. "If you could go someplace where you wouldn't be sick anymore, would you go?"

"Duh. I don't like being sick all the time."

"What if—what if Mom couldn't go with you?"

"Why wouldn't Mom come? Is she sad at me again? Does she want me to go away?"

"No, no, no. I'm just—hypothetically—"

"*Hypowhat?*"

"Pretend," Quinn answered, more sharply than she intended. "If you could not be sick anymore, but you had to leave Mom, would you go?"

"I don't think so," Riley said. "Mom would be sad, and I wouldn't know anyone."

"What if Mom wouldn't remember?"

"Why wouldn't she remember? Is something wrong with Mom?"

"Nothing is wrong, Riley. I just—if I found a place where your heart would be okay, and mom wouldn't be sad about us leaving, would you want to live there?"

"You mean like a sacrifice? Like Grit?"

"Kind of, yes."

Riley shifted under the comforter. She started to speak, then turned away from Quinn.

"I don't want to talk about this anymore. We're a family. All of us. I don't want to think about one of us not being here. I—"

"It's okay, boo," Quinn interrupted. "I didn't mean to upset you. Go to sleep. You'll feel better in the morning."

Quinn leaned over and kissed Riley on the forehead, hoping that Riley couldn't feel the wet streaks on her cheeks. She rose from the bed, grabbing a hoodie on her way out of the room. As soon as her mother was asleep, she would sneak back to the butterfly garden, back to the other realm.

CHAPTER FIFTEEN

"Going somewhere?" Jane asked, seeing Quinn exit the girls' bedroom with a hoodie in hand. She could see Quinn's grip on the jacket tighten.

"What? No, just picking up a little," Quinn said, her voice thready and high-pitched.

Jane watched Quinn walk to the hall closet and hang the hoodie on an empty hook. She knew that Quinn was hiding something, but decided to not to push. Instead, she played along.

"Oh, that's great. I haven't had a chance to clean up the kitchen. Would you mind putting the food away so I can get started on the dishes?"

"Sure," Quinn shrugged, glancing at the front door before going into the kitchen.

Jane continued to watch as Quinn pulled plastic containers from the cabinet and shovel the remaining food from each pot into a separate dish. She clicked the lids shut, then placed them in the refrigerator.

"Anything else, Mom?"

The question startled Jane a bit. Quinn was helpful with Riley, but she rarely volunteered for chores on school nights.

"Don't you have some research to do?"

"Yeah, but I can do that later."

"Are you sure, honey? I don't want you to be up all night."

"I won't, Mom. Promise," Quinn replied, raising her right hand as though taking an oath. "I'm sure you're tired too. What else needs to be done?"

Jane thought for a moment. "Well, the towels are about finished. They'll need to be folded and put away so they don't get that musty smell from the dryer."

"No problem. I can take care of that while you wash dishes."

"Thanks. You're a big help, you know."

"Just trying to make things a little easier for you."

"I love you," Jane said, pulling Quinn into her arms and kissing her on the head. Jane hadn't noticed, but Quinn was nearly as tall as she was. In another few months, she thought, she'd be eye to eye with her daughter.

"Love you too, Mom." Quinn pulled away from her mother and went to retrieve the towels from the dryer, which had begun to buzz loudly.

Quinn carried the basket of warm towels to the living room, where she folded each one as precisely as she could, first in half long ways, then into thirds along the folded edge. Her mom wasn't particular about how the towels were folded; Quinn, on the other hand, couldn't stand to see a stack of towels hanging over the edge of the shelf in the bathroom she shared with Riley. As she folded, Quinn listened for the start of the dishwasher, which would signal that her mother had gone to bed. The grandfather clock in the living room chimed ten, then eleven. She had folded all the towels and put them away, but she still heard nothing from the kitchen to indicate that her mom had gone to bed. She tiptoed toward her mother's room to check to see if she had slipped into bed while Quinn was in the bathroom. Sure enough, the kitchen was dark, and Quinn didn't see any light coming from beneath her mother's bedroom door. She pressed her ear to the door and listened. Total silence. Her chest thumped, and she felt dizzy with excitement. She tiptoed back toward the hall closet, took her jacket from the hanger, and eased open the front door.

The night air was thick, sticking in Quinn's throat like a wrong answer. The moon was full, which lit her path to the butterfly garden. She felt an inexplicable sense of dread warring with her excitement, as though she had become the flag at the center of a rope, with her family on one end and the other realm on the other. The closer Quinn got to the butterfly garden, the more at peace she felt. *If this were a game*, she thought, *the butterfly garden would be the taped off square in the middle, the point of perfect balance between this life and the other realm.* The thought relaxed Quinn's shoulders and Quinn sensed that a riddle had just become clear. *Riley is the flag, not me. I'm the rope, the only thing connecting Riley to the other realm.* Or was she? Quinn recalled a field day in fifth grade when the tug-of-war had been called a draw after she and her friends had pulled the rope until it split in two. Her face mimicked the shadows at the edge of the garden, and she wondered how long before she broke herself.

Once at the pond, Quinn zipped her jacket, took a deep breath, and jumped feetfirst into the water. This time she crossed her arms over chest in an X with each hand gripping the opposite shoulder. That was how she had learned to enter the water without making a splash. In this instance, Quinn discovered, she moved between the realms much faster. She also hit the cracked ground harder, knocking the wind from her chest. She gasped for air without thinking, causing her to choke and cough uncontrollably. Thankfully Quinn had stuffed a bottle of water into her jacket pocket. She took a long gulp, then closed her eyes and tried to slow her heart. This time, her breaths were deliberately shallow, allowing her to fill her lungs without drawing too much of the atmosphere into her mouth or nose.

The moons were beginning to rise. Quinn knew that navigating the other realm would be difficult in the dim night. She looked around, getting her bearings. She saw small pulses of red and yellow at the edge of the horizon. Hoping that the light was from fires inside the cave, Quinn started toward them. Riding with Meelie on the giant chicken had been swift, if a little unbelievable, but she struggled to cross the desert on foot. Her heart started to race as she realized that she wouldn't get to the cave before the night overtook her. She was dizzy. Her chest burned, and her legs were heavy. Even her eyes had begun to water. Just as Quinn started to panic, a stream of indigo butterflies swarmed around her. The light from their wings was mesmerizing. Unable to think or see clearly, Quinn wandered with the insects as if she were bobbing in a stream. Some of the butterflies landed on her arms and shoulders, while others flitted a few inches in front of her face.

She tried to focus on their wings, but she couldn't keep her eyes open. She stumbled, bracing herself for another hard landing, but none came. Instead, her stomach lurched like when she rode roller coasters. Quinn stretched out her hands, searching for the ground, but she felt only air. She couldn't get any footing, either. Her body leaned forward, somehow frozen midfall, but Quinn was sure that she was still moving forward. She forced her eyes open and saw that she was ten or twenty feet off the ground. She was, in fact, bobbing in a fantastic river of butterflies. As they carried her along, Quinn succumbed to exhaustion. When she woke, she found herself at the mouth of the cave.

Everyone inside was asleep, so Quinn picked her way through the people as quietly as she could, straining to make out their faces as she passed. She noticed a group of children huddled together in a far corner. Strangely, they were the only ones in the cavern who hadn't gathered around a fire. Next to them, Quinn saw Meelie's hen. A little farther off, Meelie slept beside a small patch of burning wood. Each time the bark popped, the youngest girl in the huddle of children jumped and buried her face in the oldest girl's back.

Meelie didn't seem to notice Quinn, who was still trying not to wake anyone as she approached. When she passed Pidge, though, the hen turned and gave a loud squawk. This roused two of the children, who turned and smiled groggily at Quinn. She waved at them, and they beckoned her over. She tiptoed toward them before kneeling down to introduce herself.

"I'm Betty," the younger girl, who Quinn guessed was about five years old, responded. "That's Martha," she continued, pointing to the other girl, "my older sister."

"Oh, wow. So you—did you both—"

"Die? Heavens, no. Though folks sure tried to tell mama and papa that for some time," Martha answered.

"We come through when someone set our house on fire," Betty jumped in.

"How many of you are there?" Quinn asked.

"Five of us here, five back home. 'Course we don't hear much about 'em, so I can't say if they're still alive."

Martha looked a few years younger than Quinn, but she recognized the anguish in Martha's voice, the sort of grief that makes a home in the body.

"How long have you been here?" Quinn asked. Remembering her first conversation with Meelie, she told them what year it was.

"Well, I'll be. I suppose this is our seventieth anniversary then."

"You've been here for seventy years? All five of you?"

Betty nodded. Martha looked like she was near tears. She

pinched the bridge of her nose and straightened up. "Well enough about us. How did you come through?"

Quinn told them about the letters and the butterfly house and how Meelie had come across her in the desert her first time in the other realm.

"First time? You mean, you've been through more than once?" Betty's eyes sparkled with curiosity. She moved closer to Quinn, staring at her the way Quinn sometimes stared at her math homework.

"Yes," Quinn responded with hesitation.

"I wish I could go home even for a minute, just to say goodbye to mama and the others."

"Couldn't you? I thought everyone had a choice here?"

"Oh, no. The other realm doesn't work the same way for everyone. Most folks come through water, but we come through fire. When we tried to go back like folks said, we couldn't find a portal anywhere. We're the only ones in this place who can touch the bottom, so to speak." Martha clasped her hands together and looked away, shutting her eyes tight. "Meelie and the other refugees, they've got a kinship with water. They feel connected to their previous life, like water is a channel between the world they knew and the world they chose. That's what they say, anyway. But we aren't foolish enough to go jumping into a bonfire just to see what's on the other end. Lord knows what might happen."

"I heard one of the missing say that she could watch the surface of a pond like a television, only everything she saw was from her family back home. Don't work for us, though. We can't go back."

"Did Meelie take you to see Aimee?" Quinn asked.

"Oh, sure. She thinks we can't return, because we died in the fire. She thinks that bodies can die in one place or the other, but that death severs any connection between the two worlds."

The whole time Martha spoke, she stared at the teleido-scope around Quinn's neck. Quinn shifted her weight several times, uncomfortable with Martha's gaze and anxious to move on to her friend. She didn't want to be rude, but she had come back to the other realm with a purpose. As soon as Betty yawned, Quinn rose and excused herself, thanking the girls for being so welcoming, before creeping past Pidge.

"Meelie," Quinn whispered.

"Man alive," Meelie said, her shoulders tensing, "you can't go sneaking up on an old woman like that, Quinn. Almost gave me a heart attack."

The phrase sounded odd coming from someone her mother's age. Quinn realized how entrenched her concept of time was. Meelie *looked* young, but she had lived more than a century. That was bound to have some effect on the body, she supposed.

"Sorry. I was trying not to wake anyone."

"What are you doing here anyway? I thought for sure you'd gone back for good."

"Funny you ask—"

"Is your sister okay?" Meelie interrupted. "You figure out what that flower you found was all about?"

"Sort of. I'm still not sure how, exactly, but I put the bulb next to her while she was sleeping, and the doctors haven't found anything wrong with her since."

"Then you shouldn't be here. Didn't Aimee tell you not to come back?"

Quinn was taken aback by Meelie's harsh tone. "Well, I mean—I guess so, yeah. She said I should either stay with Riley or come straight back here."

"And you didn't come straight back, did you?"

"No—" Quinn trailed off.

"Hells bells, Quinn!"

"I just—I'm doing a school project, and I wanted to talk to you about some the details."

"You're here for a school project?" Meelie looked genuinely baffled.

"Well, no. Not just that."

"Then what? Your family will notice you're gone this time. Hell, they're probably worried sick already. What's so important that you had to come back?"

"Wait, what do you mean my family knows I'm gone? What about time moving in a circle and all that?"

"That's only true for first-timers. Good grief. What did you and Aimee talk about out there on that boat? I thought she told you all this?"

Quinn thought back to the conversation.

"I may have—" Quinn sighed. "I cut her off. She was talking about how I should leave Riley and my mom without saying goodbye and I just got upset so I told her I didn't want—"

"Woah, woah. Slow down. Take a breath," Meelie broke in.

Quinn was in tears now. "Is that why my mom keeps forgetting things and why Riley doesn't want my help anymore?"

"All I know is that moving back and forth between this life and the other doesn't end well, at least not as far as I've seen."

"Is that why you never went back when your plane crashed?"

Meelie's jaw twitched in the firelight. "Doing that research, I see."

"Not really. At least, not on purpose." Quinn chose her words carefully. "My teacher, she assigned all of us someone from history, and I got your name and—" Quinn stared at the fire. "Meelie, you said you didn't have a reason to go back, but you had a younger sister just like I do."

Meelie looked at Quinn with glassy eyes, the red flames flicking inside them. "I suppose what I meant is that I had a better reason to stay." She tossed a small log into the fire. "At least I thought I did."

Quinn scooted closer to Meelie and leaned on her shoulder. "So you haven't seen your sister since you disap—since you got here?"

"No." Meelie's voice was soft, but distant. "Not for lack of trying on her part, I'll say that. She and my husband sure turned the world upside down trying to find me and my plane, or so I hear."

Quinn was overcome by a sudden wave of fear. If Meelie hadn't gone home, how could she? Quinn wasn't half as brave or wise as Meelie—she couldn't even drive. How was she supposed to handle what one of the greatest pilots in history couldn't face?

"Is—is going home that bad?" Her voice shook.

"I told you, Quinn, I don't know anything about that except what I'm told," Meelie snapped. "And if folks are right, you shouldn't have come back. You shouldn't be here at all."

Then Meelie did something that Quinn hadn't expected: she kicked sand over the fire, donned her pilot's cap, yanked on the reins of her hen, and stormed out of the cave.

Despite the children sleeping nearby, who seemed unbothered by the heated exchange, Quinn felt completely alone. Coming back had been a mistake. This place wasn't a second home. The other realm wasn't any kind of home. Angry with herself, Quinn stood up and walked to the mouth of the cave. The moons were starting to descend, creating a wonderful gradient of reds and purples in the sky.

Quinn looked out at the desert, debating whether or not to strike out now or wait until morning. Behind her, someone stirred. Quinn shuffled out into the dawn, ducking to the right in case whoever had moved was watching the cave entrance. Meelie's reaction had made Quinn anxious to get home, but her curiosity was, unsurprisingly, winning the internal debate, which drew her away from the cave, away from the pond that would take her back. Quinn wasn't sure how many days she would have to walk to get to the ocean, but she would have to find Aimee if she had any hope of understanding what had happened with Meelie or what to expect when she returned to Riley and her mother.

CHAPTER SIXTEEN

"Quinn, Riley—let's go!" Jane shouted.

She was already running late, and she hadn't seen or heard either of the girls all morning. She checked the clock in the kitchen to see if the power had gone out, but the time matched that on her watch. Frustrated, she walked to their bedroom door and knocked loudly.

"Girls, get a move on!"

Riley opened the door still in her pajamas.

"Why so early?" she murmured, wiping sleep from her eyes.

"You're not even dressed yet? What have you been doing all morning?"

"I just woke up."

"Why didn't you get up when your alarm went off?"

"My alarm didn't go off."

"And Quinn didn't tell you to get ready for school?"

"No. I think she's still asleep."

"Quinn! Let's go. I don't have time for this!" Jane said, moving past Riley into the bedroom. She flicked on the light and saw Quinn's empty bed, the covers and sheets still tucked in from the morning before. Teetering between panic and anger, she turned to Riley.

"Where is your sister?"

"I don't know," Riley shrugged. "She told me a story, then I went to sleep."

"Okay, baby. Go brush your teeth. I'll set out some clothes for you." Jane tried to control the worry in her voice.

Once Riley had left the doorway, she pulled clothes from the dresser and set them on Riley's bed. She remembered Quinn's odd behavior the night before and instinctively checked the coat closet. Sure enough, the jacket that Quinn had hung up was gone. Quinn had clearly planned to sneak out.

Jane wanted to be angry, but Quinn typically didn't lie or sneak out at night, and Jane was more worried than irritated. Where had Quinn been going so late at night, and why hadn't she been honest with Jane? Why hadn't she come home? Was she hurt? The questions tumbled over almost as quickly as her heart pounded. She would have to call in to work and tell them that Quinn was missing. And the police. Jane wondered if they would even look for Quinn. She hadn't been gone for very long; in fact, Jane realized, they may not consider Quinn missing at all. Taking her jacket meant that Quinn left of her own will. Would the police call her a runaway? The thought terrified Jane. She knew better than to think that Quinn really had run away—wherever Quinn was, she wouldn't leave Riley for very long—but the police would have to investigate. They would have to talk to Riley. And maybe Child Services. As alarmed as Jane was, she decided to tell her boss that Riley was having one of her bad days, and she would try to find Quinn herself before contacting the authorities.

Jane pulled into the drop-off lane at Riley's school faster than she should have. She tried not to make eye contact with the crossing guard, who was clearly peeved.

"Have a good day, sweetie," Jane said, flashing a smile. She hoped that Riley couldn't hear the fear in her voice.

"Is Quinn going to walk me home?"

"How about I pick you up today, and we can all go for frozen yogurt?" Jane didn't know if she would be able to find

Quinn before Riley's school let out, and she didn't want Riley waiting if Quinn didn't show.

"Okay."

"Everything all right, baby?"

"Yeah. Just tired, I guess."

"Maybe you slept too long."

"Maybe," Riley shrugged.

Jane had noticed Riley dragging that morning, and Riley hadn't touched her breakfast. Neither observation was particularly noteworthy, except that Riley had been a ball of energy and a virtually bottomless pit for the past couple months. Riley's sudden reversion worried Jane. *I knew I couldn't trust her recovery*, she thought. She watched Riley walk into the school, her small feet barely lifting off the ground as she trudged through the doors. *The other shoe always falls.*

Jane was running through last night's conversation with Quinn as she pulled away from Riley's school. She would have to call Quinn's school and tell them that Quinn was sick. Otherwise the truancy officers would be notified, and Jane would have to admit that she didn't know where her daughter was. She dialed the school's phone number, steering her car toward home. Perhaps Quinn had already returned, Jane hoped. Of course, Quinn would have hell to pay either way. What was she thinking disappearing in the middle of the night like that? Jane was having a difficult time suppressing her worry. The more she thought about Quinn, the more convinced she became that Quinn would not have deliberately left Riley to get herself ready. She was a teenager, so a certain amount of rebellion was expected, but Quinn watched over Riley like a mother hen.

Jane pulled into her driveway and hurried into the house,

but every room was dark. The house was eerily quiet. Butter-fly hadn't barked, or even come to greet her at the door. He wasn't a particularly rambunctious dog, but he made a habit of racing to the door at the slightest squeak of the hinge.

"Butterfly," Jane called.

When he didn't come, she went into the kitchen for a pouch of treats. She unzipped the pouch as loudly as she could. "Who wants a treat?"

That must have roused Butterfly. Jane could hear his nails clicking on the hardwood as he barreled into the kitchen. For all his gentleness, Butterfly forgot his size where food was involved. Jane bent down and stroked his head while he chomped on the treats she had scattered for him.

"Where's Quinn, boy? Have you seen her this morning?"

Butterfly looked up, then let out a soft whine. He nuzzled his head into Jane's chest.

"I know. I'm worried too. What do you say we go and look for her?"

Jane walked to the front door and pulled Butterfly's leash from a hook. As soon as Butterfly heard the clip thump against the wall, he ran to Jane, who bent down and attached the leash to his collar. She didn't really know where to start, but she reasoned that Quinn had left on foot. She couldn't drive yet, and, as far as Jane knew, Quinn didn't have any friends older than her. Jane led Butterfly onto the porch and shut the door behind her, careful not to lock the deadbolt in case Quinn had forgotten her house key. The two of them turned toward the butterfly garden out of habit. That was as good a place to look as any, Jane figured.

CHAPTER SEVENTEEN

O nce her eyes adjusted, Quinn found that night in the other realm wasn't that dark at all. Rather, the twin moons turned the sky the color of grape juice, and the desert sand glittered whenever the wind shifted. Curious, she took several steps away from the cave wall and kicked a patch of sand. Ripples of light immediately spread out from her foot in the direction she had swung her leg. That settled things. Quinn would be able to move through the desert easily enough, so she had no reason to wait until morning. She crept back into the cave and swiped a few marshmallow cakes from the closest campsite before deciding on a direction and setting out into the night.

As she walked, Quinn ruminated over her conversation with Meelie. What had she said to get under Meelie's skin? She had stormed off before Quinn could explain that she hadn't just come back for the school project. Despite her best efforts, Quinn couldn't convince herself that Riley was simply sick. She was too familiar with the rattle in her sister's lungs. Riley was declining again, and Quinn didn't know how quickly she would deteriorate. She wanted to talk to Meelie, but she had to find Aimee. Aimee was the only one who could help her understand why her mom had been forgetting things, and where to find another one of the bulbs to help Riley. Even if Riley didn't need one yet, she would need one eventually. She had been naïve to think that she could heal her sister permanently with one trip.

How long have I been here? Quinn wondered. Without

the familiar routines of home, she had trouble estimating how much time had elapsed. What if Riley woke up to an empty room? What if her mother had already noticed that she was gone? Quinn felt sick. She wasn't the type to rush into things without thinking. She should have known that coming back to the other realm was foolish. Aimee had tried to warn her, but Quinn had refused to listen. Now she was blindly wandering the desert. She had left her sister alone and her mother to worry. She tried not to feel guilty, but of course that only made things worse. Quinn simply wasn't accustomed to putting her own desires ahead of her family. She was so preoccupied with self-loathing that she didn't notice the sound of waves crashing until the water rushed over her feet. She had found the ocean. Now to find Aimee.

Quinn scanned the horizon as she walked. The moons were beginning to fade, and the ocean took on an iridescent hue that shifted between deep blues and rich purples as the water moved. If the day was beginning here in the other realm, Quinn reasoned that she had been gone for at least ten hours. Her mother would be awake, Riley may already be at school. Was her mother worried? *That's a stupid question. Of course she's worried. She thinks I'm missing.* Quinn's fingers were numb, and her head began to buzz. She was still chastising herself for being so reckless, for disregarding Aimee's and Meelie's warnings, for not thinking about how her disappearance would affect Riley and her mother.

"Quinn!"

Quinn looked up to see Aimee waving from a sailboat a few hundred yards from shore.

"Aimee! I'm so glad I found you!" Quinn shouted back.

All the fear and grief and guilt she had been carrying

rushed into her throat. She began to sob, straining for breath as her chest heaved up and down.

"I need your help," she called, her voice nearly inaudible.

Aimee dipped her fingers into the water, moving them as though she were playing a concerto in double time. The strange netting stretched out from the boat, this time much thicker and more tightly woven. Quinn watched as Aimee climbed onto the makeshift raft, then sat directly in the center with her legs crossed. The tide pulled her toward Quinn, who took off her socks and shoes before wading a few feet into the water.

"What are you doing here, Quinn?"

"I don't know," Quinn bawled. She recounted her conversation with Meelie as best she could, then explained her mother's memory loss and her fear that Riley was relapsing.

"I tried to warn you—" Aimee began.

"I know," Quinn interrupted. "I know. I should have listened to you, but I didn't and now I'm here, and my mother is probably panicking, and Riley is getting sick again, and—"

"Quinn, stop. What's done is done. You need to focus on what you can control." Aimee was stern, yet her words comforted Quinn. The benefit of three hundred years of wisdom, no doubt.

"You mean Riley?" Quinn wiped her eyes, trying hard to regain her composure.

"Yes. If her heart is giving out, you must find a new one and get back to her as quickly as possible."

"But how? I didn't find the bulb last time. One just appeared."

"Do you remember what else was nearby?"

Quinn told her about the butterflies with red-and-black wings that had led her home.

"Then that's where you start. Find those butterflies. Maybe they'll lead you to another heart flower."

"But . . . what if they don't?"

"You can only work with what you know. You must always move forward. You can't change direction if you're standing still."

Quinn wasn't convinced, but what choice did she have? Those butterflies were her best chance at finding a new heart and, most importantly, the way home. Just as Quinn turned to leave, Aimee called after her and tossed something onto the shore. Quinn bent down to inspect the ropes. She saw that Aimee had been busy weaving while they talked. In her hands, Quinn held her very own butterfly net.

Quinn turned the butterfly net over in her fingers. Most of the net was woven tightly, but the rope was light and flexible. One end came to a broad point, while the other had a rigid circular opening. There was a small length of rope extending from the opening which Quinn could use to secure a stick or pole, if she could find one. She scanned the beach as she walked, looking for anything that might work. The sand was empty of debris, but Quinn saw familiar scratches every few feet—footprints from Meelie's chicken! Quinn had a surge of energy and began to run, following the scratches.

"Meelie!" Quinn shouted, her chest heaving.

She swung her head back and forth, looking for any sign of her friend. She had forgotten how thick the air was in the other realm, and she hadn't gone far when she began to wheeze. Her lungs burned. She stopped, raising her hands above her head to try to catch her breath. Meelie was no-where in sight. Once again, Quinn was entirely alone.

Quinn fell to her knees and sobbed. She knew that she should be searching for the red-and-black butterflies, for heart flowers and the mystical pond that would take her home, but all she could think about was how quiet and bare the other realm was. The cave had been filled with people, yet no one had noticed Quinn and Meelie fighting. No one had stirred when Quinn set out into the night. Aimee had been helpful, but she clearly preferred solitude. Why else would she stay on a boat for centuries? And Meelie. Who could tell with Meelie? One minute she acted like a cross between a grandmother and a friend, and the next she was putting out the fire and storming into the darkness.

"Well, I'll say this, bunny. You're anything but a quitter."

Quinn looked up to see Meelie, who was perched atop her chicken.

"Meelie! I'm so sorry—" she started, trying to quell her tears. "—I didn't mean to upset you. I was just—"

"Not at all," Meelie broke in. "That was my own damn fault. I keep to myself around here, and I'm afraid I'm not accustomed to folks knowing about my sister."

Quinn could see that Meelie had been crying. Her eyes were streaked with red and the skin around them was swollen.

"I just want to understand, Meelie. Why didn't you go back to her? Were you two not close?"

"We were inseparable."

"Then why? Did something happen? Did you have a fight?"

Meelie bit her lip. "No, we didn't have a fight."

She stared past Quinn, watching the waves crest and disappear into the loam.

"I stayed for much more selfish reasons. Reasons I haven't told anybody here. I don't know why I'm telling you now, except that you strike me as the sort to figure things out anyway, so I might as well speak plain."

Quinn walked closer to the chicken, and Meelie held out a hand.

"My mother says I get my stubbornness from my father," Quinn said. She wrapped her arms around Meelie's waist.

"It's a long story, kid. And I imagine you need to get home fast as you can."

"Then let's get started."

CHAPTER EIGHTEEN

Butterfly tugged at the leash, barking hysterically. "What's wrong, boy?"

Jane was in a jog trying to keep up with Butterfly, who was desperately weaving through the park toward the butterfly garden. They were crossing through the gate when her phone rang. "Quinn?" she said into the receiver.

"No, ma'am. This is Patricia Cline with the front office at Star Creek Elementary School. I'm calling to speak with Riley Willow's mother."

"I'm Riley's mother." Jane could feel her pulse quicken. She sat down on a bench, tightening her grip on Butterfly's leash. "Is everything okay? What's happened?"

"Oh, nothing to worry about, ma'am. Your daughter is in the nurse's office. She's running a small fever and asked us to call you."

"But she's—nothing happened? She just doesn't feel well?"

Jane was torn. She preferred to keep Riley close when she was ill. She often couldn't tell when Riley had a simple cold or when her heart was working too hard. Still, her worry for Quinn was swelling in her stomach. She just knew that Quinn wouldn't leave on her own, not for this long and not without telling Jane.

"That's correct, ma'am."

"So she doesn't need to come home?" The words were sour in Jane's mouth. She'd never been forced to choose between her two daughters.

"We really do prefer students with even a small fever to stay at home for at least twenty-four hours."

An entire day, Jane thought. How would she explain that Quinn was missing? No, she had to keep searching.

"I'm sorry. I'm not able to pick her up at the moment—ouch!"

Butterfly ripped free and barreled toward the pond at the center of the butterfly garden.

"Damn it, Butterfly!"

Jane ran after him, still clutching the phone. When he reached the pond, he stopped and began barking frantically. Jane raised the phone back to her ear, trying to catch her breath.

"Hello? Ms. Willow, are you still there?"

"Yes, I apologize. My dog, he—"

"As I was saying, Ms. Willow. We really do need someone to come pick up Riley as soon as possible. Perhaps her father is available?"

"No!" Jane's face was hot with anger. "Don't you people keep notes? My daughter has been going to your school for three years, and you still don't know that there is no father? There never has been. Damn it, I don't need this today!" She sank to the ground and sobbed into the phone.

"I'm so sorry, Ms. Willow. I don't know why that information isn't in the system. I'll make a note of that right now."

"No, no—I'm sorry—I'm just—I'm—" Jane couldn't get a full sentence out through the tears. She shut her eyes and took a long, deep breath, then said, "I'll be right there."

She hung up the phone without waiting for a reply. Once she had recomposed herself, she smoothed her jacket and led Butterfly from the garden. He kept his eyes on the pond all the way to the gate.

* * *

Jane steered into an empty space and switched off the car. She flipped the visor down and checked her face in the mirror. Sure enough, she had red splotches on her cheeks and neck, and her eyes were nearly swollen shut.

Great, she thought. *The office staff will think I'm absolutely insane.* She ran a baby wipe over her face, popped a mint into her mouth, and squared her jaw. She had been hiding her worry from Riley for years. Why should today be any different?

"Hello, I'm Jane Willow, Riley's mother," she said as she entered the main office. "I received a call to come pick her up."

"Oh, yes. I'm Patricia, the one you spoke with on the phone. Riley's in with the nurse. I'll go get her for you."

Jane paced. She still didn't know what she was going to tell Riley when she asked about Quinn. She glanced at the clock: 10:30 a.m. Quinn's school usually didn't let out until half past three, which meant she had about five hours to think of something believable, six if she lied and said that Quinn was staying after school to do research.

"Hey, mama," Riley said, rounding the corner.

"Hey, sweetie. How are you feeling?"

She felt Riley's forehead with the back of her hand, then brushed a strand of hair from her daughter's face.

"I'm really tired."

Jane signed Riley out, carrying her book bag as they walked to the car. In the sunlight, she could see that Riley was much paler than she had been in recent days.

"Have you been throwing up?"

"No, why?"

"I think we ought to go see Dr. Howe . . . just to be safe." She said the last few words for her own benefit, but they did nothing to ease her concern. One daughter was missing; the other could scarcely breathe.

Jane turned the key and headed for the hospital. She was in a daze, but she knew the way better than she knew the lines on her own hands. *One day,* she told herself, *I'll forget these roads entirely. Someday they'll be nothing but stray marks on a tired map, and I won't remember them at all.*

But not today. Today, her daughter was already sleeping in the backseat. Today, as so many days before, she would carry Riley to a cold bed covered in white paper. Today, she dreamed only of a world without purple. A world where blue and red never fought for her daughter's air.

CHAPTER NINETEEN

Quinn plopped onto a flat rock and raised her hands above her head, trying to catch her breath. She and Meelie had been searching the caves for the pool Quinn had used to get home, but without the red butterflies to lead them, they weren't having much luck. Quinn's feet were beginning to blister; she couldn't imagine how Meelie was feeling with her leather boots. They would have ridden Pidge, but the rocky ground and narrow passages were too much for her, and so they left her at the mouth of the cave with Betty's and Martha's other siblings. Betty and Martha, for their part, had volunteered to help search the caves.

"You okay, bunny?"

"I'm fine," Quinn wheezed. "Just need a minute." She couldn't help but laugh at the irony. "Do people ever get used to the air here?"

"Oh, I don't know. I never did pay much mind myself. I suppose I was built for an atmosphere like this after all that time in the clouds."

As they walked, Meelie told Quinn all sorts of stories about her life before the crash. She went on and on about the planes she'd flown, different types of engines and cockpits. Quinn couldn't follow most of the lingo, but she noticed a tremor in Meelie's voice when she recalled her sister. The two had a lot in common with Quinn and Riley: they were best friends, and Meelie felt a strong urge to protect her younger sister, which confused Quinn.

"How come you never went back?" she asked, picking

pebbles from the ground and tossing them down a passage to one side.

"Quinn . . ."

"I just don't understand. You loved your sister same as me. Why didn't you want to see her again?"

Meelie sighed. "Pidge wasn't the one I didn't want to see."

"Then who?"

"Everybody else."

Quinn rolled her eyes.

"We all have ghosts, you know," Meelie said.

"What are yours?"

"History. All that history."

"But people love you. You're in all kinds of books. You're a hero."

"Because I stayed here."

Quinn frowned, tossing another pebble into the blackness.

"I'm sorry," Meelie said. "I don't mean to speak in riddles. There's just—I'm a hero because of the way I left, don't you see? No one would remember a pilot who crashed in the ocean and lived out her life on some farm. We bury our heroes; the living, that's who we forget. And what a tomb I made of that sea."

"So, you left your family because you wanted to die a hero?"

"Not my best moment, I admit."

"But you were already a hero, the greatest woman pilot ever."

Meelie kicked at the ground. "I wasn't the best. And plenty of folks knew better, too. But the papers—they were kind to me. That crash—I'd have never lived that down."

"I don't understand."

"Damn it, kid. I don't want to talk about that life anymore!" She stormed into the dark passage without waiting for Quinn.

Quinn rose and chased after her. "Come on, Meelie. Wait up!"

The passage was so dark that Quinn could hardly see her own hands. She was still running when she bumped into Martha, her figure outlined by a faint, purple fog. Quinn followed her gaze to the wall on her left. She could make out a small square that appeared to have been polished down, almost like a plaque or sign. In the center of the square, she saw a message:

In your absence, she fades. Find your way home
this night, for today may well be her last.

She collapsed against Martha and began to sob, unable to ignore the image of Riley lying in a hospital bed, her mother bent over the railing, both wondering where she had gone. Quinn had been so foolish to return to the other realm, and now she was wandering without so much as a clue as to how she would get home, much less find another heart flower to take with her.

"It's all right, Quinn. We're going to search every bit of this place for them heart flowers. Won't stop for nothing," Betty whispered, wrapping her arms around the two older girls.

"Betty—"

"You heard her, Quinn. We haven't got much in the way of family, and that we do got is worth any amount of looking. Go ahead and have yourself a cry if you need to, but we aren't going anywhere. You're family, now."

"But how will we—"

"We'll figure this out. I promise." Martha pulled Quinn in close, cradling her head as she cried just as Jane often did after Riley had gone to bed. Martha, Quinn could tell, had been a sort of mother to her siblings in the other realm.

"Say, where is Meelie?" Betty asked.

"I pushed her a little too hard about her old life," Quinn admitted. "She went off that way."

Quinn pointed farther down the path. Martha and Betty followed her gaze, and all three stood absolutely still, listening to the unmistakeable echo of sobs reverberating off the cave walls.

"We'll give her a few minutes to calm down. She don't like talking about where she's been, that's for certain. She calms down quick enough, though. I imagine most folks here have got a bit of ghost they can't give up."

Meelie came back before long and took Quinn into her arms. Quinn's tears stained her bomber jacket, but she didn't move until her back went stiff. Martha and Betty had offered to keep searching the caves while Meelie thought through strategies in her head. One thing was certain: they couldn't keep wandering the caves like a couple of lost pups. Her feet were killing her; judging from the way Quinn was limping, she wasn't faring any better. They needed to find a swarm of red butterflies, and they needed to move quickly.

She told Quinn that their best bet would be to leave the caves and go into the desert. They'd be able to ride Pidge, so they could cover more ground in half the time, and she was pretty certain there weren't any butterflies lurking in the depths of the cave. They'd have seen *something* by now.

Quinn didn't have the energy to protest, so she followed along as Meelie picked her way back toward the mouth of the cave. She could hear Quinn's feet dragging behind her. The rocks ripping across the dirt sounded like gears in a bad engine. They had got themselves in a mess, running on emotion when the situation called for anything but. Meelie felt she was as much to blame as Quinn. Quinn was coming to terms with having to leave her family, and Meelie was caught up in a selfish decision she'd made nearly a century ago. Maybe she ought to tell Quinn everything, from that first flight across the deep-blue Atlantic to the Oklahoma Derby that showed her for what she was, to that last desperate attempt to put everything behind her.

"What have you heard about me, bunny?"

"What?"

"You said you got started on some research. So, what do you know?"

"Well, um—oh! I read that you were the first woman to fly across the ocean."

"That right there is why I stayed."

Quinn looked at her, clearly perplexed.

"That's not the way things happened, and folks ought to know that. Hell, I wrote about the whole trip, told them all I didn't touch the controls one time. I was little more than cargo, kid. Some hero. But when you die, everything goes rose-colored."

"And you think people would have seen you differently after your crash?"

"They would have seen me the way other woman pilots had seen me for years: a two-bit aviator riding the tails of sponsorship and newspaper clippings to a spot in history."

"They really thought that?"

"They sure did, and who could blame them? They were right." Meelie trudged along in silence, staring at the rocky floor of the cave. "You ever heard of the Oklahoma Derby?"

"No, I haven't."

"The year was 1929, and someone had a mind to have all the best woman pilots race each other straight up the middle of the country. Most folks were excited. The whole thing stirred up quite a buzz, so of course I had to enter even though racing meant going head-to-head with women I knew full well could out fly me. And that's exactly what they did. I came in fourth place—would have come in fifth if Marvel, rest her soul, hadn't died in a crash. Maybe even further back than that, what with Pancho and Ruth hitting the ground, too."

"But that was just one race, Meelie."

"No. I flew a better, faster plane. The papers talked like I hung the moon myself. But those other women, they knew I wasn't anything special. Only reason they kept their comments to themselves is I brought a lot of attention to women in the cockpit, and we all wanted to see folks give women flyers the same respect they gave men."

"So you gave up your life, your sister, because you wanted people to remember you as better than you were?"

"That's right."

"And no one here knows?"

"Surely not."

"Why'd you tell me?"

"You're in a rough spot, bunny. And I suspect you don't have much say in the matter anymore. So listen: if you come back for good, you have family here. I want you to know that. We aren't blood, of course, but you won't be alone. Not so long as I'm around."

Quinn didn't have a chance to respond. They rounded a bend and found themselves back at the mouth of the cave. Dozens of people Quinn had never seen were milling about, folding blankets and dousing fires. Meelie stepped in front of her, leading the way to the children with whom she'd left Pidge.

"Quinn, have you met the rest of Martha's and Betty's family?"

Quinn held her hand out to the oldest, one of two boys. "Not really," she said softly. "Just Martha and Betty."

"Go on," Martha said as she and Betty stepped close to the group. "Don't be rude, now. Tell her your names."

The three children introduced themselves. Every one of them looked younger than Quinn. They didn't say much other than their names: Maurice, Louis, and Jennie. Once she had shaken each of their hands, the five huddled together almost reflexively. Any warmth that Martha and Betty had shown earlier was gone. Again, Martha stared at Quinn's teleidoscope.

"Do you want to look through the lens?" Quinn offered, slipping the lanyard over her head.

"Are you sure?" Martha asked, her voice soft and unsteady.

Quinn nodded and handed the teleidoscope to Martha, who lifted the lens to her eye.

"Looks like you've used one before," Quinn observed.

"What is that thing anyway?" Meelie asked.

"A teleidoscope, like a kaleidoscope without stained glass or a marble to look at."

"They didn't have anything like this when I was a kid," Martha added.

Quinn was perplexed by Martha's comment. Martha had known which side to look through, and she had aimed the tube at a small fire almost immediately.

"You must be a natural," Quinn remarked.

"What? Oh, no. I met a man once who makes them. He don't live here in the caves, but he comes by sometimes. Poor guy can't remember anything from his life before the other realm except how to make these doohickeys."

Martha handed the teleidoscope back to Quinn, then dug through her blanket. "Here, you can have this one." She handed Quinn an almost identical, larger version of her teleidoscope. "I have too many, anyway," Martha added, pushing the tube into Quinn's hand.

"Thanks," Quinn replied, unable to hide her confusion. Who was this man, and how had her father come across one of his contraptions?

Meelie waited until they were out of earshot before explaining to Quinn that they had all shown up together, the only ones she knew of who came to the other realm through fire. Quinn decided not to tell her that she had already talked with Martha and Betty about how they'd come to the other realm. Sometimes a shared secret is the only thing that connects two people, and Quinn knew she would need friends if she came to the other realm permanently.

"How long have they been here?" she asked, feigning ignorance.

"Oh, I'm not certain of the year, but I imagine they've been here almost as long as I have."

"And their parents?"

"Not one of them has said a word about their life back home."

"They've been here almost eighty years, and no one knows what happened to their parents?"

"Nope."

Quinn's stomach turned.

"They probably died believing that they'd finally get to see their children again. But they won't. This place is a curse, Meelie. Nothing here but a lot of souls who didn't have the decency to die when they were buried."

Meelie couldn't fault Quinn for being so bleak. She was fifteen and trapped. Her sister was a world away. And if they didn't move quickly, she might not even get to say goodbye.

CHAPTER TWENTY

J ane paced the carpet in front of the receptionist, trying
not to eavesdrop on her conversation with Dr. Howe. Between Quinn's disappearance and Riley's sudden downturn,
she had completely forgotten that he was on vacation and
wouldn't return until the end of the week.

"Yes, she's here in the office," the receptionist said, making eye contact with Jane. "Yes, sir. One moment." She motioned for Jane.

"Dr. Howe would like to speak to you."

Jane took the phone from her and raised the speaker to
her ear. "Dr. Howe, I'm so sorry—"

"Don't worry," he cut in. "I gather that Riley is in pretty
bad shape. Can you tell me more about her symptoms?"

Jane relayed what the nurse had told her, as well as the
lethargy and raspy voice she'd noticed on the ride over.

"You said her skin is pale, too?"

"Yes. And clammy."

"Now, Jane, I don't want you to worry. I can't get back
until tomorrow, but I'm going to have Riley admitted for observation overnight. I'm sure she'll be fine, but I'd feel safer if
we were monitoring her until I arrive."

Jane drew in a breath. "Okay."

"You'll be able to stay with her, of course."

"Do you think I should?"

The question stuck in her throat. Riley had never stayed
in the hospital by herself. Normally, the nurses would have
had to pull Jane from the room to get her to leave. But today

was different. Quinn had been missing for at least twelve hours now, and Jane was having a hard time masking her concern.

"That's really up to you. If I remember, you don't live far, and the nurses will call if there's any indication that Riley needs you."

Jane handed the phone back to the receptionist, who moved her fingers across the keyboard as she listened to Dr. Howe on the other end of the line.

"Dr. Howe would like to admit Riley for observation," she reiterated after hanging up the phone. "He mentioned that you won't be staying with her tonight. Is that correct?"

"Yes, I—"

"That will be fine. We will need you to stay until we get your daughter settled into a room, of course."

"Of course, I—"

"Very well. Someone will call for Riley when we're ready to take her back."

Jane was wracked with guilt, and the receptionist's curt interruptions had done nothing to ease her mind. The thought of leaving Riley by herself made her physically sick, but what else could she do? Quinn was her daughter too, and something must be wrong for her to be gone so long without so much as a phone call to let Jane know where she was. She had intended to get Quinn a cell phone when Quinn began driving, but now she regretted not getting one for Quinn sooner.

"Damn it, Quinn," she muttered under her breath. "Where the hell are you?"

"Did you say something, mama?" Riley asked, looking up from the floor where she was working on a puzzle.

"No, baby. Just thinking out loud."

Riley went back to her puzzle. Jane envied her innocence,

the way she could smile and busy herself with whatever the doctor's office had scattered in the waiting room. Or was that courage? Jane sometimes wondered if Riley understood a good deal more than she let on, but put on a mask to spare her mother. She sat watching her youngest daughter arranging the pieces, coughing each time her shoulders rose for a deep breath.

"Riley? Riley Willow?"

Jane looked up to see a woman in pink scrubs scanning the room.

"Come on, Riley," Jane said, hurrying her daughter toward the nurse.

Once in the room, Jane explained that she wouldn't be able to stay the night with Riley.

"You know I'm just a few minutes away. If you need me for anything at all, someone will call me and I'll come right back."

"I'll be okay," Riley assured her, smiling.

Jane fought back tears as she leaned over to kiss Riley on the forehead. "I'll see you in the morning."

She turned and left the room, barely able to hold herself together as she made her way back to her car. As soon as she closed the door, she began to sob. The sun was beginning to dip below the horizon, and a storm was moving in fast. Jane studied the sky, which looked almost regal with indigo hues and towering wall clouds.

At home, Jane let Butterfly out. She went to fill his bowl, but found that he hadn't eaten anything since that morning. *He must sense that something is wrong,* she thought. She made herself a peanut butter and jelly sandwich, the first thing she'd eaten all day, and thought through any place Quinn might go to wait out the storm. Jane would have a hard time searching for her if the rain was heavy, but she could also be reasonably certain that Quinn wouldn't be outdoors. She had a keen sense for changes in the weather, and Jane was willing to bet that she'd have felt the electricity in the air well before the clouds formed.

She let Butterfly back in, setting a few pieces of cheese next to his bowl. He sniffed them, then ambled over to Jane and lay down at her feet. He whined and pushed his head against her leg.

"I know, buddy. I know."

Jane gathered her purse and keys, flicked on the entry light for Butterfly, and grabbed an umbrella. She had decided to make a quick run by the bakery and butterfly sanctuary before the rain started just in case she'd missed Quinn earlier. There were a number of shops and restaurants down the hill from the sanctuary, too. Jane would have to park and search them one by one. She would have to choose her words carefully when she asked if anyone had seen Quinn or someone might alert the police. Though she was getting more and more worried, she wasn't ready to spend hours at the police station going over her daughter's behavior and possible whereabouts.

CHAPTER TWENTY-ONE

Quinn stood alone at the mouth of the cave, staring into the mulberry dusk. She felt absolutely helpless. Something had happened to Riley, and her mother was probably losing her mind with Quinn gone. The heart flower had been so easy to find last time, and the red butterflies had shown her the way home. But she had gone deep into the cave this time and saw neither. Quinn knew that she would have to go into the desert, yet the sky was already too dark to venture very far from the cave. She would be lost in a matter of minutes if she left now.

"You okay, bunny?" Meelie asked, startling Quinn.

"No, Meelie. No, I'm not. I can't stand feeling helpless. My family needs me, and I can't do a damn thing. I'm just stuck waiting for the day to break while Riley could be dying! What if I don't get back in time, Meelie? What if she dies wondering where I've gone? I promised I'd never leave her. I promised—"

Meelie wrapped an arm around Quinn and pulled her close. They both looked out at the sky, which had gone black seemingly in a moment.

"Hold on," Quinn shouted, jumping to her feet.

"What's the matter, hon?"

"That swarm of butterflies, the ones that glow, does that swarm pass by here every night?"

"Yeah. Some sort of migratory thing, I guess."

Quinn held out the net Aimee had woven for her.

"I'm going to need a stick, Meelie.'

"I don't follow."

"I'm going to catch some of the butterflies and use them like a lantern."

"Quinn, that sounds awful risky."

"I can't just sit here, Meelie. I have to do something. I have to try."

"Well, no sense going alone. Let me get my things."

Quinn waited anxiously for Meelie to return. She squinted at the darkness and felt sure she had seen a purple flash in the distance.

"Meelie, hurry!" she shouted over her shoulder. "They're coming!"

She didn't know what to do. If she missed the butterflies, there'd be little hope of searching for a heart flower tonight, but she knew she was safer with Meelie. Besides, she didn't yet have a stick for the net. The purple haze grew brighter on the horizon. To her right, Quinn heard a scratching noise. She turned to see Meelie's hen, which must have wandered over while she was lost in thought. In an instant, Quinn was on Pidge's back. She let out a loud squawk, but didn't fight her as she positioned herself.

"Come on!" Quinn urged, digging her heels into Pidge's ribs.

She tore out into the desert with such speed that Quinn nearly lost her balance. She dug her hands into the feathers at the base of Pidge's neck, turning her head toward the butterfly swarm. As they got closer, the light intensified.

"God," Quinn gasped. "There must be thousands of them."

She squeezed her legs tight and let go of Pidge's feathers with her hands, then raised the net high above her head. Pidge barreled straight into the butterflies. Quinn swept the net down through the swarm, gathering as many butterflies as she could before closing her hands tightly around the base of the net. The rope flexed against the butterflies trying to keep up with the rest of the group. Quinn twisted the net several times. Her fingers were already going numb. She knew there was no way that she could keep the net closed for long, not without a stick or something to tie the net shut, so she leaned into Pidge and turned her back toward the cave. With any luck, Meelie would be waiting for them, and she'd have found something Quinn could use to secure her catch.

"You can't just take off like that," Meelie scolded.

Pidge sulked toward her. Quinn didn't budge, worried that the slightest movement would release the butterflies from her net.

"Did you find a stick? Or something I could use to tie this shut?"

Meelie produced a long pole and a small piece of rope.

"That's perfect!"

"I told you I'd be right back. What were you thinking, running off into the night alone?"

Quinn handed Meelie the net, careful not to let go of the closed end until Meelie had tied the net shut with a length of rope.

"I wasn't thinking. I saw the migration, and I just went after the butterflies. I couldn't risk losing them. We'd have been stuck here all night."

"Or we'd have made a torch and been fine."

Quinn bit her lip. "That seems . . . easy. Why didn't I think of that?"

"Heaven knows, bunny. Makes a whole lot more sense than this bag of butterflies."

Quinn had to laugh. Something about the other realm and all the magic there had caused her to skip right over the simplest solution. "Maybe this is better," she argued. "You said they move in some sort of pattern. Let's follow them and see where they go."

"Why would we do that?"

"Well, we don't have any idea where to look for a heart flower. If we're going to wander around the desert, shouldn't we at least let these things lead the way?"

Meelie thought for a moment. "I suppose so. If there's danger, they're a heck of a lot more likely to move away from a threat than toward something that could harm them. Let's give the plan a shot." She handed the net, now secured and fastened to the pole, back to Quinn. "Scoot," she ordered, climbing onto Pidge.

Quinn slid back on Pidge, putting one arm around Meelie's waist and holding the pole with her other.

"Wedge that thing down into my boot. That'll take some pressure off your arm."

Quinn did as she was told.

Above them, the butterflies strained to break free.

"All right, now. Follow that light," Meelie said to Pidge, nudging the animal sharply with her heel.

The three of them bounced across the desert, watching the glowing captives bend and stretch the net. They couldn't see more than a few hundred feet in front of them. They were completely at the mercy of the butterflies and their instinctive flight.

"Where do you think they're going?" Quinn asked.

"Who knows?"

"How long do you think before we get there?"

"Could take all night. Or we could be there any minute. Hard to say, bunny. We're just along for the ride."

The thought made Quinn feel helpless again. After years with Riley's illness and the countless hospital visits, Quinn

was used to feeling this way. She had learned almost immediately that she couldn't control her sister's sickness. But this
was different. The one thing Quinn had always relied on, the
one constant between them, was that she never left Riley's
side on a bad night. She was always there.

"Riley must be so scared," she thought out loud. "She
shouldn't be alone tonight."

"We'll get you back, bunny. That's a promise sure as I'm
sitting on this hen. I won't rest till you're home."

Just then, Quinn had a realization that made her stomach
drop.

"Meelie, what if these butterflies are going somewhere
we can't follow?"

"What do you mean?"

"You said yourself that this hen can't fly."

"Speak plain, bunny."

"These things don't know that."

"They could take us right off a cliff—"

"Or straight into the ocean—"

"And we wouldn't have the foggiest idea until—" Meelie
trailed off.

The two of them held tighter to Pidge and to each other,
training their eyes on the expanse before them. The night was
so dark that the world seemed to end, as though the desert
was a universe expanding beneath their feet. Above them,
the butterflies glowed, the closest thing they had to starlight.
They could only guess at what lay ahead, reluctant explorers
in an uncharted night.

CHAPTER TWENTY-TWO

Riley awoke with a start. She looked down to see an IV running from her hand. The nurses had always struggled to hit the veins in her arm. Sure enough, she saw that she had a cotton ball taped to each one.

"Quinn? Mom?"

Neither responded.

Riley searched for the bedside remote, then flicked on the overhead lights. The room was completely empty. She tried not to panic. Quinn had probably just stepped out to find a snack, or maybe she was in the bathroom.

She glanced over to the bathroom door and saw light peeking from within, which calmed her for a moment. Of course that's where she was. Quinn never left her alone in the hospital, especially when she was sleeping. She settled back onto her pillow and waited, staring at the light like the glow was a bridge to some other world. Her eyes began to water.

None of this was fair. Not to her. Not to her family. Adults always talked about how they wished they could be kids again, but that was a lie. No one wanted to stay a kid forever. No one wanted to be born knowing that they'd never grow up. Her heart was a time bomb, her life a children's story. Even at seven, she knew as well as anyone that when people spoke of her, there would only ever be one chapter, a handful of pages and a few pictures to remember her by.

To remember. What sort of kid woke in the middle of the night wondering how her family would remember her? She tried to push the thoughts from her head, turning again to the light beneath the bathroom door. How long had Quinn been in there? The minutes felt like lifetimes.

"Lifetimes I'll never have," Riley whispered to herself.

She rolled her eyes and groaned.

"Enough," she said, pushing herself to a sitting position.

"Quinn!" she shouted toward the bathroom.

No response.

"Quinn! Answer me!"

Still nothing.

"I need to pee!"

Silence.

Riley growled, her frustration vibrating at the base of her throat before she doubled over, wheezing. Once she'd caught her breath, she gripped the IV stand and slid down the bed until her feet planted on the floor. She felt weak, barely able to support herself. Her legs were heavy, so she shuffled her way to the bathroom. Once there, she banged on the door.

"Quinn, hurry up!"

She pressed her ear to the door, but heard nothing. No water running. No rustling of clothes. Just a loud, lonely silence. She turned the handle and was surprised to find the door unlocked. Stepping inside, she stared into a bright, yet empty, bathroom. For the first time, Riley felt alone. No, she didn't *feel* alone. She *was* alone.

"Riley? Riley, can you hear me?"

Someone was shouting. The words echoed in her ear. She tried to open her eyes, but the light made them burn. Her throat ached, and her head was rattling like an old farmhouse in an earthquake.

"Riley? Can you hear me?"

"Yeah," she muttered.

Her mouth felt sticky and hot. She braced herself with

her hands. The surface was cold and hard, not at all like the scratchy hospital sheets she was used to. She tried to sit up, which made her head throb.

"Careful, sweetie. You took a bad spill."

Riley felt a hand on her back.

"Slowly, now," the voice said. "We don't want you to fall again."

"What happened?" Riley asked, forcing her eyes open.

She looked around, taking a moment to process the scene. She was on the bathroom floor. Next to her, blood was on the grout between tiles.

"You don't remember?"

Riley searched her thoughts, frowning at the dull pulse inside her head.

"Quinn—I was looking for Quinn."

"And Quinn is?"

"My sister," Riley answered, confused that her nurse wouldn't know that. "Haven't you met her?"

"I'm sorry, sweetie. I didn't realize you had a sister."

"Did you just get here?" Riley asked.

Shift change could be confusing at the hospital. Nurses sometimes forget to warn those taking over Riley's room that Quinn would be staying with her.

"No, I've been here all night. I helped you change into your gown, remember?"

"So, my sister —she hasn't been here at all?"

"I'm afraid not."

"What about my mom?"

"She said that she had to go take care of something. She should be back soon. Would you like me to call her for you?"

Something was very wrong. Quinn was missing. Her mother was gone. They had never just left her in a hospital room. Riley's heart started to beat faster, making her feel dizzy.

"I don't feel so good," she whispered.

"Do you need to throw up?"

"No. Can you help me back to my bed? I think I need to lie down?"

"Of course, sweetie. Just as soon as we get you out of this gown."

That's when the smell hit Riley. She was soaked in urine. She ripped the wet clothing from her body and clenched her fists, refusing to succumb to the tears returning to her.

The nurse bent closer to her, putting Riley's arms around her neck before scooping her off the floor. For an older woman, she was surprisingly strong. Riley had never been very heavy, but the nurse lifted her and strode to the bed with ease. She lowered Riley back onto the mattress slowly, careful not to let go until Riley's head was supported by the pillow.

"Now just sit tight, sweetie. I'm going to get a sponge bath ready, and something to clean up that nasty cut on your head."

Riley put a hand to her head. The hair was warm and wet. She looked at her fingers which were now red with blood. She tried not to cry, but she couldn't prevent the tears. She was scared and alone. Why had her family left her? What was so important that Quinn hadn't even visited? The questions made her tired. She closed her eyes, drifting off.

"Oh, I'm so sorry," the nurse said, reentering the room with gauze and alcohol wipes. "I know you're tired, but I can't let you sleep. Not just yet."

"Why not?"

"You hit your head pretty hard. We need to check a few things before I can let you sleep."

"What are you checking for?"

"Don't you worry about that, sweetie. We'll take good care of you."

"I'm not stupid," Riley snapped. "I may be a kid, but I'm in the hospital all the time. If you're going to test me for something, I want to know what the test is for." She was yelling now.

"Sweetie, I'm sorry. I shouldn't have dismissed you like that."

Riley glared at her for a moment, then burst into tears. She wanted to be angry. She wanted to yell. But inside all she felt was scared.

The nurse leaned onto the bed, hugging her. "Hey, now. You're going to be okay."

"I'm sorry," Riley sniffled.

"Don't worry. We nurses are used to being yelled at."

"I'm just—I don't understand—why would my mom leave me here? And where is my sister? I'm only seven. I'm not supposed to be by myself."

"I'm sure whatever their reason, they'll be here very soon. I'll try to reach your mom just as soon as I get you cleaned up, okay?"

"Okay," Riley choked between sobs. "Thanks."

"That's what I'm here for, sweetie." She smiled at Riley, then began wiping the blood from her forehead.

Riley closed her eyes again, wincing as the alcohol trickled into the cut. She focused on the cold burn of the sanitizing squares and the spongy softness of the gauze, trying not to think about where her family had gone. Before long, she was slipping into sleep again.

CHAPTER TWENTY-THREE

Quinn and Meelie had been in the desert for what felt like days. Their water was gone, and their legs were beginning to cramp. Quinn was having muscle spasms in her forearm from gripping the pole, yet she refused to relax her fingers. The butterflies were stronger than she imagined, and she was convinced that they'd take off into the sky in an instant if they could. That pole was her only hope of saving Riley; without a butterfly net, they'd be forced to set up camp in the desert until the sky was bright enough to navigate.

"You okay back there?" Meelie asked, breaking the silence that had settled between them.

"I'm sore, but I'm managing. How much farther do you think they'll take us?"

Meelie peered up at the sky. "Hard to say. The night's still young."

"Do you have any clue where we are?"

"I surely don't. Truth is, there's a lot to this place that I never bothered to learn. I wouldn't be surprised if I've only seen a sliver of this world."

"How big is this place, anyway?"

"I can't say for sure. I know back home the chickens could cover seven or eight miles in an hour. Figuring that this one here is a whole lot bigger, she can probably cover at least twice that. I've gone as many as five hours in any one direction, so that works out to . . ." Meelie trailed off, drawing numbers in front of her.

"About eight hundred miles of desert," Quinn broke in.

Meelie whistled. "Man alive. You sure that math is right?"

"Pretty sure. I'm in Algebra 2 right now."

"Algebra 2? Your school has more than one kind of algebra?"

"Well, no. The math is the same, but the second class covers more complicated types of problems."

"Wow. Most girls I knew had already quit school by the time they were your age, kid. But that was a different time, then. Few people cared if we girls had finished school. Most jobs offered to women didn't require much education anyhow."

"Did you finish high school?"

"I did. Bounced around a bit to get there, but I managed. Mother even set me up at a junior college for a bit. Didn't stick, though."

"Why not?"

"You know about the Great War?"

"You mean World War I? Or World War II?"

"I'd forgot all about there being a second war," Meelie said, her voice cracking. "Should have seen that one coming with that man in Germany riling up all of Europe." She went quiet.

"So you quit college because of the war?"

"I guess you could say that. I went to visit my sister around Christmastime, and the hospitals were just full of our boys from the war. I couldn't stand the idea of not helping, so I left school and started volunteering at a hospital with the Red Cross."

"Do you ever regret not graduating from college?"

"Not for one minute. The hospitals are where I got an itch for flying, listening to the boys and all their stories about the Royal Flying Corps."

"I never pictured myself dropping out of high school."

"Why would you do that?"

"I can't exactly help Riley *and* finish school back home."

"I hadn't thought of that."

Quinn was looking off to the left, trying to work out a cramp forming in her neck. "Uh, Meelie?"

"What's wrong, bunny?"

Quinn raised her hand and pointed to the ground. There was a definitive edge, beyond which everything went black, and the edge was closing in on them. They shifted their eyes in front of Pidge, trying hard to see what they were running toward. Darkness opened up ahead of them like a pool of black tar.

"This must be a cliff!" Quinn shouted. "What are we going to do?"

"Hold on, bunny! I don't think we'll be able to slow down in time."

Meelie bent down, talking to Pidge. "Now or never, old girl."

She tugged on Pidge's wings with both hands. Pidge stiffened, bawking frantically. "Get ready, Quinn!"

Pidge ran straight off the cliff, clawing for dirt and twisting her body.

"Fly, damn it. Fly!"

Meelie pushed and pulled Pidge's wings in desperation.

Quinn looked below them; she couldn't see anything. They could be twenty feet in the air or twenty stories. She thought about bracing for impact just as Pidge began flapping her wings. Her muscles were tense, but her stomach had begun to settle. They were in a controlled descent, which was better than nothing. Hopefully, she thought, they'd find something solid to stand on at the end of the fall.

Meelie let out a guttural yell and pumped her fists in the air.

"Not the smoothest takeoff I've ever been a part of, but we're in the air, Quinn. We're flying!"

Quinn had to laugh. Whatever waited for them at the bottom paled in the wake of Meelie's joy. Quinn could feel the energy pulsing through Meelie's entire body.

"I've spent the better part of a century on the ground, bunny."

"I guess sometimes you just have to close your eyes and jump."

"Ain't that the truth."

Quinn closed her eyes. The wind howled in her ears. Or was that Meelie shouting again? Quinn didn't care. She stuck out her tongue to taste the air. For the third time that night, her stomach dropped.

"Meelie," she whispered.

"I know. No mistaking that smell."

The air around them was cool, damp, and unmistakably sweet. They were gliding over the ocean with no way to tell when they'd hit the water, or how far from shore they already were.

CHAPTER TWENTY-FOUR

The nurse entered Riley's room to find her sleeping again. She walked over to the hospital bed and put a hand over Riley's, then gently shook her. Riley stirred, but didn't open her eyes. The nurse shook harder, clearing her throat for emphasis. Riley groaned and opened her eyes.

"Where's my sister?"

"I'm sure she'll be here soon."

"Oh."

"I just got off the phone with your mom. She said that she spoke with you earlier this evening about her having to leave the hospital for a bit, and that you were okay with her going home. Does that sound right?"

Riley thought back to when she was admitted. "Yeah. I guess I got confused."

"That's okay, sweetie. Do you want her to come in? She sounded very worried about you."

"Oh, no. I'm okay, now," Riley lied.

"Are you sure? Really, I don't mind calling her again."

Riley wanted to be strong for her mother, and she knew something must be wrong with Quinn if she hadn't even stopped by, but she was also scared. She couldn't remember the last time she had fallen. She'd been fine just a few days ago. Now she felt as weak as she ever had, she couldn't think straight, and she couldn't even remember hitting her head.

"Well, um, I would like to see her, if she's not too busy."

The nurse brushed hair from Riley's face, then offered again to call Jane for her. Riley nodded, smiling weakly. The nurse started to leave the room. Wary of being alone, Riley asked if she could make the call from the bedside phone. That way, Riley would be able to talk her mother if she was available. The nurse obliged, picking up the bedside phone and dialing a series of numbers. She then put the receiver to her ear.

"Ms. Willow? Sorry to call again so soon. Riley was hoping to speak with you?"

She paused.

"Yes, ma'am."

Another pause.

"No, we're still waiting for the results on that."

Riley was having a hard time following the one-sided conversation. She knew they were talking about her, but she felt frightened not knowing what her mother was saying. She was lost in thought when the nurse handed her the phone.

"Mama?"

"Yes, baby. I'm here. Are you okay?"

"I fell," Riley said. "My head hurts."

"I know, baby. I'm really sorry I wasn't there to help you to the bathroom."

"Where's Quinn?"

Jane didn't answer. Riley could hear thunder and heavy rain drops. Was her mother outside?

"Are you walking Butterfly?"

"In a storm? Of course not."

"But you're outside. I can hear the wind."

"Everything is fine, baby. Your sister is fine. Butterfly is fine." Jane's tone was sharp, which made Riley cry.

"Sorry, mama," Riley sniffed. "I didn't mean to make you mad."

Jane was quiet again. When she finally spoke, her voice was shaky.

"No, you didn't make me mad. Mama's just worried. I didn't mean to snap at you. I'll be there soon, okay?"

"You don't have to come. I'll be okay."

"Don't be silly. I'm on my way. Do you need anything?"

Riley shook her head, then handed the phone back to the nurse.

"Ms. Willow? I think maybe Riley's head is beginning to hurt. I'm going to give her a little something . . . Yes, ma'am. We'll see you soon, then."

The nurse put the receiver back on the dock and turned to Riley. "Are you okay, sweetie?"

Riley nodded, clamping her eyes shut to slow the tears.

"How about some Jell-O?"

Riley nodded again. "Do you have strawberry?"

"I'll go check," the nurse said, walking toward the door.

"Thank you," Riley called after her.

The nurse returned a few minutes later with a cup of red Jell-O and a spoon.

"Good news," she said. "I just spoke with the doctor, and you're cleared to sleep if you're still tired."

"What about the tests?"

"Your vitals look good, and Dr. Howe will be here in the morning. I don't think there's anything that can't wait until then."

"Okay," Riley said, taking another bite of Jell-O. She was tired, but she wanted to be awake when her mother got there. The nurse checked Riley's IV and various monitors, then updated the whiteboard with her current vitals. Riley turned and watched the monitors after the nurse had left the room. She'd been around them enough to know what they measured, and she focused her attention on the one recording the oxygenation of her blood.

During checkups, her numbers were usually in the low nineties. Dr. Howe had once told her that her numbers would always be lower than her sister, but anything over ninety was an A-plus in his book. If her numbers were in the high eighties, Dr. Howe ran extra tests and sometimes admitted her for a day or two. Tonight, the machine bounced from eighty to eighty-two. Her eyes were growing heavy. She fought to keep them open, but she was losing. Just before she fell asleep, she thought she saw the number drop to seventy-nine. Somewhere far off, Riley heard the rhythmic metronome of a patient in distress.

CHAPTER TWENTY-FIVE

The sky was beginning to shift like a new bruise to a deep blue. The butterflies were beginning to fade; their glow disappearing into the fog that surrounded Meelie and Quinn. Night was giving way to day, yet Quinn could see even less now than when she had set out from the cave. Quinn and Meelie huddled close on the back of Pidge, who had figured out how to glide, trying to stay warm as they were carried farther and farther out to sea.

Meelie had plenty of experience flying over the water, but she wasn't accustomed to flying blindly. Pidge was hard enough to steer on the ground. Now that she had figured her way into the air, she resisted Meelie's direction at every turn. Meelie didn't want to worry Quinn, so she kept her thoughts to herself. In truth, she was starting to wonder what would happen when they hit the water. She'd seen enough chickens in her day to know that they weren't fond of being forced to swim.

"What do you think drives the butterflies out this far night after night?" asked Quinn.

"I don't know. I'm sure not in a hurry to spend a night in the desert, though, after seeing how far they'll go to avoid the open plain. Must be something mighty fearful out there."

The fog felt wet on Meelie's face, and she wondered if they'd flown right into a storm without noticing. She held out her hand to test for raindrops, then realized that the water wasn't so much as falling as collecting on all sides of her hand at once. She bent low and trained her ear on the void below. What she heard was the unmistakable song of a whale pod. In that moment, she knew two things for certain: they were much closer to the water than she had realized, and they were definitely too far from shore to swim back.

"We're going to hit the water before long, bunny. I want you to be ready to jump because this hen is going to cast a kitten when she realizes she's in the middle of the ocean."

"What about the butterflies?"

"Wherever they're trying to go, we're going to have to find on our own. You'll need both hands to swim. These waves can get bigger than you and me in a hurry."

Quinn wrapped her free arm tighter around Meelie's waist. She was trying not to panic. She'd spent too many summers watching *Shark Week* to swim in the middle of an ocean. What if whitetips heard Pidge thrashing and swarmed them? *Killers of the deep*, television hosts would call them. But maybe there weren't any sharks in this ocean. Aimee had lived out here for centuries without any problem.

"You ready?" Meelie shouted.

"No!" Quinn answered. "What if there are sharks?"

"We stick close, and we kick anything that gets near, you hear?"

"I'm scared!"

"I am too, bunny. But we've got two choices: we can go under, or we can fight."

Quinn took a deep breath.

"On my count! One, two, three, jump!"

The two leapt from Pidge's back. Quinn had a vice grip on the pole, but the net broke free when they hit the water. Quinn was shocked at the force of the impact. She felt a bruise forming up and down the length of her body almost instantly.

"Quinn, call out!"

"I'm here!" She spun around, searching for Meelie among the waves. She caught sight of her a few yards away and began to swim toward her.

"There you are!" Meelie said when their eyes met.

"What's that sound?"

"I think that might be a whale pod."

Wonderful, thought Quinn. If this ocean had whales, she would put money on there being sharks too.

"Quinn, look out!"

Quinn stopped swimming, stiffening her body. Right in front of her, she saw an enormous, gray blowhole. A burst of water shot into the air. As she watched, the whale dove back under the waves, a wide tail slapping the surface before the animal submerged again. Were there more she couldn't see? What else was swimming in the water beneath them? She was too terrified to move.

"Meelie, what are we going to do?"

"We stick together." Meelie was still making her way toward Quinn. When she was close enough to touch her, she pulled a length of rope from the water and tied herself to Quinn.

"Where did you get that?"

"Tucked a piece into my belt before we left the cave. You never know when you'll need a little rope."

"Okay. What now?"

Meelie shielded her eyes and scanned the horizon for any sign of land. Before she could make a complete circle, she caught sight of Pidge, who was frantically slapping her wings against the waves.

"Crazy old bird. I don't know why chickens hate being in the water even though they don't sink or anything. Look at her, bobbing up and down like a buoy."

This gave Quinn an idea. They couldn't get too close to Pidge without risking a smack to the head, but perhaps they could somehow attach themselves to her and prod her along with the pole.

"You got anymore rope hiding in your pockets?"

"What have you got in mind?"

Quinn explained the plan while Meelie fished another length of rope from some hidden pocket beneath the water. They were testing various knots when Quinn saw the first fin. The color and shape were different than anything she'd seen on television, but she was certain that a shark was now circling them. She tugged the rope around her waist, pulling Meelie closer to her.

"What do you see, bunny?"

Quinn pointed at the fin.

"Okay, let's put our backs together. We need as wide a range of vision as possible."

She turned and pushed against the water, until she felt Quinn's shoulder blades digging into her back.

"What do you see?"

"There's at least three of them."

"I see two on this side. That makes five."

"Any idea what they are?"

"No. The sharks back home have sharper dorsal fins, and they're usually some shade of gray. These are almost green."

Quinn dipped beneath the surface to try and get a look at them. They were long and lean like she expected, but their noses were broad like a bull shark. That was odd. Broad noses usually meant powerful, aggressive breeds, but those breeds rarely scavenged in the open ocean. Their bodies were strange too, covered in dark patches that would have made them almost invisible in shallow water.

"Meelie, I don't think we're that far from shore."

"What makes you say that?"

Quinn explained what she'd seen and what she knew about the sharks on television. She was no expert, but what she said made sense. Besides, large whales were known to migrate just a few hundred yards from shore.

"Well if we're going to make a move, now's the time."

Meelie pointed at one of the sharks.

"That one is closing in, and the others aren't far behind."

"Won't be long before they get brave enough for a test bite," Quinn agreed.

They bobbed closer to Pidge, tossing the looped end of the rope toward her neck like a lasso. Meelie timed the toss perfectly, and the loop slipped onto Pidge in a single motion.

"Nice shot!"

"Okay, bunny. Let's see if this plan of yours is going to work."

Quinn pushed the pole into Pidge's left side. She squawked, but didn't budge. Quinn poked her again, a little harder than before.

"Maybe she doesn't know to kick her legs?"

Quinn thought for a moment, then went under water and aimed the pole at one of Pidge's legs, then the other. She poked the hen's feet one after the other. Pidge was clearly annoyed and kicked back at the pole. Before long, she realized she was moving through the water and began to kick on her own. Quinn broke the surface to see Meelie, white-faced, kicking against the water. Quinn could see a dorsal fin just a few feet away. The sharks were getting bold. If Pidge didn't pick up the pace, they'd never make land in time. Quinn positioned herself directly in front of Meelie, gripped the pole tight in her hands, and thrust with all the strength she could muster. If these sharks wanted a fight, she was ready to give them one they'd remember.

CHAPTER TWENTY-SIX

Jane pulled into a parking spot at the hospital and turned off the engine. She still hadn't heard from Quinn, and no one she had talked to had seen Quinn that night. The rain had passed, but the sky was still an eerie blue-green and littered with sheet lightning. Thunder growled menacingly, tree branches littered the roads and sidewalks, and the leaves still clinging to life swished like an angry shoreline. Jane closed her eyes, breathing deeply for several minutes, trying to collect herself before she went in.

The nurse had told her that Riley had fallen and hit her head. Jane felt terrible for leaving Riley by herself. She'd convinced herself that Riley would sleep through the night, yet she knew that Riley woke up often when she stayed for overnight observations. Truthfully, Quinn was so diligent about calming Riley down and helping her back to sleep that Jane was rarely even aware that the girls had woken up.

She wiped her eyes and ran a hand through her hair, still damp from the rain. Hopefully, she thought, Riley would be asleep again, and Jane could slip in without calling attention to her rain-soaked clothes. She really should have stopped to change; Riley sounded so despondent, though, and Jane wanted to get back to her as quickly as possible.

Inside the hospital, Jane first wanted to find the nurse assigned to Riley and get caught up on Riley's condition. As she entered the children's wing, she heard the telltale beeping of a patient in trouble. Someone in scrubs pushed past her and headed straight for Riley's room. Jane quickened her pace, trying to swallow the lump that was already forming in her throat. She reached the room to see several nurses and a doctor checking various machines, rattling off instructions and confirming dosages. At the center of everything was Riley, fast asleep. Was she asleep? Of course she was. She had to be. Jane scanned the machines, trying to locate the source of the incessant alarm. Heart rate was low, but not enough to trigger this response. Blood pressure was also lower than normal. Then she saw the blue number: Riley's oxygenation was in the seventies. She was dangerously hypoxic.

Jane could see, even from a distance, that Riley's skin was pale. Her lips and fingertips had a distinct blue tint. And her head, oh, her poor head. Jane saw a large bandage with a small spot of blood soaking through. How could she have left Riley alone? This was all her fault. If she'd been there, she could have helped Riley to the bathroom. She would have noticed Riley's oxygenation levels dropping. Yes, this was her fault. And Quinn's. How could she just disappear? Quinn knew how much the two of them needed her.

One of the nurses was running an oxygen line for Riley. Jane stared at the machine, which was still wailing. The number began to slowly climb back into the eighties. After a few minutes, the machine went silent. Some of the nurses began to trickle out. Riley's heart rate and blood pressure were still low though, and her oxygenation seemed to be plateauing around eighty-five. That wasn't odd for Riley, but the combination made Jane feel uneasy.

"Is Dr. Howe back, yet?" she asked.

"Oh, you must be Ms. Willow. I'm Wendy. Dr. Howe is still trying to get back. The storm slowed him down a bit."

"What's wrong with Riley? Why are her numbers so low?"

"Well, the oxygenation is a byproduct of her stenosis, of course. Her heart is having a harder and harder time cycling oxygen-rich blood to the rest of her body. The others are a result of her fall."

"How can you be sure? Couldn't they have caused the fall in the first place?"

"That's certainly possible, but her readouts don't show a clear dip until after I cleaned her up. I wouldn't worry too much about that. She should be stable now, and Dr. Howe will be here soon enough to talk about long-term options."

Wendy updated the whiteboard, then exited the room.

Jane carried a chair over to Riley's bed. She couldn't believe that Riley had slept through the machine's alarm, much less the people surrounding her. *Poor kid must be absolutely exhausted*, Jane thought. She tried not to dwell, but she knew that Riley's energy levels were directly tied to her heart. She and Quinn had gauged Riley's health on the length and frequency of her naps for as long as Jane could remember.

She took Riley's hand in hers. The fingers were frigid, so she rubbed them between her palms. Then she took Riley's other hand and did the same. She noticed that gooseflesh had formed over most of Riley's exposed skin, so she went to the closet and searched for more blankets. The only option was a thin, scratchy throw blanket that had clearly seen too many beds over the years. Still, a thin blanket was better than nothing. Jane unfolded the throw and stretched the blanket over Riley's body, tucking in the edges to hold in the heat.

Riley stirred. "Mama?"

"I'm here, baby."

"Where did you go?"

"I had to take care of a few things, remember?"

"You were looking for Quinn, weren't you?"

"What makes you say that?"

"I was thinking about this morning and how you said that Quinn had to go to school early. But she never leaves without telling me. And when I woke up, she wasn't here. She wouldn't do that, mama. Something is wrong, and you don't want to tell me."

Jane sighed. "I'm just trying to protect you, Riley. You shouldn't have to worry about anything like this. You're just a child."

"Do you ever wonder why Quinn and I get along so much better than you and I? She doesn't treat me like a kid. She knows better. I understand a lot more than you think I do."

"I'm not saying that you can't understand. I just don't know what's wrong, or if anything is wrong. What I do know is that no matter what happens, I'm helpless. I can't change anything or fix anything or—"

"Mom, if Quinn is missing, there's a reason. She's always here. Every doctor's appointment. Every trip to the hospital. She doesn't even skip baths or bedtime stories. She's there for me. Always."

"Sometimes people just want to be alone for a while."

"No one wants to be alone. Not really. They just get tired of people needing them. That's what Quinn told me. Isn't that why you disappear into your room most nights?"

Jane fought back tears.

Riley's face softened. She pulled the blanket tighter around her body, changing the subject. "I'm so cold, mama. Why do they keep these rooms so cold?"

"Let me go ask for another blanket."

Riley nodded.

Jane left the room, scanning the nurses' desk for Wendy, but she saw no one. Too anxious to linger, she began to wander the halls, peering in on patients and into open supply rooms. All the nurses were either busy or hiding. She wanted to ask Wendy more about Riley's fall and the contusion on her head. As she searched, she came across a closet with various bed linens. She decided to take a heavy blanket for Riley. No sense waiting for a nurse to get one later, after all. Walking back to Riley's room, she caught sight of Wendy slipping a jacket over her scrubs at the far end of the hall. Before Jane could speak, the nurse pushed open the large, wooden doors and disappeared into the main hospital. Jane was too late.

CHAPTER TWENTY-SEVEN

Quinn and Meelie took turns slamming the stick into the sharks when they passed too close. Pidge was still swimming, though they couldn't be sure if they were headed toward shore or farther out to sea. Quinn had worried that Pidge would be easy prey for the sharks, but they must have been deterred by the frantic beating of her wings on the water's surface, because they rarely came close. Meelie had taken the brunt of their curiosity, and she shoved several away just as they bared their teeth for an exploratory bite. Her fear had startled Quinn initially, and Quinn realized that she hadn't thought much about how death worked in the other realm. Since no one aged, she had assumed that people simply didn't die. She had been foolhardy in her quest for the heart flower, stupidly believing that she was invincible here. To Quinn's credit, Meelie couldn't remember if she had seen anyone buried since coming to the other realm.

"They're trying to wear us down, get us too tired to fight back!" Quinn shouted.

"The plan is working!" Meelie panted, handing Quinn the pole.

The two rotated so that Meelie faced Pidge and Quinn faced out into the open water. They were more vulnerable to the front and counted on Pidge to keep the sharks at bay when they circled around. Quinn noticed that the sharks moved in a distinct pattern, and a different shark went in for a bite each time the group circled. They worked as a pack, taking turns and gliding through the water at a slow pace in order to conserve energy. If Quinn and Meelie had been working to stay afloat, they'd have long since gone under. Luckily, Pidge was pulling them along quickly enough to stay above water without expending much energy. When Pidge tired out, they would be an easy meal for the sharks.

"Meelie, do you see that?" Quinn yelled, pointing to her left.

Meelie spun around long enough to glimpse a towering shadow against the horizon. "What is that? A boat?"

"Sure looks like one," Quinn answered, relieved.

"I hope so! This hen is slowing down. We won't last much longer on our own."

Quinn turned just in time to see one of the sharks move in on Pidge. As soon as the shark closed in, Pidge moved her head up and down against the water like a piston, driving her beak into the shark's back.

"That thing has more fight than I thought!" Quinn exclaimed.

She turned back toward the shadow she'd seen. This time the object was close enough to be sure: a large clipper ship was headed straight for them.

Quinn began to wave the stick through the air and shout, trying to signal the captain. Meelie joined in. Even Pidge began to squawk loudly. The three were making such a big ruckus that the sharks dropped back, widening their circle.

"Look at that! They're skittish!" Unlike the sharks Quinn had seen on television, these seemed scared of loud noise and big movements. "They must be true scavengers, not used to prey fighting back!"

Encouraged, the pair whooped and yelled even louder, smacking the waves with both hands. They were surrounded by white froth. The ominous, green fins grew smaller and smaller, until Quinn could scarcely find them between the waves.

The ship continued to head straight for them. Quinn guessed that the vessel was about a mile away now, too far to hear them yell. Day was approaching quickly, but the light was still too faint for them to be seen. They had to do something to get the boat's attention.

"Meelie, let me see your flight goggles," she said. "I'm going to try to catch a little light. Hopefully someone on that ship notices before they pass us by."

Meelie handed her the goggles.

"I'm plumb out of rope, bunny."

Quinn began to untie the piece holding them together.

"Are you sure about this? If we get separated by even a few yards—"

"We have to try, Meelie!"

Quinn fastened the goggles to the pole as tightly as she could, then held the contraption up out of the water, testing various angles until the glass lenses caught a bit of light. The task would have been much easier if the other realm had a definitive sun; without one, Quinn was forced to bend and turn the goggles constantly. Rather than a bright flash of light, she was making an indigo ripple that seemed to hover just above them.

The boat was closing in quickly, and the trio began to make as much noise as possible. They waved their arms in wide semicircles, sometimes prodding Pidge to make her squawk when their throats began to ache. They still couldn't tell if anyone on board was standing watch, or if the captain had taken notice of their position, but the ship maintained its heading. They'd either be rescued or run over.

"Meelie, I think that's Aimee at the wheel!"

Meelie followed her gaze.

"I think you're right! Sure looks like she upgraded from that old dinghy!"

"Hey! Help!"

"Ahoy there!"

"Please!"

The two yelled until their tongues swelled and their throats burned.

"Meelie, Quinn—is that you?"

Quinn recognized the voice immediately.

"I knew that boat had to be you, Aimee!"

"What in the world are you two doing out here?"

"That's a long story, old friend, and one I'd be glad to share if you can help us aboard!"

"Of course!"

Aimee moved swiftly to slow the ship, casting a wide net off the side. Meelie and Quinn swam toward the ship, pulling Pidge behind them.

"I don't think we're going to get Pidge to swim onto this net, Quinn!"

Quinn nodded, then disappeared beneath the water. She gripped one end of the net with both hands and kicked her feet hard against the surface. She dove deeper, the net still in her hands, until she was sure she was clear of Pidge's feet, then swam away from the boat. When she resurfaced, she tugged on the net until every strand was taut. Pidge wasn't perfectly in the center, but Quinn had given enough space on each side for Aimee to scoop them up.

"How do you plan to get us out of the water?" Meelie shouted toward Aimee. "Anybody else up there?"

"No. Just me. Hang on!"

Aimee tossed them one end of a long rope.

"See if you can loop that through the corners of the net!"

Quinn swam around the net, weaving the end of the rope

as Aimee had instructed. Once she had looped in all four corners, she swam close to the ship. The deck was too high for Quinn to throw Aimee the rope, so she tied the end to her pole and held the pole as far out of the water as she could. Aimee leaned over the edge, straining to grasp the pole, but she couldn't quite reach. Meelie swam over, dove under, then pushed Quinn up out of the water.

"There we are!"

"Now that's teamwork," Quinn grinned.

Aimee disappeared from view.

"Okay," she called, still out of sight, "I'm going to haul the net up. Get a good grip!"

Quinn and Meelie did as they were told, locking their arms and legs around the edge of the net. They watched as the four corners of the net lifted out of the water, closing in until the net looked like a teardrop. Pidge flailed inside, squished between the sides. Slowly, the three rose out of the water until they were high enough to see Aimee. She had used one of the masts and the ship's wheel as a makeshift pulley.

"Okay. We're out of the water. Now how do we get to the ship?" Meelie yelled.

Aimee scratched her head. "Oh, I've got an idea!" She ran below deck. Quinn could hear metal clanging and objects being tossed about. A few minutes later, Aimee emerged with a small anchor and another piece of rope.

"I'm going to hook the top of the net and then pull you in!"

"Banana oil!" Meelie shouted.

Quinn's face drained of color. "And what if you miss?"

"Never got anywhere without a little risk, right?" Aimee chuckled.

Meelie and Quinn looked at each other, then back at the anchor. They closed their eyes and braced for the worst. They felt a hard jolt, then a swinging sensation. Quinn opened one eye just enough to see the net rocking back and forth like a pendulum. She followed the motion to the top of the net. Aimee had hooked them on the first try.

"She got us, Meelie!"

Meelie warily opened her eyes and looked up, then let out a long breath.

Once aboard the ship, they freed Pidge from the net. She immediately took off running in circles around the deck, so Meelie tied her to one of the masts while Quinn relayed the night's adventure to Aimee. When she finished, she was in tears. Their one hope, their one clue, had vanished into the night. They had no way of knowing where the butterflies were going, or if they'd even find a heart flower there, but she had to do something.

Absentmindedly, she pulled the teleidoscope Martha had given her from her pocket and put the lens to her eye. She half-expected to see Meelie and Pidge bouncing through the desert; instead, Quinn was startled by bright, white light. She winced and squinted, searching the accosting glow for any shapes or flecks of color. As her eyes adjusted, she saw what looked like a curtain, then a bed. Three figures: the smallest was lying down in the bed while another bent over her; the third figure was seated beneath the curtains. The standing figure moved one arm and the scene dimmed enough for Quinn to see the room clearly. Riley was back in the hospital, and she was stuck in the middle of an ocean a world away.

CHAPTER TWENTY-EIGHT

Riley woke up famished, so Jane had gone on a quest for something more digestible than the powdered eggs and gummy meat the hospital offered. While she was gone, Riley rummaged through Quinn's backpack, which her mother must have brought in with her. She didn't know why her mother needed Quinn's backpack, but there was nothing else to do in the room, so she figured a little snooping wouldn't hurt. There were a number of loose pages, a binder, and several books on Amelia Earhart. Quinn must have been using them for her research.

She pulled one of the books from the backpack and began to read. Riley had always been an advanced reader, probably because she'd been listening to Quinn's bedtime stories for most of her life. Reading was one of the few things Riley was allowed to do in the hospital, so she pushed for her mother to teach her when she was just three years old. Now she was at least three grade levels ahead of the other kids in her class. Of course, that wouldn't last for very long, Riley thought gloomily. Most of them would be reading long after Riley died.

"What have you got there?" a nurse asked, entering the room.

"Who are you?"

"I'm your nurse, hon."

"What happened to the other lady?"

"Wendy? Oh, she had the night shift. I'll be with you during the day today."

"Okay," Riley said, going back to the book in her hands.

The nurse tried to make small talk while she fiddled with the machines, but Riley was too absorbed in the words on the page. Quinn had bookmarked a chapter about a plane crash. Riley hadn't been on a plane before. She hadn't even considered what flying must be like. Would she be scared?

That was a tough question. Everyone she met had fears, but Riley's life didn't leave much room for them. She was dying. When you really think about folks, almost everyone's fears are really just a fear of death, and why should Riley fear the one thing in her life that she had always known was coming? But if that were true, why had she been so scared the night before? Because, she realized, she had been alone. Everybody knew: the only thing scarier than dying is dying alone.

"Sorry that took so long," her mother said, startling Riley from her thoughts. "I wasn't sure what you wanted, so I got a little of everything."

Riley set the book down on her lap and looked through the bag her mother had set on her bed. "Did you get anything to drink?"

"Of course," Jane said, smiling. "I picked up one of those sunrise smoothies you like."

"Yes!" Riley shouted, raising her arms in the air.

The best thing about being in the hospital was that her mother often splurged on her favorite foods. She took the cup from her mother, then pulled two burritos wrapped in foil from the bag.

"Thanks, mama."

"Of course. Has Dr. Howe been in?"

"No. Just some nurse. Not the lady from before. A different one."

Riley spread salsa on the tip of her burrito, then took a

bite. Her mother often made fun of her love for spicy food. She'd started eating salsa when she was just eighteen months old. Quinn gave her a taste as a joke, figuring Riley would go crazy when her tongue began to burn. Instead, Riley dunked her entire fist into the salsa and licked her fingers.

After she'd finished her first burrito, she asked, "Any word from Quinn?"

Her mother looked away. "No, nothing yet."

"Do you think she's okay?"

Jane chewed her lip. "I'm sure she's fine."

Riley stared at her. "You're not supposed to do that."

"What?"

"Lie to family. That's our promise, remember? No lies, even when the truth hurts."

Jane sighed. Before she had a chance to speak again, Dr. Howe entered the room. He had bags under his eyes and a massive paper cup in one hand. Steam wafted from the opening on the lid, filling the room with the smell of burnt coffee.

"Good morning, Riley. How are we feeling?"

"I've been better," Riley admitted.

"I can see that. What on earth did you do to your head?"

Jane updated Dr. Howe on the symptoms she and Quinn had noticed, as well as the events of the night before. When she described the nurses surrounding Riley, Riley reached for her hand.

"I don't remember any of that, mama."

"I know. You slept right through."

Dr. Howe reviewed the notes on his clipboard, comparing the numbers in front of him with those on the machines.

"Well, looks like the oxygen is helping, but not by much."

"So what's the plan? Another valvuloplasty?"

"That was just a stopgap." He looked at Riley and frowned. "Perhaps we should discuss this outside?"

"No," Riley insisted. "I don't like when you talk about me where I can't hear."

Dr. Howe looked to Jane, who nodded. "I'm afraid we've run out of options."

"So, I'm not going to get better this time?"

Dr. Howe spoke slowly, lingering on each word.

"What I'm saying is that there's nothing more I can do for you."

Riley tried not to get angry, but she couldn't hold her tongue anymore. No one ever wanted to come right out and tell her she was going to die even though everyone knew. They had known from the moment she was born. Her entire life was a timeline with a definitive end. So why wasn't Dr. Howe telling her the truth, that this was her last visit to the hospital, that she wouldn't go back to school or ever walk Butterfly at the park again? Why was he avoiding looking at her? All her frustration came tumbling out of her.

"I'm not a child, you know! I'm seven years old, and I've been dying my whole freaking life. The least you could do is tell me!"

Jane gasped, her eyes wide and glassy. "Riley!"

"That's all right, Ms. Willow. She's correct." Dr. Howe turned to Riley. "I'm sorry. I shouldn't have avoided your question. The truth is, I don't want to believe that you're dying, so I have a hard time saying those words out loud. But you're right. You deserve an honest answer."

Dr. Howe paused, pain washing over his face.

"You don't qualify for a transplant, but you'll die without one."

"Thank you for being honest," Riley said. "Now I'm tired. I'm going to sleep."

She turned away from her mother, facing the large glass

wall at the end of her room, and closed her eyes. She had had enough of doctors for one day.

"I'm so sorry," she heard her mother say. "I think this whole situation is really starting to hit home for her."

"That's quite all right, Ms. Willow. She's scared and an-gry. Most of us are when we're facing death. No one likes to feel helpless. No one wants to just lay down and die."

Riley heard her mother begin to cry. She wished they would go away, but she didn't want to upset her mother any more than she already had. She was just so angry. Angry with Quinn for not being there. Angry with her mother for crying. Angry with the nurses for pretending everything was going to be okay. Angry with her heart. That stupid, wasted heart that had haunted her every day of her entire life.

CHAPTER TWENTY-NINE

Quinn was relieved to learn that Aimee knew exactly where the butterflies went each night and that she had turned the ship in that direction as soon as she'd heard Quinn's story. Now Meelie was attempting to calm Pidge down while Aimee stood at the captain's wheel. Quinn sat alone, scanning the horizon for the island Aimee had described. She was trying not to give in to hopelessness, but she was beginning to lose faith in her ability to save Riley. For all she knew, Riley was already gone, and her mother was collapsing with no one there to lean on. Quinn was the rock. She was the strong one. And she'd abandon her family for a fool's quest.

To make matters worse, Aimee had explained more about the effects of moving between her home and the other realm. Each time Quinn returned to the other realm, memories of her existence on Earth would disappear. The first memories to fade were the most personal, which made the effects hard for people to notice. Some even dismissed the forgetfulness as normal. However, the more a person traveled back and forth, the more of them vanished. Eventually, the only thing most loved ones would have left was the vague recollection of a name, perhaps one that had been considered for a new baby and then forgotten, an almost child.

The moons had all but disappeared into the sea; the sky was clear enough for Quinn to see several miles in every direction. Waves tumbled over one another in the wind, filling the water with jade-colored foam. *If the other realm had a sun*, Quinn thought, *the surface would look like a vast field of precious green stones.* But because she could see no sun, there was only the distance between her and Riley. She and Meelie had searched all night only to find themselves in the middle of an ocean so immense that even Aimee, afloat for three centuries, hadn't charted the entire thing.

"There!" Aimee shouted.

"Where?" Quinn followed Aimee's hand, straining to see what had caught her attention.

"I see them," Meelie shouted, "portside off the bow!"

Quinn ran to Meelie and followed her gaze. Far off, just above the horizon, a patch of sky shimmered and seemed to move very slowly across the front of the ship.

"That's just a mirage," she mumbled, slumping down onto the deck.

"Get up, bunny. Use your head. That's no mirage. You have to have sunlight for all that."

Quinn turned the words over in her head. Meelie was right. And if the shimmering cloud was not a mirage, then something really was moving up ahead. Had Aimee found the butterflies already?

"Mind yourselves!" Aimee hollered. "You'll want to grab hold and button down!"

Quinn peered over the side of the ship to see swells slapping at the wood. The closer they got to the mysterious cloud, the larger the waves grew. Ocean spray was already dampening her hair and jacket. Any other time, Quinn might have been terrified, but she was too focused on getting back to Riley to dwell on the heavy pitching and swaying of the ship. Aimee, for her part, looked as serene and ethereal as she had the day Quinn first met her.

Meelie rushed to tie Pidge to the center mast, then scrambled up the steps to Aimee. Quinn couldn't help but notice Meelie's white-knuckled fists. From the waist up, she was the epitome of strength, yet Quinn noticed her legs trembling the way Riley's did when she sat before a new slide for the first time. *The line between cowardice and courage,* Quinn thought, *is crossed in a single step.* When the time came, would her feet fall forward or back? She couldn't be sure, but she hoped—for Riley's sake—that she wouldn't hesitate.

"Hard to port!" Aimee bellowed.

Quinn was jolted from her thoughts just in time to shield her head with her hands before careening across the deck, narrowly avoiding a panicked Pidge clawing at the base of the mast and tugging hard on the rope that bound her.

"A little more warning!" Quinn shouted, once her words had returned to her.

"All these shoals might as well be a slalom," Meelie huffed, pulling herself up.

"What on earth is a slalom?" Aimee asked, confusion overtaking her brow.

"A type of downhill skiing, if I recall."

"Skiing?"

"Look out!" Quinn interjected as the stern crashed into a cresting wave.

Water blanketed the deck, sending Pidge further into a frenzy. Quinn, who was sopping wet, wiped her eyes and began making her way up to Meelie and Aimee, who had managed to stay dry thus far.

"Won't be long, now," Aimee assured them.

"How can you be sure?" Quinn asked. "I don't see any island nearby."

"When are you going to learn? This place isn't like your home. Don't just look at what's in front of you; see what's really there."

"What does that even mean?" Quinn snapped. She was in

no mood for riddles. She'd had enough of the other realm. "I just want to get home to my sister before—"

Meelie tried to embrace Quinn, but Quinn pushed her away.

"Look, I really appreciate you helping me, but Riley is dying, and a hug won't save her! Nothing can."

"You can't let go of hope, bunny."

"Don't talk to me about hope. Your sister had hope. Every day for the rest of her life, she looked out into an ocean just like this one and hoped. Do you know what she got for all her hope? Nothing."

Meelie stared at her. Quinn stared back, but she couldn't look into Meelie's eyes, red and glistening with sorrow. She stormed back down to the lower deck. She was already drenched anyway. At least there she could be alone.

"Meelie—" Aimee started.

"She's not wrong," Meelie interrupted. "Almost eighty years I've been waiting to hear those words. Sure didn't figure she'd be the one to say them, though."

"Quinn certainly is spirited."

"Got to give her credit for that. How many would have given up already? How many would have stared off that cliff and never jumped?"

Quinn listened from the deck below, her back to the women so they couldn't see her own eyes filling with tears.

"And still so young," Aimee continued.

"That one? Applesauce. Look at her. Why, she never had a chance in the world. Young? That ended the day her sister was born."

"You could say the same about most the people here, I guess."

"At least she won't be alone in her grief."

"If she stays."

"What do you mean, if she stays?"

"I'm not sure she'll risk leaving Riley again."

"Aimee, if she doesn't come back—"

"Riley will die."

Quinn could feel their eyes on her back, but she didn't dare turn around. What could she say, anyway? Aimee was right: Quinn had no intention of leaving Riley. Not this time. Besides, she hadn't even found a heart to take back. This time, she wasn't going home to be her sister's savior. She was going home to say goodbye.

The ship rocked violently as Aimee steered through the shoals. Quinn had inched her way to the bow and now huddled into the crook, her shoulders slamming into the hard wood every time they hit a wave. Her eyes were locked on Aimee, who had gone silent. Lines creased her face, telling the story her agelessness could not. Her story was not as simple as she had pretended, that much Quinn could see. The question was, why had she banished herself to the ocean for more than three centuries? If she ever got home, Quinn would do her best to find an answer.

"Okay, Quinn. The island is just up ahead!" Aimee shouted down.

Quinn stood and turned to face the water, but she still couldn't see anything resembling an island. Instinctively, she leaned down and peered into the waves breaking against the ship. Beneath her, the ocean floor was sloping upward until the shoals disappeared completely. The water looked shallow enough for Quinn to swim, and in an instant she was over the ship's edge.

"Quinn! What in Kansas are you doing?" Meelie shouted.

Quinn looked up to see Aimee turning the captain's wheel hard. She could hear the ship straining under the sudden change of direction; Meelie and Aimee braced themselves as one side of the ship rose out of the water, their eyes locked on the masts tilting toward the surface of the ocean. Quinn swam with all her strength, desperately trying to get clear before the port side slammed back into the sea. In moments, she was dragged backward by a powerful undertow, then propelled forward by a large, rolling wave. Just as she heard the ship break the surface, she felt sand against her knees. She stood up to find that the water was only a few feet deep, hitting her square in the hips.

She trudged toward an invisible shore, but her lower half remained submerged. She was beginning to feel like she was walking in circles. Had she jumped too early? Had she managed to strand herself on a sandbar? Quinn turned to see Aimee's ship anchored several hundred yards away, unable to get any closer to shore without damaging the ship. She squinted, but couldn't make out the silhouettes of either woman on the deck. Then she saw a smaller boat inching toward her. Between her and the vessel, she noticed a strangely dark patch of water that seemed to be glowing. She dropped the rest of her body into the water and began to swim again. She had learned enough about the other realm to know that all good things gave off light.

CHAPTER THIRTY

The nurses had moved Riley into a new room with a couch that converted into a bed so that Jane could sleep more comfortably. Of course she couldn't sleep with her daughter lying a few feet away, switching between throaty sobs and angry outbursts. She pulled a chair close to Riley, resting her hand on Riley's while she slept. Riley's hand felt much bigger than Jane remembered. In her mind, Riley was still small enough to carry to bed, small enough to fit her whole hand inside Jane's palm while they crossed the street. Somewhere along the way, her little girl had gotten much older than she realized, much older than a seven-year-old ever should be.

Jane tried not to stare at the machines looming over her daughter's small body, but the neon numbers were too bright to ignore in the otherwise dark room. Riley's oxygen levels had plateaued at eighty-five percent, low enough to require constant monitoring, but not low enough to cause significant internal damage. If the levels dipped below eighty percent, Riley would be at risk of long-term damage to her brain and heart, among other things. Though her levels had remained constant for nearly two hours, Jane was unable to look away. She was consumed by a sense of dread. The thunderstorm and Quinn's disappearance were just too ominous to ignore; she could feel in her gut that something terrible was just around the corner.

Quinn made her way through the hospital as quietly as she could, trying not to draw attention to herself, which was dif-

ficult considering the ruddy-amber glow emanating from beneath her hoodie. She had been too frantic to worry about
changing clothes, but she regretted her decision the moment
her shoes hit the hospital floor. Every few steps, the rubber
soles made loud, squeaking sounds, and she was leaving a
slippery trail behind her as she walked. She avoided eye contact by pulling the hood down over her eyes and locking her
gaze on the strikingly-white linoleum.

"Excuse me, sir. Sir?" one nurse shouted after her.

"Ma'am, can I help you find someone?" another pressed.

Quinn ignored the questions, looking up only long
enough to track her progress toward Riley's room, which she
had gotten from a receptionist at the front desk. The hospital
felt like a maze, which reminded her of the day Riley had
been born, of all the turns and strange names that had forever
etched themselves into her memory.

One more corner and Quinn found herself standing outside Riley's room. All the lights were off, allowing Quinn
to read the numbers on the monitors that surrounded her
sister. On the far side, she saw her mother bent over Riley,
her shoulders slowly rising and falling. She was sleeping, not
crying. She had gotten back to her sister in time. She gritted
her teeth, mustering every bit of resolve she had to keep from
falling to her knees and sobbing right there in the hallway.

Quinn could feel the bulb pulsing against her chest exactly as she had the first time she had saved Riley. This time,
she was overwhelmed by the knowledge that what she felt
was, or would soon be, her sister's heartbeat. For a moment,
they were closer than they ever would be again. She closed
her eyes, trying to memorize the rhythm. Her fingers tapped
against her thigh as she mouthed the beats until her whole
body felt stiff and began to ache. She refocused her eyes
and peered into the room, checking to see that her mother

was still asleep. She felt the pangs of grief at how small Jane looked curled up next to Riley. She saw in her mother's body the same fear and helplessness that she had seen so often in her sister. Jane would never recover from losing Riley. The truth was right there in her body language. Quinn moved quickly, positioning herself on the near side of Riley, opposite her mother.

She unzipped her hoodie and eased the bulb from the makeshift cradle, concealing the radiance with Riley's bedsheet. As slowly and deliberately as she could, Quinn moved the bulb to her sister's chest until she had positioned the new heart above the telltale red freckle. Light swelled until the room resembled the horizon at dawn. Her eyes instinctively darted to her mother, but Jane didn't stir. Even Riley, whose entire upper body was ablaze, didn't move an inch. Quinn stared at her sister until all the light had left the room again, save the inescapable machines shouting in the dark. The last thing Quinn saw as she slipped into slumber were the blue numbers of the oximeter rising just above ninety percent, her hand already draped over Jane's in her sister's lap.

"What are you doing?" Jane yelled. "Get your hands off my daughter!"

Quinn snapped up, rubbing her eyes. The room was sunlit now, and she immediately missed the subtleness of daylight in the other realm. Had the morning always been so assaulting and harsh?

"Nurse! Get this girl away from Riley!"

Several nurses rushed into the room, pulling Quinn away from the bed.

"Mom! W-what's wrong with you?" Quinn stammered. "Let me go. She's my sister!" Quinn twisted against the nurses.

"Security!' one of them called into the hallway.

"We don't need security. Let me go! Riley is my sister. Mom! Tell them!"

"How did she get in here?" Jane fumed. "Don't you people have protocols to protect your patients against things like this? What sort of hospital just lets strangers squat in hospital rooms?"

"What's happening?" Riley groaned.

"Riley!" Quinn freed herself from the nurses and rushed to her sister.

"Why is everyone shouting?" she asked groggily.

"Riley, do you know this girl?" Jane interjected.

"Of course. She's my sister. Duh. I've got a bad heart, Mom, not a brain problem."

"What are you talking about?" Jane's voice wavered now.

The nurses looked at one another, their confusion written across their faces.

"Everything okay in here?" Dr. Howe asked, entering the room. "I see you found Quinn," he added, putting a hand on Quinn's shoulder.

Jane stared at him, then Riley, then Quinn. Her eyes were hazy, and Quinn could see her jaw muscles pulsing.

"I'm sorry, Quinn. I don't—I must have—"

"No, you're right," Quinn interrupted. "Sorry I disappeared on you two."

"Ms. Willow, have any other doctors visited Riley?" Dr. Howe broke in.

"No, why?"

"Her oxygen levels are rising," he answered, motioning to the oximeter. "If they continue to climb, her oxygen saturation will be in the normal range within a few hours. That's twice now," he said, turning to Riley, "you've battled back from what I believed, frankly, to be insurmountable. If

I didn't know better, I'd say you have some sort of miracle worker looking out for you."

Quinn caught herself fidgeting with the zipper of her hoodie and shoved her hands into her pockets. "So, she's going to be okay?" she asked Dr. Howe, who was scouring the line graph readouts from various machines.

"She certainly seems to be rebounding, but I'm hesitant to release her just yet. We've seen this once before, and she took a sharp turn for the worse. We can't risk that happening at home. With your permission, Ms. Willow, we'll keep Riley under observation for a couple days. That should give me a chance to better understand her recovery, and we can ensure that her heart will continue to circulate the oxygenated blood properly."

"Yes, of course," Jane responded, her expression still perplexed.

Quinn felt like she was being studied by her mother and turned her attention to Riley. "What do you say I grab a sleeping bag and camp right here until you can come home?"

"That sounds fun," her sister beamed. "Do you have any new stories for me?"

Quinn grinned. "I'm working on one I think you'll love, but the ending isn't quite ready yet."

By now, most of the nurses had trickled out of the room, though one lingered near Dr. Howe, who was using a red pen to draw circles around various points on the graphs he had pulled from the machines. Quinn studied his face, which was creased with confusion. She wondered if he was aware that he was talking to himself, mumbling about how he could think of no logical reason for Riley's sudden improvement. He had seen miraculous recoveries before, he said, but never twice in the same patient. He must have felt Quinn staring because he snatched up the readouts and turned sharply, then dismissed himself from the room. Jane didn't seem to notice his departure. She was draped over Riley's lap, cooing the way she used to when Riley was a baby. Quinn knew the sound well, and she knew that her mother would be difficult to rouse anytime soon. Riley, too, had drifted off again.

Might as well run home while they sleep, she reasoned. Her entire body ached, and her eyes had been burning for so long that she had almost forgotten what they felt like on a normal day. Still, her clothes were damp and beginning to stiffen, she smelled like week-old seawater, and she hadn't eaten much besides moon fruit and Meelie's flat cakes since she had left for the other realm. She could keep herself awake a little while longer for a hot shower and a hamburger or two. Besides, she wanted to dig deeper into her research on Meelie, and she was determined to find out more about Aimee's life before the other realm. She kissed Riley on the forehead, then began to leave. Not wanting to worry her mother any more than she already had, she left a note on the dry erase board for her: *Hungry. Soggy. Be back soon.* She drew a butterfly beneath the message. She tiptoed to the door, took one more look at her weary family, and left the room without a sound.

CHAPTER THIRTY-ONE

Quinn patted her pockets for the house key, but they were empty. She would have to retrieve the spare key from the walkway behind the house. Her mother kept one underneath a large stepping stone in the backyard because Butterfly often slept or played there during the day, and she figured that few intruders would think to go around back to look for a key. She scanned the street, not wanting give anyone the impression that she was trying to break into the house. Seeing no one, Quinn trudged through the muddy strip of grass toward the back fence. She was almost to the gate when Butterfly began barking furiously and jumping into the fence.

"Quiet!" Quinn whispered as sternly as she could. "Do you want to get the cops called on me?"

She continued toward the gate, shushing Butterfly, but he refused to calm down. She peered through the gap between two fence posts and called Butterfly to her. He responded by lunging at her, his teeth bared. Quinn jumped back just before his body slammed against the posts. He was barking even louder now, his paws slapping the wood each time he launched himself forward. The entire panel shook. Quinn continued to shush Butterfly, but he was too worked up to hear her. Then Quinn remembered her last return from the other realm. Aimee had explained to her that visiting the other realm would erase certain memories from her family's minds; she hadn't considered that Butterfly had memories too. Had he forgotten who she was already? If so, entering the backyard would be dangerous.

Quinn leaned against the house, considering how she might get into the house without Butterfly attacking her or drawing more attention than he already had. She couldn't risk pulling the screen off any window in the front; perhaps one of the side windows was unlocked. She made her way along the brick, stepping quietly so that Butterfly would not rush back into the house to meet her. Her mother's bedroom was locked. Luckily, the window in Riley's and her bathroom was unlocked. Since the opening was at least six feet off the ground, they weren't as diligent about securing that window.

She pushed up the sleeves of her jacket, scraped the soles of her sneakers against the brick, then scooted back to give herself a little room. Counting down in her head, Quinn took three quick strides toward the window, pressed her foot against the brick and pushed up hard. She caught the ledge with her fingertips. Holding herself up with one hand, she ripped through the screen with her other and pulled hard on the frame. The brick was already tearing at her skin, and she could feel her arm beginning to tremble. She pressed the palm of her free hand flat against the glass, then pried the window up until she had enough space to grip the underside and push the window all the way open. As soon as she did so, her fingers gave out, causing her to tumble to the ground. Undeterred, she cleaned her shoes one more time, backed up to the neighbor's wall, and ran hard toward the opening. This time, she raised her foot higher off the ground, leapt upward, and flung her right arm over the windowpane. Quinn tensed her muscles and pulled herself through the window.

Once inside, she eased her way to the bathroom floor. Butterfly would be inside in an instant if he heard someone walking around. She removed her shoes and socks, then tiptoed to the back door. She could hear Butterfly barking outside, right where she had left him. Preferring speed to stealth, she slammed the doggy door down and flipped the lock. Butterfly barreled across the yard, pawing at the hard plastic that now blocked him from entering the house.

"Sorry, bud. I love you, but I've got to get cleaned up and back to the hospital before Riley wakes up."

Quinn unlocked the front door and retrieved the mangled screen from the side of the house to be safe. She took a longer shower than she intended, scrubbing her body three times to get the salt from the ocean off her skin and out of her hair. Refreshed, she gathered clothes for the next few days. When she found her backpack, she saw that someone had rummaged through her research. Riley had a habit of nosing around, which Quinn didn't usually mind. Today, though, her sister's curiosity had her on edge. Had she written anything about the other realm in her notes? She couldn't be sure until she got back to the hospital and talked with Riley. She shoved her tablet into the bag, grabbed the duffel with her clothes, and slipped out of the house.

Back at the hospital, Quinn's thoughts were clearer than they had been in days, allowing her to navigate the labyrinthine halls with ease. She walked quickly, weaving to avoid the nurses and doctors making their rounds. Within a few minutes, she was outside Riley's room, watching her family through the window. What she saw touched her, but also hollowed her: Jane was sitting with her legs crossed at the end of Riley's bed, tallying the points from her latest turn at Yahtzee.

She was shocked; she and her mother played the game every Friday night when Quinn was first learning to count, but the box had been moved to the top shelf of Jane's closet, a place Quinn had once called the graveyard for games of probability. Her mother had not been amused, Quinn remembered, and sent her to her room for the rest of the weekend. Now that she was a bit older and more mature, Quinn understood that probabilities made Jane spiral. To her mother, probability was the enemy of hope, and Jane desperately needed hope.

Quinn watched as Riley scooped the dice into the cup, then made a wide circle with her hands as she shook the cup. Satisfied, she slammed the cup onto the bed, then lifted the rim just enough to peek under.

"Three fives!" Riley shouted, clapping wildly.

Jane smiled, penciling in Riley's points. She mouthed something that Quinn couldn't make out, but she assumed Riley had just won the game because they started to place the scorecards and dice into the dusty game box. After they had cleared everything from the bed, Jane lay down next to Riley and stroked her hair until Riley fell asleep. Jane closed her own eyes, resting her head above Riley's on the pillow. They looked almost serene despite the harsh white light and crowd of monitors around them. *Happy*, Quinn thought. *They looked happy.* That should have relieved Quinn, but instead she wondered if they would be better off if she decided to stay in the other realm.

"Don't be ridiculous," she muttered to herself.

"I'm sorry, ma'am. Did you say something?"

Quinn turned to see a nurse behind her. She shook her head, then turned her attention back to the hospital room. The backpack dug into her shoulders, and the duffel bag seemed to get heavier every minute. She tried to move into the room, but her legs were stiff and aching, so she stood there, a window away from the family she had shielded, the mother and daughter who had finally learned to find strength within themselves. Quinn let the bag drop to the floor, then eased herself down and sat cross-legged outside the room. Everything she cherished was lying in that hospital bed, yet they didn't even know she had been gone. Had she been so easy to forget? Then she thought of Meelie, and Aimee, and the strange children who had made the other realm their home, and she realized that she missed them. They had become a family of sorts to her as well. They knew her sadness. They knew her struggle. They knew her sister's name. If something happened to Quinn, she genuinely believed that they would take care of Riley and her mother. Perhaps the other realm wasn't as lonely as Quinn had imagined. Someday, she too might even call the caves her home.

CHAPTER THIRTY-TWO

That evening, Jane asked Riley if she was okay with just Quinn staying that night. She wanted to shower and get a good night's sleep before returning to work the following day. Riley seemed to have rebounded, and her numbers were holding steady, at least for the moment, and Jane hadn't been in the office in nearly a week. Riley assured Jane that she would be fine and that Quinn would take care of anything she needed just as she always had. Before Jane left, though, Riley begged for a break from hospital food. Her mother made a quick run for burritos and chips, then left for home.

Riley was still getting her strength back and got tired easily, so Quinn turned on the television for her and retrieved one of the Amelia Earhart books from her backpack. She kept a spiral notebook and pen nearby to take notes, but she quickly became so immersed in reading about Earhart that she forgot the assignment altogether.

"What are you reading?" Riley asked awhile later, startling Quinn.

"Just a book for class," she replied nonchalantly.

"What is the story about?"

"This isn't a story. Well, I guess there's a story, but not like you're used to. I mean—okay, so this story is true, right? Remember that woman I was talking about at dinner one night, Amelia Earhart? She decided that she wanted to fly planes, only some people didn't want her to."

"Why?"

"She was too outspoken about the need for women pi-

lots, which I guess was controversial at the time. I can't figure out why so many people would resist the idea of female
pilots, though, especially during a war. Even if the military
didn't want to send women into battle, which I think is a little ridiculous anyway, they could have used women to deliver
supplies to camps in safe zones, or to help with mail service
while men were overseas."

"So what did she do?"

"That's the coolest thing about her. She just did her own
thing: flew planes and wrote a book and encouraged other
women to learn how to fly, too. She was the first woman to
fly across the Atlantic Ocean. Some people said that wasn't
special because she was just in the plane, not the one actually
flying, so then she flew across the same ocean all by herself. People really started to like her after the war. Maybe she
didn't talk as much about women soldiers, or maybe people
just had more to worry about when the country ran out of
money. I don't know. I'm still reading."

Riley was quiet for a few minutes.

"What was your dad like?" she asked, the question growing until every corner of the room felt heavy and full.

"You mean our dad?" Quinn corrected.

"I don't have a dad," Riley shrugged.

"Of course you do."

"Can you call someone dad if you've never met him?"

Quinn had expected her to ask about their father eventually. In fact, she was surprised that Riley hadn't asked when
she was young and all her friends were doing Father's Day
crafts at school, but Riley just made pictures of Quinn, her
mother, and Butterfly. Really, that was the only version of
family Riley knew.

"I don't know how to answer that, boo."

"I'm not sad or anything. I just—maybe I could miss him

if I knew what he was like or how he smelled or when he went away."

"You know, I can't remember exactly when dad left. He left me this teleidoscope," Quinn gestured to the object hanging at her neck, "on the day you were born. But I remember a trip not too long before then. Mom was really big and couldn't hike very far into the mountains without getting dizzy. Dad was there. At least, I think he was."

"Was he nice?"

"Oh, definitely. Dad was the biggest goof. He lived to laugh."

"Then why did he leave?"

Quinn thought for a long time. "I—I can't remember. I think he had to go somewhere for work, and he just—I guess he couldn't find his way back home."

"Do you think he left because of me?"

"No way, sis. Wherever he is, I imagine his saddest thought every single day is that he doesn't get to know you."

Quinn studied Riley's face, which seemed to slump in the way her whole body did after running on the playground.

"Hey, do you want to help me find stuff about some other people I'm researching?" she asked, trying to get Riley's mind off their father.

"Okay!"

Hopefully Riley could at least find information about who the children were in the other realm. They knew everything about her from talking to Meelie, yet Quinn knew almost nothing about them. The idea that she could miss people whose names she didn't remember, or who lived decades or even hundreds of years ago, was difficult for Quinn to embrace and accept.

She pulled the computer from her backpack, plugged the cord into the bedside outlet, and then connected to the hospital's wireless network. Next, she wrote down several phrases on a piece of paper: *five children; disappeared; kids missing; unsolved; never found.*

"So the first thing you'll do," she explained, "is type one or two of the phrases into the search bar." Quinn pointed to the search bar, then typed: *five children + disappeared.*

"Why did you use a plus sign with words?"

"If you use the plus sign, you can find things that have both of the phrases you type. Sometimes, we find too many websites to read all of them. This is one way to filter them, or see only the ones that talk about what we're looking for."

Riley nodded, then furrowed her brow and began to scan the search results. Quinn smiled at the look of concentration on her face. Perhaps research was a little more than Riley was used to, but Quinn figured Riley would get a kick out of helping, and she would have to learn how to do Internet searches eventually. When she got to middle school, teachers would be assigning research projects in almost every class.

"When," Quinn whispered to herself, letting the notion take shape in her mind.

She was used to saying "if" when she thought of Riley's future, but that didn't feel right anymore. She looked over at Riley, whose face was illuminated by the laptop. Her baby sister was growing up. Most people probably dread the day their kids learn how to use the Internet, but things are different when you don't think your kid will live long enough to need an e-mail address. Families with dying children don't live the way other families do. They are all part of a larger culture, one built on grief and desperation. How would her family adapt if Riley stayed healthy? Quinn didn't have an answer; the question was intriguing, though. She decided that she would have to spend some time looking into how other families moved on once kids had beaten cancer or gotten a transplant. Not at the moment, though. At the moment, all she wanted was to know more about the people she had left behind in the other realm.

"You finding anything interesting?" she asked.

"Some."

"Can you be more specific?" Quinn pressed.

"Oh, sorry. Um—I see a lot of stuff with the name Sodder. I can't really understand most of the words, but I found fire and Sodder and children in a lot of the little paragraphs under the links. Is that what you were looking for?"

"Fire? Do you see anything about what caught on fire, or what happened to the five kids?"

"The family had ten kids, not five. Oh, no—their house burned down on Christmas. That's so sad!"

"Wait, *ten* kids?"

Quinn put her book on the chair and walked around to look at the screen. She began mouthing the words to herself as she read.

"Read out loud," implored Riley. "I want to know, too!"

"This says that the house caught on fire. Most of the older kids, and the baby, got out of the house, but three girls and two boys were stuck upstairs. No one could get through to the fire department. Someone had thrown the family's ladder down a ditch away from the house, so the father couldn't get to the kids who were trapped, and they couldn't get down. Whoa—someone cut the phone line on purpose. After everything had burned, the fire department said the house had electrical problems, and none of the children could be found, except a lot of people saw the Christmas lights on—that doesn't make any sense. How could a power surge cause the fire if the lights stayed on? Sounds like some people think the fire was started on purpose to get back at the dad or something. Oh, the fire wasn't hot enough to burn up the kids.

The mom and dad always believed that the missing kids were still alive because the firefighters never found any bones or anything. They just . . . disappeared."

"That's so sad. And on Christmas? Why would your teacher want you to learn about this?"

Quinn thought for a minute. "I'm trying to learn about people who went missing. My project is about Amelia Earhart. She disappeared trying to fly around the world. The Sodder children disappeared, too. They didn't go missing in the same way, but I guess learning how different people disappeared and what happened after will help me understand Amelia Earhart more."

"How can people just stop being there?"

Quinn took a deep breath. She wasn't ready for this conversation. Though she was honest with Riley about death, she didn't spend much time on the people who keep living after someone dies. She was afraid that Riley would have a harder time with her condition if she knew that her family would have to go on without her. And why should she carry that? Knowing that Jane and Quinn would be heartbroken wouldn't change anything. They were going to mourn Riley no matter what. Unless, of course, this butterfly heart healed Riley for good.

"I think that's enough research for today. Why don't you get some sleep?"

She moved the computer from Riley's lap to the table beside the couch. She left the cord plugged in, but closed the lid, casting the entire room in darkness. They had been so engrossed in the Sodder children that neither one had noticed the sun go down. That meant that Riley had missed dinner, too. Quinn offered to walk to a fast-food place; neither of them was really hungry, though, and they decided that sleep was much more appealing than another greasy meal in a paper bag. Quinn lay down on the couch, spreading one of the rough hospital blankets over her body. She started to say good night, but she could already hear Riley cooing in her bed. She closed her own eyes and rested her head on a fresh hoodie she had balled and wedged into the crook of the sofa.

Jane stopped by the next morning with breakfast casserole. Quinn and Riley were so hungry after missing dinner that they tore into the meal immediately. Though the dish was easy enough to make, Quinn considered the concoction of eggs, shredded potatoes, and breakfast sausage a real treat. She thanked Jane for the food, but her mother didn't seem to hear her. In fact, she didn't seem to see her, either. Every time she looked Quinn's way, her expression would go flat again. What was worse was that she didn't just stare through Quinn; she stared at her. Quinn began to feel like she was being studied, scrutinized.

"Mom, are you still upset with me for taking off?"

"What?" Jane responded, looking confused. "Did you go somewhere?"

Quinn wasn't sure how to answer the question. On the one hand, she didn't believe that her mother had forgotten her disappearance. On the other, she would rather not have to lie more than she already had about her whereabouts. She decided not to say anything unless her mother pressed.

"Oh," Jane said, pulling an envelope from her purse, "I finally got around to printing some of the pictures from Christmas last year. Do you want to look at them with me?" she asked, turning to Riley.

"Yeah!"

Jane scooted close to Riley, leaving little room for Quinn to sit with them. She decided to stand. That would at least give her a better vantage point for the pictures. As her mother thumbed through the prints, Quinn was absent from the images. Riley noticed, too.

"How come Quinn isn't in any of the pictures, Mama?"

"Isn't she? I didn't realize. I guess she was doing something else while we opened presents."

"No. She was there. I remember because she read to me from the butterfly guide from Santa. The words were too big, and you were in the kitchen making gingerbread pancakes with chocolate chips. We wanted to sit by the fire, but Butterfly wouldn't move his big butt, so we laid on him like a giant pillow, and she told me about the pictures. That's when I saw the question mark butterfly with the funny-shaped wings."

Jane suggested that perhaps Quinn had been in the bathroom while she was taking pictures, or that she had gotten up late and missed the first part of Christmas. Quinn distinctly remembered Riley waking her up before her mother, bounding from her bed to Quinn's pillow with a high-pitched "Eeeeeee! Christmas morning!" The sound was so jarring that Butterfly had left the room huffing. They had decided not to wake Jane until the fire was built—something Quinn had been practicing that winter—and a pot of coffee was brewing. Jane was always more amicable on Christmas when she had a good cup of coffee and a warm perch beneath the mantel.

Quinn could no longer ignore her mother's behavior, or the fact that she had been looking at Quinn for the last two days like she was a stranger. Her conversation with Meelie echoed in her mind. Going back to the other realm had been a terrible idea, one that Meelie and Aimee had tried to warn her about. As usual, her stubbornness had gotten the better of her. Now, she would have to accept the consequences of her actions. Whatever bond she'd had with her mother, things were different now. The two of them would coexist, but Quinn suspected that they would not snuggle in the easy chair or sit and talk through the tears on the really bad days. She was no longer her mother's confidant. Selfishly, Quinn was bothered by the fact that her mother would no longer need her. Quinn had spent most of Riley's life perfecting her role as the protector of the family. Now, Jane sat with her shoulders squared and seemed to carry Riley's condition with strength rather than grace.

Where Jane had been the empathetic one, the one who was often overcome with joy or grief, Quinn had been the stoic one, rallying the troops after each defeat. Their roles had switched, and Quinn discovered that she wasn't very well equipped to carry the emotional side of things for her family. How would she ever learn to lean on others? She had walled up her feelings before Riley's first birthday. Vulnerability was not her strong suit, yet she couldn't bear for Riley to see only strength. Her sister had to know, had to see, that being overcome by grief or defeat or even joy was a part of being human.

The adjustment would take a lot of work, work that Quinn wasn't prepared to do yet. Instead, she excused herself from the room and carried her computer to the lobby where she e-mailed her teachers to explain her absence and request missing assignments. Most of her teachers were terrible with e-mail, sometimes not responding for weeks. Still, sending an e-mail was her only option short of calling each teacher individually from the hospital room—that sounded awful. She also appreciated having a paper trail in case some teachers had forgotten arrangements she'd made with them, or never provided the missing work for her to complete.

Most of the e-mails were generic but, with her English teacher, she expounded on all the information she had read about Amelia Earhart and the Sodder children. She also suggested that her presentation would reflect not just one infamous disappearance, but the culture of disappearance. She wanted to use the project to start a conversation about how people don't want to be remembered as they were, but as they strived to be. For their part, most mourners are happy to oblige, establishing an almost legendary heroism to people who, in life, were often uninspiring or downright cruel. She stayed gone until she was sure that her mother left for work, then bought a few donuts and headed back to Riley's room. When she arrived, Riley was fast asleep again. Unlike the first heart flower, this one seemed to be taking longer for Riley's body to accept.

CHAPTER THIRTY-THREE

D r. Howe stopped by after lunch. Quinn asked question after question, assuring him that she would report everything back to her mother. He obliged, explaining that he hadn't seen any further improvement in Riley's blood oxygen levels, which may explain why she didn't have much energy or appetite. She was stable, but he was hesitant to release her until her numbers were a little further into the normal range. Of course, he understood that staying in the hospital complicated things for Quinn and Jane, who didn't have anyone else to stay with Riley during the day. Quinn was grateful for the information, and said that she'd much rather be with her sister than sitting in school.

She actually preferred to do her work alone, so she figured she would be fine as long as she continued to communicate with her teachers. Thus far, only two had written back: English and Physics. Her English teacher was intrigued by the idea of researching multiple disappearances, but she insisted that Quinn's presentation remain focused on Amelia Earhart because she wouldn't have time to impersonate multiple characters for parents.

Physics was in the middle of an egg-dropping contest, one that sounded both fun and impossible to Quinn. She was supposed to construct an escape pod out of balsa wood, cotton, toothpicks, and hot glue, then drop the contraption from at least three stories with an egg inside. If the egg survived, she would get an A. If the egg broke, she would get an F. Since her teacher would accept video, Quinn decided that the project would be a fun way to spend time with Riley the next day. She messaged her mom and asked her to bring the supplies to the hospital that evening.

"Quinn, I meant to ask you," Jane started, setting the project supplies on the ground near the door, "did you lock Butterfly out of the house when you went home to shower?"

Quinn explained that he had been acting oddly, and she was genuinely frightened by his behavior. This seemed to satisfy Jane, who turned to Riley and spent the rest of the evening talking with her. Quinn felt more and more like the outsider in her family, someone who was accepted but not well-liked. Riley didn't ignore her maliciously, of course; in fact, she hadn't shown any indication that her memories of Quinn were fading. Unlike Jane, Riley was also still clearly attached to Quinn. For whatever reason, the effects of her visit to the other realm didn't appear to have any impact on Quinn's and Riley's relationship. She excused herself from the room, not giving a reason for Quinn's departure. Riley waved, then yelled after Quinn to bring back hot chocolate. Jane didn't notice her leave. She was too engrossed in the puzzle she and Riley had spread across the hospital bed.

The crisp, evening air felt wonderful on Quinn's face. This was her favorite weather because she could basically live in hoodies. And everything smelled like cinnamon and pears, which made her feel warm even when the evening air cut through her jacket. She decided to walk to the park across from the hospital. The city kept lights strung on every branch year-round, so every night felt like Christmas. The entire park was illuminated, each white bulb mimicking a firefly. Normally she wouldn't walk through the park at night. To-night, though, the full moon made the bike and pedestrian paths just as bright, maybe even brighter, as they were at noon.

Quinn considered her last conversation with Aimee, who had tried to explain to her that Quinn must make a choice: either she could go back to the other realm, or she could accept her sister's condition and spend what time they had left together. Aimee mentioned something else, about the need for balance between the two worlds, but Quinn hadn't understood what she was trying to say. But how could she possibly know what would happen if Quinn continued to move between the two worlds? She didn't remember seeing any sort of guide or instruction book in the other realm. Everything she had learned came from two women who had been too scared to leave, or from the strange etchings that sometimes appeared when she was lost. None of the etchings had warned her not to stay with Riley. They hadn't said anything about not coming back, either.

Her mind spun. She wanted to believe that her friends were wrong, that she could continue to live with her family and heal Riley at the same time, yet she had to admit that Aimee had been right about her family—at least her mother—forgetting her. And Meelie had been right that returning the second time would only make things worse. Did they get lucky, or did they understand the other realm more than Quinn wanted to believe? She couldn't think of a single answer that would ease her mind. Either way, Jane didn't look at her with any sort of affection anymore, and Riley was still stuck in the hospital. Quinn wondered if her mother would even miss her if she left for the other realm. Meelie had not returned to this world so that she would be remembered, or at least the best parts of her would be. Would Quinn become a hero to her mother if she left and never came back? Did she even want to be a hero? That question was surprisingly easy to answer: Quinn had no desire to be a hero. If she had, she would have told her family about the other realm and explained why Riley was suddenly getting better, but she hadn't. Saving Riley was her secret, one she planned to keep to herself as long as she could.

Back at the hospital, Jane had fallen asleep on the couch. Riley was half-watching a documentary about uncontacted tribes in South America. Quinn carried a chair over to her, pulled a bag of cinnamon-roasted almonds from her jacket pocket, and handed them to Riley. One of the few things the two sisters enjoyed about winter was the smell of freshly roasted nuts wafting through shopping centers. Each year, they lamented about why people refuse to roast nuts and cook with pumpkin after the holiday season.

Riley excitedly snatched the bag from Quinn. "Where did you find these?" she chirped. "I thought those people in the aprons only made them at Christmas."

"Quiet," Quinn whispered. "You don't want to wake mom. Then you'll have to share!"

Riley snickered.

"How long has she been asleep anyway?"

Riley thought for a minute, audibly sucking the cinnamon and sugar from the almond in her mouth. She guessed that Jane had lain down at least an hour ago because the documentary was almost over, then she went on a tangent about how scared the people on the television must have been when they first saw things like cameras and cellular phones.

"Did they think people were magic?" she wondered aloud. "How else could they explain pictures and videos and sounds coming from tiny boxes?"

Quinn laughed. That was Riley, constantly asking the most logical, unanswerable questions. Her curiosity didn't match her age. Quinn imagined that she would be curious, too, if she grew up knowing that she only had a limited time to learn everything there was to learn in the world.

"Are you tired, or do you want to help me with some more research? I want to learn more about that Aimee character you looked up yesterday. How long ago did she live, what happened to her, what's her fascination with boats and water, was she magic—"

Quinn realized her slip as soon as the words left her mouth. She was hoping that Riley hadn't noticed, but she had no such luck. Riley flipped off the television.

"How do you know she liked boats or the ocean? What makes you think she's magic? And why have you been so weird, anyway? You and Mom both—like you're mad or being mean about something. You keep leaving when you see mom, won't play games with us—I don't understand?"

Quinn took a deep breath. She hated lying to Riley, but she knew she had to. She told her sister that she had argued with their mom one night after Riley went to bed, and that Quinn had sneaked out after they fought so she could clear her head.

"That's why I didn't go to school the day you got sick, and why she couldn't find me . . . if she even looked for me. Anyway, things just feel weird right now. I'm sure they'll get back to normal when we leave the hospital. You know neither of us is really cut out for the all the people and sounds here. I promise. Everything will be fine when we get you home."

"What if I never go home?"

"You will," Quinn said, squeezing Riley's hand. "One way or another, you will."

"How do you know?"

"I'm your big sister, kid. Nothing in this world or any other is going to keep me from taking care of you."

CHAPTER THIRTY-FOUR

Riley had trouble sleeping that night, so Quinn suggested that they do more research for her project. Reading about strangers was a welcome distraction for Riley, and Quinn still wanted to know more about the mysterious Aimee. She had very few details to get them started, so they spent quite awhile scouring the Internet for information. To start, she typed in the phrase: *Aimee + disappeared + ocean.*

"There's something!" Riley exclaimed, pointing at an entry for a woman named Aimee du buc de Rivery.

"Looks like she lived in the eighteenth century, the 1700s. She was from a wealthy French family who lived on an island, and she went to school in France," Quinn read aloud. "When she was nineteen, she was traveling back home from France, and her boat disappeared."

"That's all the page says?"

Quinn returned to the search results and clicked on the next link, which took her to an article discussing several theories about what happened to de Rivery after her boat sank.

"Looks like folks are split on what happened next. Her boat definitely sank. No one seems to disagree about that. Some people believe that the boat was attacked, and that Aimee was kidnapped by pirates and sold as a concubine."

"What's that?"

Quinn wasn't sure, so she typed the word into a new window. The definition was too much for Riley, so Quinn paraphrased.

"Basically," she said, "a concubine is like a female slave.

But a lot of historians have been unable to find any evidence to suggest that Aimee was even captured, though, so maybe she got away."

Quinn knew what had happened, or at least Aimee's version of events, but she couldn't tell Riley without explaining her adventures in the other realm. Instead, she told Riley that she would rather believe that Aimee was the type of person who couldn't be captured, who would sooner go down with the ship than live under someone else's control. Riley wanted to know more about pirates, so Quinn told her some of the stories she had read when she was younger, but the image of crazed men jumping onto ships and waving swords scared Riley. She changed the subject, asking Quinn to describe the ocean instead. The family had hoped to take a trip to the coast one summer; however, Riley's health had forced them to stay close to home. Quinn had gone with her mother once before, when Jane was pregnant. She tried to downplay the majesty and immensity of that much water, but Riley knew what she was doing and pushed her to just be honest.

"I might not get to see the ocean. That's okay. I just want to know what the waves feel like, how the sand feels on your toes, if you can see fish swimming around. Mama talks about the smell of the ocean when she lights her candles—does the water smell different than bath water or rivers? Remember when we went to the river, and I said the air smelled funny, then you pointed to all the fish and said they were taking a bath? Is the ocean like that?"

The truth was that Quinn had been afraid to get in the water as child. Besides, where they had gone the water was murky and green. She hadn't been able to see anything. The shells on the beach hurt her feet. She was hot almost immediately. From what she remembered, her first trip to the ocean had been a disaster. But Riley wanted majesty, and that's exactly what Quinn gave her. She described the water in the other realm, how the whole surface glowed purple. She spent a long time talking about the sharks there and the way every living thing turned incandescent when the two moons rose. Riley hung on every word, getting especially excited about the sharks. She was almost as fascinated with sharks as she was with butterflies. That night, they fell asleep watching a show about sharks that glow in the dark. Naturally, Riley wanted one for herself.

Quinn was yanked from sleep by a shrill alarm. She jumped from the chair, immediately checking the various readouts to see what was wrong with Riley. Her heart rate was in the fifties: bradycardia. Jane was already at the door, shouting for a doctor. Quinn tried to rouse Riley, but she couldn't get her sister to open her eyes or answer her pleas. They had seen low heart rates before, almost always in the day or two before a procedure. This time felt different, though. This time, everyone was aware that Riley wouldn't have a procedure. She would have to bounce back on her own.

Nurses rushed into the room, clearing Jane and Quinn away from the hospital bed. They strained to see over the nurses, who were fast at work. One tapped Riley repeatedly on the cheek and spoke to her in a loud voice. Another cleared her chest of clothing and placed two leads on either side of her heart. Quinn had long been impressed with how efficiently nurses work. They had to trust each other completely, at least in moments of crisis. Quinn knew this because the nurses rarely spoke when they were trying to revive a patient.

A woman entered the room wearing a white coat. She introduced herself quickly, not even taking the time to glance at Quinn and Jane as she assessed the situation. Riley was still in bradycardia. The doctor ordered one of the nurses to inject something into Riley's IV, then pressed her stethoscope between the leads. She looked at her watch while she listened, then moved her fingers to the edge of the stethoscope. She felt around for what seemed like an eternity, listening at each place her fingers had been. By the time she turned to look at Jane, Riley was awake and her heart rate was climbing back into the seventies.

"Are you aware of the stenosis?"

Jane nodded.

"Then I assume you're familiar with the term bradycardia. We've stabilized Riley with blood thinners, but this is a temporary solution. She'll need a procedure to correct the issue; otherwise, her heart rate will remain low, and she'll be at risk for further cardiac distress. The procedure is called a valvuloplasty. I'll make a note of that on the chart for her pediatrician."

"Thank you," Jane interrupted.

Quinn could tell from the sound of her voice that Jane was trying not to be rude, but her frustration was showing through. Whenever a new doctor worked with Riley, they went over the same information. Dr. Howe was meticulous with his notes, which made Jane even more upset when doctors appeared oblivious to Riley's medical condition and history.

"Well that's a heck of a way to wake up." Riley laughed, then began to cough violently.

"Quiet, sweetie. Give yourself a minute," Jane said.

Quinn offered to go to the cafeteria and hunt down a decent cereal for them. She slipped on her shoes, grabbing a disposable toothbrush on her way out the door. The hospital was enormous, with the children's wing on the opposite end from the cafeteria. Quinn didn't really understand the design; kids usually had more visitors than older patients, which meant more people who would eventually want something to eat. She preferred walking the first floor, the maintenance floor, since most of the people she encountered were working and tended to leave her alone. She enjoyed seeing how long she could hold her breath as she passed by the laundry area; the air smelled like disinfectant and burned her eyes, so the game was born out of necessity. Her personal record was seventy-five steps, which she had later timed at roughly two minutes. Two minutes without oxygen before her head began to swim.

Quinn reentered the room to see Dr. Howe sitting with his hand on Jane's shoulder. Riley ignored them, flipping through channels on the television. Quinn spread out three cereal options before Riley even though they both knew which cereal Riley would choose: Cinnamon Toast Crunch, her absolute favorite. Quinn emptied the contents into a paper bowl her mother had brought, poured milk from a bottle they kept stashed in the hospital refrigerator, and dropped into the chair closest to Riley. She wanted to hear what Dr. Howe was saying, but didn't want to leave her sister by herself.

She tried to watch the television, but she couldn't focus. So she retrieved the shopping bag her mother had brought and began unpacking the supplies for the egg experiment that she and Riley were going to build that afternoon. She laid out the pieces by type: balsa wood in one stack, cotton balls in another, then toothpicks, and finally the hot-glue gun from home. Quinn had no idea how to construct an escape pod from the items before her. If she were being honest, she didn't really care about the grade. She just thought that building something with Riley would be a good distraction, and they could secretly drop the pod from a hospital window when they were ready to test their design.

Jane started to cry. Neither Riley nor Quinn could ignore the conversation any longer. They turned their attention to Dr. Howe. Then Riley pushed Dr. Howe to share the details of his talk with Jane, reminding him that she deserved to know. Quinn was shocked by Riley's assertiveness. She took a moment to recover, then beamed with pride.

"As I said to your mother," Dr. Howe began, "the brief recovery we saw appears to have been an illusion. Your heart is, quite frankly, deteriorating—breaking down—from all the extra stress that your stenosis has caused. To put things another way: your heart is tired. Now we all know that you don't qualify for a transplant, and you have too much scar tissue built up around the valve for a valvuloplasty."

"So I'm dying?"

"Yes, I'm afraid so."

"How long?" she asked, her voice small and tight.

"If I were to guess . . . days. Maybe a week."

Jane began to sob. Quinn just stared at the doctor, trying to figure out what to do. What he was saying didn't make any sense. The other realm was supposed to fix problems. Had she caused Riley's rapid deterioration? Was she to blame for bringing the heart flowers back without fully understanding them? She didn't want to blame herself; she and her mother had been waiting for this inexorable day of quietus for seven years. All Quinn had wanted to do was give Riley a long life, let her do things like go on a date and learn to drive and get married. Quinn had ridden a giant hen, she'd chased butterflies across a desert and over a cliff and over the seas. She'd fought sharks. And for what? Riley, despite all Quinn's efforts, was still dying.

The frustration boiled over, causing Quinn to scream out loud. When she opened her eyes, Jane was cradling Riley in her lap. She turned to Quinn, her eyes and cheeks still flushed from the tears. Instead of the empty stare that had haunted her since her return from the other realm, Quinn saw desperation. What she felt she saw in her mother's eyes was a plea. Jane was begging her to save Riley. She got up, grabbed her hoodie, and left the hospital.

Quinn wasn't sure where she was going when she walked through the sliding glass doors and into the cool, night air. She wanted to break open the sky for having the audacity to hold up everything but her sister. She cursed every god she could remember for creating a world full of grief. She cursed the other realm for giving her hope, the universe for having more questions than answers, Aimee for her nonsense about balance. What did balance have to do with saving her sister, anyway? The universe. Aimee. Balance. The rest of the conversation was suddenly clear. Quinn had been foolish. She had been reckless. And now Riley was paying the price.

She finally understood why the heart flowers weren't working: she had to stay in the other realm. That's what Aimee had meant about balance. If Quinn was going to take a heart from the other realm, then she would have to leave something there. Meelie had been trying to tell her all along, but she had been too stubborn to listen. She couldn't have both. Either she could save Riley, or she could be with her for her final days. She had to decide which daughter her mother would lose.

Quinn looked up to see that she had wandered right back to the hospital, through the glass doors, to Riley's room. The lights were off, so Quinn couldn't see what her mother and sister were doing. She cupped her hands around both eyes, peering through the glass. Inside, she saw nothing. No one on the couch or in the bed. Even the school supplies had disappeared from the table where she'd arranged them. Where had they gone? They had to have known she was coming back. Or had her mother forgotten about her again?

"Excuse me, are you Quinn Willow?" a nurse asked, walking up behind Quinn.

"Yes, I am."

"Your sister wanted me to tell you that they decided to go home. Your mother thought that that would make for a more comfortable transition. A lot of people have an easier time moving on at home—oh, listen to me—I'm so sorry, dear. I—this must be such a difficult thing for you. I've seen you two together. She really looks up to you, you know. If not for you, I imagine that girl would have given up a long time ago."

"Thank you," was all Quinn could manage, her throat was so constricted.

For the third time in twelve hours, she weaved through the hospital and out into the darkness. If her mother had packed up their things and left without Quinn, she certainly wouldn't miss her. But she would miss Riley. In every realm, in every version of the future that Quinn could imagine, Jane needed Riley to survive. The only real question Quinn had ever needed to answer was whether or not *she* could live without Riley.

By the time Quinn got home, Jane and Riley were asleep. She had thought to move the spare key to the front of the house, which made slipping in a bit quieter. That was the plan, anyway, but as soon as Butterfly heard the door, he came around the corner in a frenzy. This time, Quinn understood his fear. He was forgetting her, just like her mother. Her only hope of avoiding an attack was a mangled toy she'd stuffed in her backpack, one that she and Butterfly had played with when they adopted him as puppy. She had learned that memory was tied to smell, and dogs have a keener sense of smell than humans. With any luck, that meant that Butterfly might re-member her if he smelled her on his toy.

She tossed the toy into the foyer, then pulled the door closed and crouched in the hearth. Through the door, she could hear him sniffing. As soon as she heard a squeak, she knew that Butterfly had the toy in his mouth. She eased the door open a second time, bracing herself for his fury. He dropped the toy and let out a low growl, taking slow, de-liberate steps toward her. She knelt down and held out her hand, shutting her eyes instinctively. Moments later, she felt his wet nose in her palm. He was whining and gazing at her with what looked like shame.

"You're okay, boy. I've made a mess of things around here. You just wanted to keep us safe. That's your job, now. You've got to keep this house and your family safe."

Quinn took off her shoes and walked to the bedroom, smiling at the sound of Riley cooing from her bed. She looked around the room, taking stock of all the objects she and her sister had surrounded themselves with over the years. Above her desk, she had pinned school projects spanning the last ten years. When the wall had started to fill up, she decided that she would save only her favorite piece from each year. Now, they stretched out like a timeline.

Kindergarten: a rocket ship made from toilet-paper rolls.

First grade: the black and white newspaper mosaic of her pregnant mother.

Second grade: a family collage with Riley's baby pictures.

She scanned the projects for the one she cherished most.

Eighth grade: plaster impressions of Riley's and her hands.

Of all the homework assignments and all the lessons she had ever learned, Quinn most loved squishing her fingers into the wet plaster with her sister. Jane had regretted not making impressions when they were babies, so when her history teacher had assigned an intensive research project on family, Quinn decided to get a plaster kit for her visual. Jane sat at the table and watched the timer while the plaster baked, then tried not to cry as Quinn and Riley painted their impressions. She had been so worried that Quinn might break the impressions on her way to school that she had intentionally hidden them, only to deliver them herself later that morning, something she confessed to Quinn on the day she hung them above her desk.

Quinn traced Riley's impressions with her finger, then pressed her palms into them. She couldn't help but laugh out loud when she remembered the fight that had broken out when Riley pulled her hands from the plaster and clapped them over Quinn's cheeks. They had showered three times trying to get the plaster out of their hair, which eventually turned into a water fight that left the entire bathroom floor drenched. They had to use every towel in the bathroom to soak up the puddles, then snuck the load into the washer so their mother wouldn't catch them.

Quinn's throat ached with sadness. Tears swelled and trickled down her cheeks. She knew that she had to leave. It was such an easy decision. What had finally settled in her was not that her family would carry on without her, but that she would have to carry on without them. Her only solace was that this time, at least, she would be able to leave her family on her terms, in her own way. She sat down beside Riley's bed, leaning into a pillow that was hanging over the side, and closed her eyes. Tomorrow, she decided, would be her last day on this Earth.

CHAPTER THIRTY-FIVE

Jane called both Riley's and Quinn's schools during breakfast, informing them that, due to a family emergency, the girls would be out of school for at least the next two weeks. She didn't go into detail, at least not as far as Quinn could hear. With her boss, though, Jane had to be more forthcoming. When she explained Riley's downturn, her voice cracked and she struggled to get the words out. Finally, she requested a leave of absence. After hanging up, she told the girls that she would have to go into the office for a short time to fill out paperwork. Quinn saw her wiping tears from her face. She wanted to hug her mother, to be strong for her, but Quinn understood that their relationship didn't exist anymore. Instead, she watched as Jane smoothed her clothes, put her hair in a bun, and left for the office.

Riley was too weak to do much of anything, so she and Quinn huddled under a blanket, flipping through the channels until they found a game show to occupy their attention. Butterfly wedged himself between them and soon was snoring. He had been sullen since the family returned from the hospital. Boxers have a knack for intuition, often sensing and reacting to owners with chronic illness. They had adopted Butterfly because of this, but they hadn't been prepared for the way his empathy made them feel like he was one of the family, as if he knew exactly what was happening with each of them at any given time. Many nights, he was the only one Quinn talked to about how she felt, never wanting to burden Jane or Riley. She would miss having him as a confidant, even if he did fart in his sleep and drool on her pillows.

For a while, Quinn sat listening to Riley and Butterfly sleep, then eased from beneath the blanket to begin preparing for her departure. She would have to be careful not to leave any hint that she was running away; she was sure that they would adapt to her absence, but not if Riley and Jane believed she had abandoned them. No, she would have to make her disappearance look accidental. She didn't want to leave any more work for her family than she had to, so she did her laundry and tidied all the common spaces. For once, she was thankful that the house had wood floors because running a vacuum would have drawn Riley's attention. Next, she gathered a handful of clothes, things that she hadn't worn in a while, and stuffed them into a knapsack she had gotten at school. She hated the drawstrings because they cut into her, yet every presenter who visited her school handed them out. Since she didn't use them, Jane wouldn't notice one missing from her room. Taking her own backpack or the projects from her wall would be an obvious sign that she had left on purpose. She would have to leave them behind, too.

She had compiled most of her stories in a set of spiral notebooks, which she stacked neatly on her desk. She sat down to write her last story in a leather-bound journal that her mother had given her several years ago. The pages were hand-woven cotton with honeysuckle and marigold inlays. Until now, Quinn hadn't felt that any of her stories were worth preserving in such a beautiful, permanent fashion. She spent nearly two hours on the story, sometimes writing a sentence or paragraph on scratch paper, editing, then transferring the copy to the journal. If this was to be her last gift to Riley, she wanted to make sure that every letter was perfect. She kept the door cracked, listening all the while for any indi-

cation that Riley was awake, but she didn't budge until Jane
returned from work.

"I'm sorry that took so long. I didn't realize how much
paperwork went into medical leave these days. Everything
is squared away, though, so I shouldn't have to go in again
until—" Jane's voice cracked, unable to put the inevitable
into words.

Quinn went to her and put an arm over her shoulder,
then immediately regretted the gesture. She could see on her
mother's face that she was startled by the intimacy. Luckily,
Riley pushed herself up from the floor and joined them in
their embrace. The three of them stood there, folded together
like a single prayer, none of them acknowledging the damp-
ness on their sleeves or the heaving or the incredible weight
of last times: the last Christmas together; the last birthday;
the last spaghetti dinner; the last afternoon on the swing set;
the last group hug. The finality of their family shifting from
group to pair made Quinn's legs buckle. She let go of them
and sank to the floor.

After dinner, Quinn helped Riley with her bath. Any inde-
pendence Riley might have craved in the months prior with-
ered when she grew winded trying to remove her clothes.
She leaned back in the bathtub with her eyes closed. Quinn
watched the shallow rise and fall of her shoulders. Riley
explained that she constantly felt the need to take a deep
breath, but each time she tried, she would double over
coughing. Her chest felt tight, her head swimmy as though
she could actually feel gravity pushing against her bones.
Quinn hoped that her sister didn't expect a response because she was afraid that she would crumble if she relaxed
her already-clenched jaw. Riley laid her head on Quinn's
shoulder; water soaked through Quinn's shirt and pooled on

the floor beside the tub. She started to apologize, but Quinn interrupted her.

"I'm really going to miss you, kid."

Riley didn't respond.

"For a long time, I thought I was prepared for this. You were loaned to us—that's what mom used to say. We knew you couldn't stay. But what will I do with my nights when I don't have you to bathe and listen to my stories? Will my stories die, too? I guess I wrote most of them for you, so there won't be much reason for them after—" Quinn trailed off.

"Say the words," Riley whispered. "I'm tired of avoiding them. *After I'm dead.* Let me hear you say the words."

But Quinn didn't say the words. Riley wasn't going anywhere. Quinn was the one leaving.

"You promised me a story," Riley insisted, pulling her comforter up to her chin.

Quinn nodded.

"Did you finish the ending?"

"Yeah . . ." her voice trailed off. She knew exactly how the story would end, and she was determined to tell her sister the truth. She just couldn't tell her the whole truth.

Riley gave her a sassy stare, emphasizing her wide eyes with a broad sweep of her hand.

"All right, all right. Move over, brat." Quinn slid under the covers and propped herself up facing Riley. "This one is a long one, maybe a little hard to believe, so bear with me. Everything you're about to hear is absolutely true. This is the story of the day I fell into a pond and found a whole world at the bottom."

She started at the beginning, with the note she took to the butterfly garden. Quinn recounted every detail of her time in the other realm and even got out of the bed to indicate the size of the hen that almost ran her over. When she got to the glowing butterflies, Riley gasped, clapping her hands over her mouth. She was so excited by the idea that she sat up in bed, a glimmer of her former energy coursing through her body. Quinn kept going, afraid that she would lose her nerve with any pause in the story. When she got to the part about putting a heart flower in Riley's chest, her sister instinctively touched her chest. Quinn was grateful that the lights were already off; otherwise, Riley might have searched for the red freckle. Talking about getting trapped in the ocean made her chest pound. She could hear her voice wavering, but she pressed on.

"I turned, and that's when I saw a shadowy glow between me and the small boat. So I did the only thing I could do: I dove."

"You didn't!" Riley shouted.

"I did. And I'm glad I did because that's how I found the island. You see, all the shoals and sandbars used to be the tips of mountains, but rain swallowed everything up. Except the mountains had caves in them. For whatever reason, the water couldn't enter the caves. As soon as I ducked my head under water, I saw the entrance to one of the caves shining in front of me. I had to swim down until my whole body burned. I knew I would black out if I turned back, so I swam deeper. Just as my head began to throb, I fell into the cave.

"Like most things in the other realm, almost everything I saw was luminous. That means they had light coming from inside them. Even though I didn't have a flashlight or a lantern, I could see all right. I didn't have my butterfly net anymore, though, so I had to track the swarm by the faint trail of scales that fell from their wings. I went farther and farther into the cave, which was scary because I worried that I wouldn't be able to find my way back. Knowing that you were back home in the hospital gave me strength, made me brave.

"Finally, after what felt like hours, I turned a corner, and the swarm was right in front of me! They flew in tight circles, scales trickling down like a radiant mist. Beneath the swarm, I saw a patch of heart flowers, enough to save you a hundred times over. I was so excited that I bolted for the patch, flinging myself into the bulbs. I snatched two from their stems and zipped them into my hoodie."

"Why two?"

"I just wanted to be sure, you know. What if something happened to one of the bulbs? I couldn't come home without a way to save you—you're my sister. Anyway, now that I had heart flowers, I knew that I had to find a portal to get back to you. The hard part was that portals are usually under water. Since no water can get into the caves, I couldn't see any pools or ponds anywhere. That's when I realized that I would have to swim back out into the ocean. People can't survive at the bottom of the ocean here, so I figured the same was true in the other realm. If I was going to get to a portal, I would have to go deeper into the caves. I started looking everywhere for places where the caves slopped downward. When I got to a cavern where the entire floor was flat, I figured that I had gone as far down as I could. Next, I followed the sound of rushing water until I found an opening.

"The water outside was darker than anything I've ever seen, but I could just make out a shimmer not far from the cave wall. I took breath and lunged back into the ocean. The pressure was immediate. My whole body felt like someone was squeezing me into a tiny ball. I pushed with everything I had. Then, I went black. The next thing I remember, I was passing through the portal. I came out in the middle of the river down by the park. I immediately checked my jacket for the heart flowers, then panicked because I couldn't find anything at all on my left side. That's when I remembered that I had zipped two into the jacket, so I checked my right side and found one still there. I was so glad that I had grabbed an extra bulb, or I wouldn't have come back with anything at all!

"Once I got myself out of the river, I knew I had to get to you. Even though I hadn't eaten in days, I started for the hospital. I weaved through the halls until I found your room, but I was scared to go in. You and mom were asleep. After a while, and some pestering from nurses, I crept inside, unzipped my hoodie, and put a heart flower on your chest. The rest, well, you know."

Quinn pulled one of the kaleidoscopes from her shelf and ran a finger over the lens.

"Where did you get all those things anyway?" Riley asked, her voice scratchy and soft.

"From Dad, mostly."

"Is that why you stopped collecting them after I was born?"

"I suppose. But I also had something much better to hold my attention," Quinn smiled, tousling Riley's hair. "Kaleidoscopes show people how broken things can be beautiful again. Once I met you, kid, I just didn't need the reminder."

Riley made a low, whistling sound. Quinn looked at her and saw that Riley's eyes were closed. She was fast asleep, her small, warm head nestled against Quinn's chest.

CHAPTER THIRTY-SIX

Quinn lay next to Riley well into the night, desperately trying to memorize everything about the room and her sister and her old life. She waited until the moon began to descend, then slid from the bed—a difficult task with Butterfly snoring beneath the girls. She retrieved the knapsack she had hidden in one of the pillows on her bed, feeling around blindly to make sure she had everything she needed. Leaving for the other realm inspired many questions she hadn't considered before, like what people used to brush their teeth and how she would wash her clothes. Perhaps those in the other realm chose specific people to return to her world every so often for supplies. Most answers she would have to learn the hard way, but Quinn had found a few sample toothbrushes and travel-sized toothpaste tubes from the dentist that would at least keep her teeth clean for a while.

Once she was sure that she had everything she could take without rousing suspicion, Quinn went to her desk. She pulled the leather-bound notebook from the drawer, arranging the other spirals to frame the gift for Riley. Quinn hoped that Riley's curiosity would push her to read through the spiral notebooks, but she knew that she would have to leave some sort of note or Riley would avoid the leather-bound journal. Something about the craftsmanship made the book appear more personal than the other notebooks. A note would be tricky, though, as Quinn didn't want to be too obvious about her plan to leave the family behind. Her disappearance couldn't look like a sacrifice, otherwise Riley would spend her entire life carrying the guilt of survival with her. She had been thinking about the note all day, but had yet to come up with the right words. Fearing that her mother would be awake again soon, she scribbled the only thing that came to mind:

Riley,
    This story isn't mine, but yours. You have been at the center of everything I've written, but this . . . this one is different. The words say that I saved you. That's not true. You saved me. You gave me purpose.

Love,
Your Favorite Storyteller

P.S. Did you know that a group of butterflies is called a kaleidoscope?
Never stop looking for beauty in broken things.

Quinn opened the journal to the story she had penned earlier that afternoon, using the note as a makeshift bookmark. When she closed the journal, the only word still visible was Riley's name. Surely that would be enough for her sister to at least open the journal. Next to the journal, she placed one of her favorite kaleidoscopes, one with brass tubing and two wheels speckled with shards of stained glass.

Tears welled up in Quinn's eyes. She hurried to the door, eased out into the hall with her knapsack, then crept from her house. The click of the latch on the front door sounded far away to Quinn. She leaned on the door, putting her hands flat against the polished wood. She let herself weep; anyway, better to break down on her front porch than walking along the street. The sun peeked over the horizon, smearing pink and orange across the sky. Quinn stood up, brushed herself off, and headed for the river. While she walked, she studied the dawn, committing the scene to memory. Where she was headed, light emanated not from a single point, but from within each living thing. If light really did signify hope, as her teachers had taught her, perhaps she was leaving a place with a single, finite point of hope for a world with optimism in the atmosphere.

The closer she got to the river, the more she noticed about Earth. Though many of her observations had been explained to her by science teachers over the years, she hadn't really considered the implications of the various facts. Sunflowers, for instance, followed the sun's movement throughout the day. What would a sunflower do in the other realm? Blades of grass, too, bent themselves toward their light source. The effect was so profound that some golfers even studied the lean of turf at different times of day. Was that why the land-scapes in the other realm were so barren? Certainly plants couldn't function the same way, since photosynthesis would be impossible without regular access to ultraviolet light. Quinn had been so wrapped up in the idea of living without her family that she hadn't stopped to think about the fact that she was also leaving everything she knew behind. In the other realm, she would have to learn not just how to look after herself, but also how to gather and prepare meals, how to survive at the most basic level.

Wind swirled, kicking dust into the air. Leaves and even small branches rattled to the ground around Quinn. She pulled her hood over her head and kept her eyes fixed on the ground to avoid the onslaught of dirt and debris. She could smell rain in the air again. Some streets still had puddles from the last storm, and she remembered a reporter saying that the river was already twelve feet above normal for this time of year. The temperature was cooler than usual, too. This, at least, meant that the river walk would be relatively empty. Most people avoided the parks and walking trails at the slightest hint of a cold, wet forecast. Quinn was grateful that she would be able to walk along the shore unnoticed. If anyone saw her swimming out into the water, they were sure to call the police since swimming was strictly prohibited inside the city, and for good reason: the combination of industry and wind patterns made the river prone to whirlpools. Entering the other realm would be safer at the butterfly garden, but Quinn couldn't risk a lengthy search for another heart flower. Riley was fading too quickly for that. She needed to get a bulb into her sister as fast as possible, then get back to the other realm before Riley began to deteriorate again. Her only hope was to find the portal she had come through in the river, then enter the other realm right next to the submerged caves.

Quinn hurried along the shoreline, scanning the water for any shadow or darker patch of blue that might indicate a portal at the bottom. This proved more difficult than she had anticipated, as the surface was churning in the wind. Everywhere she looked, she saw only froth and white caps. Desperate, she shut her eyes and tried to remember what she had seen on her last return. Blacking out had made her delirious, but she had a vague recollection of blue bicycles and giant anthills. Quinn racked her brain, sifting through the various parks and landmarks she had walked past a hundred times. The city had installed bike-renting stations near every park, so she hurried from one to the next. Finally, she neared a splash pad with massive green-brown hills surrounding the fountain. In her fog, she had mistaken them for anthills, but they were actually turf-covered slopes for parents to sit on while kids played.

Quinn jogged ahead with renewed fervor. Her heart was

pounding as she stared out at the river. She was a strong swimmer, but the churning water threatened to form a vortex any minute. If she wasn't careful, she could be pushed to the bottom of the river far from the portal or, worse yet, carried down river by the current. She decided to leave her hoodie behind so that she would have a greater range of motion and less drag. Quinn wedged the jacket under a rock just beneath the surface, hoping that would be enough to conceal her entry into the water. Next, she tucked the knapsack inside her shirt, tightening the rope against her shoulders. Behind her, traffic had picked up as folks streamed to work. She thought of her mother, probably sipping from an old coffee mug at the table in silence. She thought of Riley curled around Butterfly, cooing into his fur. And then, seeing a gap in the traffic, she leapt into the river.

The water was colder than she expected. Her arms sprouted gooseflesh within seconds, but she wasn't deterred. Quinn gritted her teeth, digging in hard with each stroke, taking a short breath every time she plunged her right arm into the water. Since she had come to in the middle of the river on her last return, she assumed that she would need to get as far out as she could before she dove down to the bottom. Her arms and lungs burned, and her strokes were becoming less pronounced. She looked back to see that was she a mere ten yards from shore. She still had at least forty yards to go if she was going to get to the deepest part of the river. To make matters worse, the current was beginning to spin around her. She kicked off her shoes, took a deep breath, and pushed forward.

Quinn's deliberate strokes devolved into a slow paddle aided by frantic kicks. Her entire upper body ached, and she had a harder and harder time catching her breath. Each time she inhaled, spray from the angry river would hit the back of her throat. She was twenty or so yards from where she had come through on her last return, and the water seemed to counter every effort to go farther. Desperate, she decided to try swimming beneath the surface; perhaps the current would be more manageable if she could go deep enough. Quinn paused, taking several slow, deep breaths as best she could, then let herself sink. Knowing that she wouldn't be able to stay under for long, she combined strong breaststrokes with short, rapid kicks. She moved through the water with ease. Even with her eyes closed, she could sense that she was nearing the portal from the intermittent bursts of frigid water around her. She had been under for nearly two minutes. Quinn's ears popped, and her head throbbed. She saw pricks of light in the blackness behind her eyes. Her body was turning on her, hungry for oxygen. And then she heard a familiar sound: the pulse of a heart flower. Without hesitation, she angled her body toward the sound and descended. She opened her eyes; in front of her, almost close enough to touch, she saw the faint glow of a bulb. The bulb she had lost when she came back from the other realm. One more hard kick, and she had the heart flower in her hand. Her body jerked. Something inside her forced a breath, filling her mouth and lungs with water. She clutched her chest, but she couldn't cough. The last thing she felt before losing consciousness was the sudden, very cold, tug of the vortex.

CHAPTER THIRTY-SEVEN

Meelie stood at the edge of the cave, looking out into the deep sea. She had been searching the submerged island for days, but Quinn was nowhere to be found. Aimee would be returning soon with the children. Together, Meelie hoped they could check every nook and cranny for her lost friend. That had been the plan, at least. But now, staring at a patch of black water in the midst of so much midnight blue, Meelie wondered if Quinn had found her way home after all. One of the chambers she'd seen certainly contained enough of the rare, magical flowers to save Riley several dozen times. Perhaps Quinn had simply gone home.

Home. The word haunted Meelie. The other realm had welcomed her, yet she had not embraced the strange world as anything but a temporary haven. Of course, she had dragged her feet for so long that she had nothing left of her old life. No one was waiting for her on the other side. She had long felt like a woman swallowed by one planet and spat out by another. The truth was that Meelie had avoided gateways her entire time in the other realm. If one of the children found one, she routed her movements so that she didn't come within half a mile of the portal. That is, until Quinn disappeared into a drowned cavern. Sure enough, her fear had been justified; only a dozen or so yards away, the dark patch called to her. Above her, Meelie heard the din of five old children trampling through the caves. She was too mesmerized by the sight in front of her to turn around, but she called to them over her shoulder. The cave had excellent acoustics, carrying her message through each chamber undistorted.

"Down here!" she shouted. "We'll start from the bottom and work our way up!"

"Sounds good," a voice cracked. "On our way."

The voice started to say something else, but Meelie had already turned her attention back to the ocean floor. The patch shivered, and Meelie heard a loud whoosh that sounded like an airplane passing too low overhead. She rubbed her eyes and peered into the abyss; what she saw frightened her to her very core: there, floating in a limp fetal position, was Quinn. Her form was almost entirely cloaked in shadow save a single glow emanating from the center of her chest.

"Sweet Mary! Quinn, are you okay?"

No response. The body was motionless, doll-like.

"Can you hear me, Quinn?" she screamed, her shrill plea clawing up through her throat and catching on her tongue.

Still nothing.

Meelie couldn't wait any longer. She thrust a hand into the water, then the other. She swam toward Quinn, fighting to conserve enough energy to get them both back into the cave. The pressure around her reminded her of high-altitude flying, the way her limbs began to ache and her brain swelled in her head. She lunged for Quinn's hand, but missed. She would have to get closer. Her air was running out, and she could feel her body filling with carbon dioxide. She kept her arms outstretched, closing her eyes to better focus on moving through the water. Moments later, she felt Quinn's fingers graze hers. Meelie shot forward, grabbing one lifeless, ice-cold wrist.

Having secured her friend, Meelie turned back to the cave. Her chest throbbed. She was locked in a battle with her natural instinct, which was telling her to take a deep breath.

She would be a fool to open her mouth at this depth, though. She shut her eyes again and kicked, then again. On the third kick, she drew close enough to hear the children. They must be waiting to see if she would get back to the cave on her own. Besides, only one of the children had a frame much larger than the typical eight-year-old. They wouldn't have the strength to rescue Meeile if she got stuck in the water. Lucky for everyone, she wasn't new to ocean floors. One more kick, and Meelie fell into the cavern, sputtering and gasping for breath. Quinn tumbled in behind her, landing face down on the rocks.

"Help her," she gasped. "She's not breathing!"

Aimee knelt over Quinn, tilting her head back to clear the airway, then blew a long breath into the young girl's lungs. She put her palms over Quinn's heart, but she didn't press down. She was transfixed by the ruddy, orange glow coming from beneath the girl's breast bone.

"Aimee!" Meelie yelled.

This startled Aimee, who shook her head, then began a series of compressions.

"Come on, Quinn," she begged. "Not like this. You're a fighter, kid. Come on!"

Quinn's eyes flitted open. Water and blood spilled from her mouth.

"Save . . . Riley . . ." she croaked. "Riley . . . not me."

Meelie looked to Aimee, who shook her head. Neither of them knew how to get to Riley, much less how to save her. They wouldn't even recognize the world waiting for them on the other side of the portal.

"Backpack—" Quinn grunted, rolling to one side.

One of the children saw a bulge underneath Quinn's shirt. She ran toward the women, yanking the hem of the girl's shirt up and pointing to the knapsack. Meelie maneuvered the straps off Quinn's shoulders, then tore open the bag. Two books fell onto the floor, followed by a plastic card with Quinn's picture in the upper-right corner. Meelie snatched the card and studied the markings.

"Is this an address?" She pointed to a series of words, holding the card for everyone to inspect.

Another of the children nodded, adding that what Meelie held was a library card. The oldest child explained that the address was for the library, which was probably very close to Quinn's house. If one of the women could get to the library, she would have a decent chance of finding Riley. Meelie asked if anyone had seen the heart flowers on the way down, but they each shook their heads. She wasn't convinced; she doubted whether most of them even knew what the heart flowers looked like. Still, they couldn't save Riley without one.

"Have you ever seen anything like this?" Aimee asked Meelie, pointing to the glowing spot on Quinn's chest.

Meelie bent down, putting her ear to the strange light.

"That's a heart flower!" she exclaimed. "Inside her. She must have pressed one against her chest as she came through the portal!"

The light was starting to fade, as did the low thump. Meelie put her mouth over Quinn's and blew, but she couldn't bring herself to pump her friend's chest. She knew what Quinn wanted. Somehow, she had to get that bulb to Riley. She had to save Quinn's sister one last time.

"I need something sharp—a rock or knife or something. Hurry!"

Aimee and the children scrambled to their feet, patting pockets and running through the massive space in search of anything that might work. Aimee was the first to find a razor-thin sliver of stone. She ran back to Meelie, handing her the find. Meelie grabbed the rock and pressed hard into Quinn's skin. Aimee stood open-mouthed for several minutes before realizing that the children were standing behind her. She ushered them away, whispering that everything would be okay. God willing, she was right.

The heart flower hadn't passed through the breastplate, yet. Meelie let out a loud sigh, tugging the bulb free of her friend's body. The glow intensified, and the rhythmic pulse filled the room.

"Someone has to get this to Riley!" she begged, turning to face the others.

"You," Aimee said. "You have to go."

Meelie started to protest, but she knew Aimee was right. She had hidden in the other realm for nearly a century. The time had come for her to face the world she'd left behind, no matter the consequences. Quinn had sacrificed her life for her sister; the least Meelie could do was sacrifice her legacy. She nodded toward Aimee, shoving the heart flower into the inside pocket of her bomber jacket. Before she had a chance to reconsider, she dove into the water, swimming with everything she had for the dark patch that Quinn had come through. She closed her eyes and entered the portal with the haunting, inescapable image of her lifeless friend, laid out on the cavern floor, pinned to her mind.

CHAPTER THIRTY-EIGHT

The river was cold and heavy, tossing Meelie about even before she broke the surface. She took a deep breath and opened her eyes, tilting her head toward the sky. The sun screamed in her face, forcing her to bury her eyes in the crook of her shoulder almost immediately. She had long forgotten how bright the day could be. Had there really been a time when she looked forward to sunlight? She couldn't imagine. Now, the sky just seemed obnoxious. Even the surface of the river was difficult to look at. Meelie squinted and pulled herself slowly toward the shore. When she was close enough to dig her hand into dirt, she dragged her body onto the grass and lay on her back. That was a bad decision. Even when she closed her eyes, she felt like she was eye-to-eye with a floodlight.

Meelie could hear children shrieking and, farther off, the strangest combination of hums and buzzes. She stood up to see that she was very near a park. Parents were scattered on impossibly perfect hills. Many of them had devices of some sort in their hands which they were either studying or holding up to the children running about. Doing a quick scan, she saw that concrete roads stretched out in every direction. Buildings lined the streets. Zooming past, Meelie saw a steady stream of vehicles. Sometimes, lights hanging over the street would change to red and the cars would line up as far back as she could see. The strangest thing was that many of the cars had only one person in them, and the drivers ranged from teenagers to geriatrics. She couldn't imagine how each one of them could afford their own vehicle, or why so many people required vehicles at all.

"I love your jacket!" someone yelled from an open window.

Meelie started to thank the stranger, only to be cut off by the roar of engines as the light turned green. She waved in the direction of the voice, but she had already lost sight of the car. Undeterred, she ambled toward the parents. The hills, she found, were made from a kind of fake grass that felt soft and springy under her feet. The texture was odd but delightful, the perfect material for kids at play. As she approached, Meelie could feel the various parents staring at her. She must have looked a fright, standing there in sopping-wet flight pants and a heavy leather jacket. No matter—she was on a mission.

"Can someone point me toward the library, please?" she inquired, looking from face to face.

"Can you be more specific?"

"How do you mean?"

One of the women explained that the city had several libraries. Meelie pulled the library card from her pocket and read the address aloud. That seemed to be enough information, as another woman pointed to the intersection and rattled off directions for Meelie. She felt fortunate that she had some experience with navigation; otherwise, she surely would have gotten lost before she even started. She repeated the directions back to make sure she understood them, then set out for the library, which the lady had said was just a dozen or so blocks from the river.

Despite being nearby, finding the building was a challenge. First, Meelie had to cross the impossibly-busy street running parallel to the river. After several missteps, she successfully reached the far side of the road. Next, she had to weave through several small side streets. She kept a close eye on the street signs, turning left here and right there, until she stood before a beautiful, red brick building with a striking glass façade. A sign out front indicated that she had arrived at the library. Inside, she showed someone at the front desk Quinn's library card.

"I found the card lying in the grass just outside," she lied. "Might I have the young woman's address so that I may return the card to her?"

The worker was hesitant, but Meelie insisted that she couldn't bear to think of a young girl distraught about losing such an important item. In the end, Meelie left the library with a new address.

Again, she wove through the city, following the library attendant's instructions exactly. She was grateful for the street signs because every house looked nearly identical to Meelie. Sure, she saw some variation in color and a few different designs, but the whole area felt very repetitive to her. Eventually, she arrived at Quinn's house and knocked on the door. She heard a large dog barking inside, but no other signs of life. She felt a wave of frustration and slammed her hands against the door, which only served to rile up the dog further. She tried the door just to be safe, but of course the handle didn't budge.

"Are you looking for Ms. Willow?" a voice called from the sidewalk.

Meelie spun around to see an older woman walking two miniature dachshunds. Again she lied, this time telling the woman that she had an urgent message for the owner of the house.

"Well, I'm afraid you just missed them. That little one, I forget her name, took a turn this morning. Poor thing, you can't imagine what she's been through, and only six years old. Mercy."

The woman prattled on for several more minutes. Meelie pounced on the first opportunity to interject, asking for the name of the hospital and directions, if the neighbor was familiar enough. To Meelie's surprise, the neighbor offered to drive her to the hospital. She was wary of climbing into one of the new-fangled vehicles with a stranger, but she had spent almost half the day tracking Riley down. If she was sick enough to be back in the hospital, Meelie had to pick up the pace. She accepted the offer and followed the neighbor to a house near the end of the street. The neighbor talked all the way to the hospital, saving Meelie the trouble of improvising any additional information.

Meelie was stunned by the size of the hospital. Even during the war, the largest hospital she had visited could house just a few hundred patients. She couldn't even describe what she saw as a single building. This hospital was more like a sprawling complex, and the entire expanse was painted a soft pink that reminded Meelie of twilight in the other realm. She could search the hospital for hours and never find Riley, she realized. Even if she could find one little girl in the sea of patients, she would need a reason to enter the hospital room. Thankfully, she had enlisted as a nurse's aide in her youth. Posing as a nurse was the perfect rouse. She decided to hunt down the appropriate clothing, then seek out Riley.

Having stumbled on a laundry room, Meelie donned a blue shirt and a blue pair of pants. The clothing looked odd and unprofessional, but she had passed numerous employees in similar garb. Besides, she didn't have time to second-guess herself. Once she looked the part, finding someone to show her to Riley was relatively easy. As she followed her escort through the maze of narrow halls, Meelie gripped the pulsing bulb in her pants pocket. She hoped this would conceal the amber glow, as well as the bulge created by the heart flower. Each time they turned a corner, her own heart quickened. Playing the part of a nurse was simple, but facing Riley would be beyond difficult. On the one hand, she would have to give the heart flower to Riley without either her or her mother noticing; on the other, she would have to interact with Quinn's family without letting them know that Quinn had died.

Finally, they stood outside a small room. Inside, Meelie saw the frail frame of a young girl, motionless save the occasional twitch of one hand. A woman sat in a chair next to the young girl, tears steadily trickling down her cheeks. The machines surrounding the two looked like a small, mournful city standing watch over Riley. She was so engrossed in the scene that she didn't notice her escort leave, yet she was standing alone. She didn't want to disrupt the moment, but she also didn't want to call attention to herself unnecessarily. Her hands were clammy and her breath short. She decided to enter before she lost her nerve.

"Good evening. I'm Ame—Amy, your nurse for the time being."

Riley opened her eyes weakly, looked at Meelie, then drifted off again.

"I thought our nurse's name was Hannah," the woman said, her voice thick with doubt.

"Oh, Hannah had an emergency. She'll be back soon. I'm just here to fill in while she takes care of a few personal things."

Meelie pretended to check the machines, then fluff Riley's pillows. She tucked the coarse hospital blanket under the small girl's frame, then put the back of her hand to Riley's forehead.

"Do you feel cold, dear?" she asked Riley.

Riley didn't respond.

"I think she needs another blanket. Would you mind terribly?" Meelie lied, motioning toward a set of linens on one wall.

The woman started to protest, but stopped herself and rose from her chair. As soon as her back was to Meelie and Riley, Meelie pulled the bulb from her pocket and placed the object on Riley's chest. Within seconds, the heart flower had disappeared under Riley's skin. Meelie quickly pulled the blanket up to Riley's neck. Just then, the mother returned with the extra blanket, which Meelie draped over Riley's torso.

"There you are, dear. You just sleep tight. You'll be back home in no time."

"Please don't do that. She knows she's too sick to be released again."

"Beg your pardon, ma'am. I suppose you're right. Then again, a little hope never hurt anybody, don't you think?"

"I don't have the strength to hope. Not again."

"May I speak out of turn?"

"You might as well. Truth is about the only thing we have left."

"I've a good mind that this little girl is stronger than any of us believes. Perhaps hope is on the menu, if only one more time."

The mother sighed, but Meelie read gratitude in her expression.

"I'm sorry," the mother said after a moment. "I'm just tired."

"Don't be so hard on yourself, dear. We have all heard of those who die with grace, but the living—well, now—putting your loved ones to rest with grace, that requires as much strength as anything."

Quinn's mother began to weep.

Meelie excused herself, scurrying from the room before she, too, succumbed to the sadness she had been holding in her jaw. She took one more look at Riley, who was beginning to stir, then made her way from the hospital. Her feet carried her back to the river, which she walked along aimlessly. She knew that she ought to get back to the other realm, but the thought of burying Quinn upon her return made her legs heavy. Eventually, she came to the spot from which she'd emerged. The wind had died down, and the water was smooth as glass. Meelie waded into the river, swam out to the middle, and dove under. The next time she took a breath, she would be over Quinn's body.

Without the sense of urgency distracting her, Meelie was much more cognizant of her surroundings as she passed back through the portal. Her limbs felt almost elastic as they were pulled taut. On every side, she saw cornflower blue dotted with white bursts of light. She must have been moving through the space quickly because the lights were blurry, and she couldn't see where they originated. Then, Meelie realized that she was without a very familiar sensation: gravity. She didn't feel grounded or held down the way she often did. Instead, her body hung suspended inside the portal. Something ancient rose from inside her, and she felt as free as she had in the cockpit. She began to weep. For more than a century, she had resisted the one thing that could take her home. Not back to her family or to the world she knew, but to that place where nothing fell, where nothing was heavy.

Meelie splashed into the ocean water more at peace than she had been since her plane crashed into the waves all those years ago. She had to fight her urge to smile as she swam toward the cave opening. The joy quickly dissipated, though, when she remembered what waited for her inside that cavernous void. Her face pushed through first, and she took a long breath, then clamped her hands on the rocky edge and let herself tumble from the water. She rubbed her eyes, then saw a pathway of glowing butterflies that wove through the cave and out of sight. Quinn and the others were already gone. She walked toward the first butterfly, inspecting the net that held the insect in place. Only one person in the other realm was capable of such craftsmanship. Aimee had left the butterflies on purpose. She wanted Meelie to follow them.

Each time Meelie came to a butterfly, she tugged on the netting and stood back, allowing them to regain their bearings and fly off. Every one of the butterflies headed in the same direction, along the path Meelie was following. She quickened her pace until she was jogging through the cave. She tripped several times, but paid no mind to the pain or the blood dripping from her shin. She would have time to tend to the wounds later. First, she had to see what Aimee had found, what all the butterflies were drawn to. She knew that she was getting close because she heard some of the children giggling and shouting at one another. In an instant, everything went dark. She had released the last butterfly, but couldn't keep up as the creature darted through the cave. Unsure of where to turn, Meelie stood as still as she could. She held her breath and listened for the children. Once her eyes adjusted, she could see a hint of orange radiating in the same direction from which the voices had come. She lowered herself to the ground, putting one hand in front of her and the other against the cave wall. Moving through the space was slow, but she inched toward the light until she found a curve in the pathway. Beyond the curve, she saw an immense cavern lit with hundreds of heart flowers. Aimee was sitting in the center of the expanse next to Quinn's body.

Meelie swallowed the lump in her throat, then entered the room. She didn't speak; she didn't know if she even could. The children saw her first and ran toward her with glee before enveloping her in hugs. She admired the way the children had held onto their youth despite their age, and she was grateful for the embrace. Aimee must have noticed the commotion because she stood and waved to Meelie, beckoning her over. Meelie steeled herself for the sight, then stepped away from the children. She could already feel the tears welling over in her eyes, but she refused to break down. Quinn died saving her sister; she wouldn't have wanted Meelie to mourn her sacrifice. Meelie's eyes were playing tricks on her, making her believe that Quinn was moving each time the light flickered. Except Aimee hadn't lit a fire. The light came from the heart flowers, and they weren't flickering at all.

"I don't understand," Meelie whispered as she approached Quinn's body. "I saw her move. How could that be when I felt her die in my hands?"

"After you left," Aimee explained, "one of the children ran off. I sent the others to go find her. When they came back, each of them was holding a butterfly. We both know that's what drove us here in the first place, so I fashioned a net and let the little things guide us. Before long, we came to this room. I told the children that Quinn was gone and that heart flowers couldn't save her, but they insisted we try. So, we picked a bulb and made our way back to Quinn. I set the heart flower exactly where the last one had been. Then, strange as this sounds, we watched the bulb sink into Quinn. Her chest glowed, then faded. She started to cough. I rushed over to help sit her up. She was confused, but breathing on her own. I tell you, this one's a fighter."

"But what about the cut on her chest?" Meelie asked, running her fingers along the place where she had split her friend open. The skin was smooth and flawless except for a jagged, red line.

Aimee told Meelie how one of the children had cut her finger while they were walking through the caves, yet the wound had healed by the time they got back to Quinn. All the children had scales from the butterfly wings. They thought that maybe the butterflies themselves were magic, since they seem to look after the heart flowers, so the children rounded up as many as she could in the net, then brought them over to Quinn. As the butterflies tried to escape, scales rained down onto Quinn's chest. Everywhere the scales landed, the skin closed up. Before long, the cut from Meelie had healed until the only remnant was the red scar.

Meelie could hardly believe what Aimee was telling her, but she couldn't deny that the wound had disappeared and Quinn appeared to be sleeping. Her chest rose and fell. Her eyelids twitched. She even had a grin on her face. Meelie had to suppress her desire to wake Quinn, but she couldn't resist lying beside Quinn and putting an arm around her. Aimee draped a blanket she had been weaving over the two, then ushered the children to a far corner and quickly let loose several bed pallets and blankets. *Handy to have a friend who spontaneously produces all our woven needs*, Meelie thought to herself, before closing her eyes and succumbing to sleep.

CHAPTER THIRTY-NINE

Q uinn jerked awake, confused by her surroundings. Instinctively, she touched her chest, which was tender, as
if she had been stricken or bruised. She felt a firm line of tissue running down her torso. How long had she been asleep?
Scars took time to form, but her scar didn't make sense because her clothes were still damp from the ocean. She shifted
to see Meelie sleeping beside her. Meelie's clothes, too, appeared damp. Hearing several voices nearby, she pushed herself to a sitting position and looked around. She saw several
people sleeping in a far corner of the cavern, as well as two
children playing amongst a patch of heart flowers.

She stood up and walked toward the children, who she
now knew were the missing Sodder kids she had read about.
She wanted to say something, to ask them about the fire
and how they had come to the other realm, but she also felt
strangely uncomfortable having researched the children, almost as though she had violated some unspoken trust by digging into their past. Quinn couldn't be sure they had shared
anything about their previous life with Meelie or Aimee. She
decided to keep her newfound knowledge to herself, at least
for the immediate future. She wanted to build trust with
them. The five children accounted for more than two-thirds
of the people she knew in the other realm. Calling attention
to what she knew might jeopardize any attempt to form
friendships with them.

"Quinn, you're awake!" Betty shouted as Quinn approached.

"Am I? So this isn't a dream?" she joked half-heartedly.

The little girl giggled. Betty, the youngest among the children, was just five years old when she disappeared. Quinn knew that the children had disappeared in 1945, which meant that while Betty looked very young, she was actually more than seventy years old. Like Meelie, she spoke with a wisdom that belied her age, though the effect was much more pronounced coming from such a small child.

Martha scolded Betty for making too much noise while the others were sleeping.

"How did you all find the cave?" Quinn asked Martha.

"Aimee came to us and asked for our help when you went under," she explained. "Most of the people in the World of Forgotten—that's what I call this place—are loners, folks who chose to stay because they would rather live by themselves than return to a world that hadn't really seen them to begin with. Not us, though. We came to this world together after our house caught fire, so we latched onto Meelie pretty quickly. She's got a real mothering instinct, that one. Anyway, Aimee knew we'd be on board for a makeshift search party, so she gathered us up to help search this island. Even with the lot of us, we spent the better part of two days hunting you down."

Martha went on to describe Quinn tumbling out of the ocean, how she had stopped breathing, and Meelie's decision to pull the heart flower from her chest.

"I don't know much about what happened to Meelie while she was gone. She'll have to tell you that for herself." She continued, telling Quinn about running through the caves, finding this room full of magical bulbs, and placing one in Quinn's chest. By the time Meelie had returned, Quinn had healed almost completely.

"Thank you," Quinn responded, her voice quivering. "Sounds like I owe you my life."

"That's what family is for, right?"

Quinn could feel her face flush with sadness.

"Oh, fiddlesticks. That wasn't very couth of me. I just meant—"

"You don't need to apologize. I suppose I could use some family right about now."

Martha asked Quinn if she could give her a hug, to which Quinn consented. She felt odd hugging a stranger, but Martha put her at ease with her tender eyes and easy smile. The two of them held each other for several minutes before Betty wriggled between them and chirped about being hungry.

"Some things never change," Quinn whispered, already grateful for Betty's exuberance. Perhaps adjusting to the other realm wouldn't be as difficult as she had thought. She still had some questions, like why Quinn's mother hadn't recognized her, and why Riley appeared to be the only one whose memory wasn't affected by her trips to the other realm, but she reasoned that she would get more complete answers if she waited for Aimee to wake up, too.

While Quinn waited for Aimee to wake up, she pressed Betty and Martha for details about their life before the other realm, but they were very guarded. Quinn considered telling her new friends about the posters and conflicting accounts of the fire, about how their parents died believing that the children were still alive. She wondered, though, if that would only bring them sadness.

"Oh, you're awake," Aimee muttered, stretching her limbs.

Betty nodded toward her, gleefully relaying their morning conversation.

"Sounds like we have a lot to teach you," Aimee said, sleep still weighing on her eyes and tongue.

"I have so many questions," Quinn started, reaching for her notebook. "How do we get toothpaste? Does anybody have a washboard? What sort of—"

Aimee held up her hand.

"Give me a minute, will you? I can't even see straight yet."

"You know, I haven't seen any coffee, here. And what if you need glasses?" Quinn continued.

Martha put a finger to her lips, emphasizing the gesture with raised eyebrows. This time, Quinn complied. The longer she sat waiting, though, the sicker she felt. She still hadn't had a chance to talk to Meelie about her sister. Had she been able to get the heart flower to Riley on time? Quinn assumed that everything was okay; otherwise, Meelie would have woken her up, or not come back at all. Right? She hated the way uncertainty fed on silence, filling the void with unanswerable questions. She didn't want to wake Meelie, but she also couldn't just sit there chewing her fingernails and panicking over possibilities.

"Do we have anything to eat?" she asked, even though Martha had already told her that they didn't think to bring any food in the frenzy to find her.

Betty shook her head.

"I'm going to go see what I can find," Quinn declared, rising and walking toward the nearest mouth of the chamber. She knew that she wasn't likely to find much in the caves, but at least she could distract herself. If nothing else, she imagined that fish passed by the caves often enough; she could figure out a way to snag one. Of course, then she would need to find a way to cook the meat. No matter—the important part was the search. She had spent so much of the last few months looking for things that she had become addicted to the pursuit.

Quinn wandered through the passages, kneeling to inspect groundwater for plants and edible fish. She was grateful for the ever-present glow of heart flowers, which made navigating the cave much more manageable. She usually could see fissures in enough time to avoid them. The farther she went, however, the darker the space around her became. Lost in thought, she wandered into a dark zone. Her right foot slipped, and Quinn tumbled from the path she had been following. She grasped at hard, slimy knobs as her body slid down an incline. She could feel the skin tearing, then a fingernail catching on the rocky slope. Quinn screamed. The echo reverberated for a full thirty seconds. Panic set in. She couldn't slow her fall, and judging from the distant trill of her scream, she was nowhere near the bottom of the pit.

"Where is Quinn?" Meelie asked, rubbing the sleep from her eyes.

"She went to look for food," Betty answered, not bothering to turn around.

"By herself?"

"Yep."

Meelie shook her head, then gestured for Aimee to follow her. When they were out of earshot, she told Aimee everything that had happened during her visit to Earth. Aimee was relieved to hear that Riley's body had accepted the heart flower, and hopeful about her prediction about the healing process remaining stable if Quinn remained in the other realm. The two women agreed that they needed to find Quinn as soon as possible before her temerity got the best of her. They didn't want to alarm the others, though. Despite having been in the other realm for nearly a century, they had retained quite a lot of their youthfulness and could quickly descend into panic if the women weren't careful with their words. They decided not to share that they were worried and instead make a game of the search, calling the rescue mission the Quest for Quinn.

"Whoever finds Quinn first," Meelie explained, "will get to captain the ship with Aimee on the way back."

The children cheered, turning and taunting one another, each one proclaiming that they would win the challenge. Aimee gathered the netting and blankets she had woven while Meelie lined the children up and started the countdown. Every one of the kids was off and running before she finished the word *go*. The women chased after them. The two girls went left while the three boys headed right. Aimee veered to the left, tossing her hand up and ushering Meelie after the boys.

Meelie tried to gain ground, but her body was still taxed from her trip through the portal. Before long, the boys were beyond her field of vision, and she was forced to use their taunts as a guide. The tunnels were growing dimmer as she ran after the children, until she could see only a few feet in front of her. She heard a faint scream and tried to stop, but her boots couldn't find traction on the wet rock and she barreled into the boys, who were huddled in the middle of the path. The three of them sprawled out on the rock, collecting nicks and scrapes on every limb.

"Is everyone all right?" Meelie heaved, struggling to bring in oxygen.

The boys nodded. Together, they pointed to their ears, then farther down the path. Meelie indicated that she had heard the scream, too. They rose, careful not to make too much sound, and listened in the direction of the first scream.

"Can anyone hear me?" Quinn shouted. "Meelie! Aimee!"

She clung to the side of the hill, her bloody fingers locked onto a large piece of cave coral. Her forearms were beginning to cramp. She felt the slope beneath her for footing, but the surface was smooth and wet. Her legs hung loosely, already going numb. Terrified, she willed her eyes to adjust to the darkness so that she could better assess her position on the slope. She estimated that she was at least forty or fifty feet below the path, with another two or three hundred feet looming beneath her if she had done the math correctly. For once, her physics homework was proving useful. Of course, she didn't have a stopwatch to measure the echo of her pleas precisely, so she could be off by a dozen or so yards.

"Quinn?" a small voice called.

"Betty! Is that you?"

"Where are you?"

"Down here! I slid off the path, and I'm stuck on the side of this slope."

"Get back!" another, very stern voice shouted.

Moments later, Quinn heard something slap the rock. Aimee's voice cut through the darkness. She was trying to get a rope down to Quinn, but she was working blindly. Quinn could hear the friction of the heavy braid swinging back and forth on the slope. She thrust a hand above her head, clinging to the cave coral with her other. Her grip was waning. If she couldn't get hold of the rope soon, she would plummet to the bottom.

Quinn heard the scrape of boots and someone breathing heavily. As she flailed for the rope, she swore that the sounds were getting closer. She felt her fingers giving out and tried to switch hands, but she missed the cave coral and began to fall. Her screams felt eerily disembodied, as though the cave walls were wailing. Her only thought as her body bounced farther into the expanse was that she would never know if Meelie had been able to heal her sister.

"More slack!" a familiar voice ordered. "She's falling fast!"

Meelie must have been the one who had tried to reach her with the rope. Now she was throwing herself down the side of a cave cliff with only the hands of those above to keep her anchored. Quinn felt sick. Once again, her headstrong foolishness had put someone she cherished in danger. She pushed herself away from the slope, giving herself to the emptiness.

"Grab my waist!" Meelie instructed, slamming into Quinn and locking both arms around Quinn in a vice grip.

Above them, Aimee grunted under the sudden increase in weight. She barked for Martha and Jennie to help them haul the dangling duo up the slope. Meelie planted her feet against the rock and elbowed Quinn to do the same. Together, they walked the incline, using the momentum from each tug to gain ground. The approach seemed to alleviate some of the exertion for Aimee and others, who showed a collective surge of energy. Quinn was practically jogging along the rope just to keep pace with Meelie and the intermittent heave from the invisible rescue team. They were moving so fast that she tripped when her feet cleared the slope, causing her to roll headfirst onto the path.

"I smell blood," a voice that Quinn assumed was Jennie said, breaking through the chorus of shallow breathing.

"I don't have any shoes," Quinn answered. "I cut my feet a few times on the climb."

"Let me help," Aimee said, putting her hands on Quinn's feet.

Quinn could feel the tickle of thread forming around her mangled toes and heels. Aimee may have only picked up the one trick, but she sure put that skill to good use—who knew that sprouting rope would be such a valuable bit of magic? Quinn had underestimated how frequently she would have a need for something strong and fibrous.

"Damn it if you aren't the most stubborn girl I ever met,

bunny," Meelie scolded, untying the rope from her waist. "What's in your head, anyway? Taking off through the caves alone and with no light. You don't have a lick of sense. And don't give me that drivel about being hungry, either."

Quinn hung her head, tears dripping onto the rocky path.

"I just—I couldn't sit there anymore thinking about Riley and my mom and—I'm not strong enough for the silence, Meelie."

"Then *tell* someone. Do you see these people?" Meelie asked, gesturing to Aimee and the children. "*This* is your family, now. Every one of us carries a haunting inside. We've been where you are now, bunny. You won't last a week here if you don't trust us."

Quinn nodded.

No one said much on the way back to the boat or during the sail. Quinn, embarrassed and distraught, shut herself away below the deck. Meelie came down to check on her and bring her up to speed on Riley. As far as Meelie could tell, Quinn's sister was going to be just fine. In fact, she confided, Meelie was more worried about Quinn than she was Riley. Adjusting to the other realm was tough enough for those with no one to miss. Quinn's entire history was defined by the slow implosion of family.

Quinn, who had kept her face buried in her knees as Meelie spoke, leaned forward. She was a long way from calling the other realm home, but she knew Meelie was right. She had spent enough of her life carrying the grief of her mother and the fear of her sister. She had plenty of her own to work through, and the people before her were as good as any she had ever met. She let herself be pulled into the embrace. And then, for once, she let the tears fall without a fight.

CHAPTER FORTY

For the third time in as many months, Riley had bounced back seemingly overnight. Dr. Howe was noticeably suspect, but he informed Riley and Jane that he didn't have cause to keep Riley in the hospital. They had been monitoring her sudden recovery for the past twenty-four hours, during which she had remained stable. He had informed the nurses that she was ready to be released.

"You should be home in time for dinner," he chuckled.

Riley was excited, but Jane's concern was evident in her wrinkled forehead and tight-lipped smile.

"Are you sure that's a good idea? She'll be okay at home?"

"I can't guarantee anything, of course, but that's my belief, yes. Riley is a fighter, and her body seems determined to overcome whatever life throws her way."

Though Riley felt better than she had in weeks, Jane insisted that she lie down when they got home. Riley whined that she was sick of hospital beds, and they agreed to a compromise: Riley didn't have to lie down, but she did need to remain home for the time being.

"That way," Jane told her, "you'll at least be able to rest if you feel the need."

Riley nodded, calling to Butterfly as she skipped down the hall to her room. She closed the door behind her, then opened the window to let in some light and the crisp, evening air. Butterfly was busy sniffing Quinn's bed, then her desk. He let out a low growl. Riley went to see what he had found that was so upsetting, but the only thing out of place on the desk was a leather-bound journal and a note addressed to her. She opened the letter and read the message. The words scared her. Quinn hadn't come right out and said she was leaving, but Riley had a sick feeling in her stomach and the sense that she had seen her sister for the last time. Just as she exited her room to ask her mom about the note, Riley heard a knock at the front door.

"Ms. Willow?" a woman's voice called.

Pause.

"Ma'am, this is Officer Wayne with the police department. I need to speak with you concerning your daughter, Quinn Willow."

Riley felt her knees buckle. Had something happened to Quinn? She crept toward the end of the hall as quietly as she could and crouched down, hoping that her mother wouldn't see her when she answered the door. She heard the squeak of Jane's bedroom door, then the shuffling of feet. Her hands trembled and started to sweat, but her mother walked right past her without looking down. She heard Jane unlock the deadbolt and ease open the door.

"I'm sorry, who is this regarding?"

"Your daughter, Quinn Willow. That is your daughter, correct?"

Silence.

"Can you tell me when you last saw your daughter, ma'am?"

Riley tried to follow the exchange, but her mother's responses were too quiet for her to hear clearly. She heard the officer asking when Quinn had left the house, where she had been going, and if her mother had talked to Quinn since she left the house. The officer's voice was measured, but Riley heard a hint of grief. She could recognize the sound of sadness faster than any other tone—the curse of growing up sick. The door creaked open, and Riley heard the heavy thud of boots on the hardwood floor, then the click of the door latch. Her mother must have let Officer Wayne inside. Riley listened as the two women moved into the living room. She didn't want to let on that she was listening, but her mother and the officer were speaking in such hushed voices. Riley decided to venture into the kitchen. From there, she would be able to listen through the paper-thin dividing wall. If she was discovered, she would just say that she was looking for a snack. Nothing out of the ordinary about that.

Riley had just gotten to the kitchen when she heard her mother begin to cry. Not the controlled tears and quivering lip kind of crying, either; this was the blow-your-nose, wail-like-a-funeral-procession kind of crying.

"Are you absolutely sure?" Riley heard her mother ask, her voice thready and weak.

"Well, no. I'm sorry. I wish I could be more specific. All we know right now is that we found a jacket near the river with your name on a receipt inside. Several people reported seeing a young woman swimming across the river early this morning. We can't be certain whether or not that person was your daughter. We did find her library card floating a ways downriver. Between that and the way the jacket was pushed up under the rocks—well, we're not jumping to any conclusions, but I think you should consider the possibility that—that your daughter went out into that river on purpose."

"But . . . why would she just dive into the river like that? She knows better."

"We're still comparing witness accounts, but at least one person seemed certain that she was swimming toward something, maybe a dog or a person caught in the current."

Riley clamped a hand to her mouth, fighting back tears

of her own. A moment later, she heard the women rise from the couch. From the sound, the officer was headed to the front door again. Riley peered out from the kitchen. Seeing her window, she bolted for the hallway. Inside her room, she turned off the lights and climbed under her comforter. When her mother knocked faintly on the door, Riley pretended she was sleeping. Jane called for her, but she didn't answer. Then, her mother wedged the door open. Riley stayed as still as possible, her eyes fastened shut. She needed time to understand why Quinn had gone into the river, if she had at all. After a few moments, Jane sighed and left the room.

When she was sure that her mother was not coming back, Riley jumped from her bed and ran back to Quinn's desk. She reread the letter Quinn had left for her, then again. Each time she read the words, they felt more like her sister saying goodbye. Riley slumped to the floor, startling Butterfly, who darted beneath Quinn's bed. The ruckus caused something to fall from Quinn's shelf of kaleidoscopes, landing on the desk with a hard thud. Riley picked up the small tube and recognized the design immediately. She was holding the teleidoscope Quinn had worn for as long as Riley could remember. Riley knew that Quinn would never have forgotten to take the teleidoscope with her. Wherever her sister had gone, Riley was sure that Quinn had left it on purpose.

Riley put the lens to her eye, shifting until the light from a desk lamp illuminated the image. She expected to see a fractured montage of stained glass like the geometric images in Quinn's kaleidoscopes, but instead she saw a single image, clear and sharp as the slides in her mother's old View-Master. The sky wasn't exactly dark; the clouds reminded her of the purple stains that blueberries left on her fingers, and two spheres hovered among them. Beneath the sky, Riley saw a hulking shadow with spots of red and yellow flickering from the center. The hint of firelight reminded her of the camping trip Quinn had planned for her last summer. They didn't get to the campgrounds; as with most plans, Riley's health got in the way. Still, Quinn had built a fire in the neighbor's chiminea, and they roasted marshmallows for s'mores until their mother beckoned them inside.

She let the teleidoscope slip from her eye and settled into Quinn's desk chair, inadvertently knocking her sister's leather-bound journal to the floor. She reached for the book, untying the strap and opening the cover. Inside, she found that Quinn had written one of her stories. As she read, she realized that the story was the last one her sister had told her. She had been too weak to follow the story, but as she turned the pages she was transfixed.

Her sister often made a point of putting Riley at the center of her stories, but one thing Quinn didn't do was make herself a major character. She certainly did make herself out to be a hero. And then Riley remembered the names she and Quinn had researched in the hospital. Both women were in the story. Then Riley came to the heart flower and the red freckle on her chest. Instinctively, she pulled down the collar of her shirt and checked for a red freckle. Sure enough, she saw the spot on her chest, exactly as the story had described. Quinn hadn't been making up a story at all. She had been trying to keep Riley alive.

Riley listened for her mother's bedroom door to close that night, then got out of bed and retrieved Quinn's journal from under her mattress. She read the words over and over, trying to memorize every detail. Her plan was to convince her mother to visit the butterfly garden the following morning, then search for the note mentioned in Quinn's story. If she found the note, she would know for sure that the story was real. And if the story was real, maybe Quinn wasn't in trouble at all. Maybe she had just gone back to the other realm.

By the time her mother woke up, Riley had read through the journal five times. She hurried to the kitchen as soon as she smelled Jane's coffee, pouncing on her mother even before she sat down at the table. She rattled off all the ways she felt better, then lamented about how cooped up she had been feeling the last couple weeks. Then she closed in, begging to see the butterflies in the garden. She could see that her mother was distracted, probably thinking about Quinn and the visit from Officer Wayne, but she also saw a glimmer of relief when Riley mentioned the garden. Her mother agreed, then shooed Riley away while she finished her coffee.

Riley could hardly contain herself as they walked to the garden. She felt bad for her mother, who didn't speak for the entire walk, but she was also hopeful that she would find the note by the pond. One question remained: if she did find proof that Quinn had been visiting another world, should she tell her mother? On the one hand, she knew that her mother was upset that Quinn had gone missing again; on the other, Riley didn't know if Jane would believe her even if she showed her mother everything. They were close to the garden, and Riley skipped ahead, trying to put distance between herself and her mother so that she could investigate without being noticed. Inside, she ran to the pond, only to find a family taking pictures in front of the fixture.

"Riley?" her mother's voice called.

"Here, mom!" she called back. "By the pond!"

Riley didn't want her mother standing over her while she searched for the note, but she hoped that her words might usher the family along more quickly. Her instincts were correct, and the parents pushed their kids farther down the path. She knew that her mother would be making her way through the garden any minute. She darted into the bushes surrounding the pond and scanned for any hint of paper.

"Where are you?" Jane called.

Riley ignored her, rifling through the foliage.

"Damn it, Riley, answer me!"

This time, Riley heard a tremor of panic in her mother's voice. She poked her head from behind the bushes and laughed.

"I win!" she exclaimed.

Jane flashed a forced smile. "I didn't realize we were playing hide-and-seek," she answered. "Do you want to hide again?"

Riley nodded, then told her mother to turn her back and count. That would buy her at least a few minutes to continue looking for the note. She tiptoed back into the bushes, listening for her mother's voice. Jane was already halfway to one hundred. Riley would have to poke around very quickly or she'd be found out. She pushed closer to the pond. Right on the edge, almost completely buried, Riley saw a small, white piece of paper. She pulled the note from beneath the bushes and brushed off the dirt. On the outside, in Quinn's handwriting, was Riley's name. The message was simple: *Find Riley a new heart*. So the story was true. And if the story was true, that meant that the pond was a doorway to another world. Riley pushed up her sleeve, then felt for the bottom of the pond. She was so distracted that she didn't hear her mother finish counting.

"Riley, get away from there right now!" Jane shouted.

Riley shot up and stuffed the note into her waistband.

"Sorry, mom. I saw this butter—"

"I don't care what you saw, Riley. What were you thinking? You have no idea how deep that water is, and with Quinn—"

Jane's eyes got wide. That was the first she had mentioned anything about Quinn's disappearance to Riley.

"I mean—you just need to be more careful! Come on. This was a bad idea. We're going home."

Riley started to protest, but Jane grabbed her arm and pulled her back onto the path. She continued to scold Riley until they had nearly crossed the park. Jane was on the edge of a breakdown, while Riley was fighting the urge to scream that she was being unreasonable, that Quinn was okay. In the end, she stayed silent, letting her mother turn her anguish onto Riley because that's what Quinn would have done. Riley knew that if Quinn wasn't coming back, she would have to be the strong one for her mother.

"I can't lose two daughters. I just can't. You have to be smarter, Riley. I can't lose you, too."

"What do you mean?" Riley pried.

Jane stopped walking and sat down on a bench at the far end of the park. She patted the seat next to her. Riley tried not to notice her mother's red-streaked eyes. Jane relayed the conversation she'd had with Officer Wayne.

"The weird thing is," her mother continued, "I keep trying to picture her face, and I—I just can't. That upsets me more than her being gone. I know she was the perfect daughter. She was a hero to us both, really. She sacrificed her childhood to take care of you when I couldn't, and I remember so much about her, but I can't remember her eyes or the way she smiled. She did smile, didn't she?"

"Of course she did, mom. She was always positive."

"I tried to have her thrown out of your hospital room. Did you know that? She walked in while I was sleeping, and I didn't even recognize her. She kept telling me over and over, 'I'm your daughter,' but I didn't listen. I felt as though my mind had been emptied. The very next day, she disappeared. Do you think she left because of me? Do you think—"

Jane began to sob. Riley moved closer to her mother, putting an arm around her.

"My sister would never just leave. If she's gone, you can bet that her reason was about helping someone else."

Her mother rose, smoothing her jacket and wiping the runny mascara from her eyes. She reached for Riley's hand, then led the way back home. There, they sat without speaking. Riley wanted desperately to tell her mother about Quinn, yet something prevented her from speaking up, something about the way Jane had spoken about Quinn. The two had been at odds for months. Maybe believing that Quinn was gone had wiped that tension away. As much as Riley wanted to make her mother feel better, she wanted Quinn to be the hero Jane had described. She was that hero, even if the things her sister had done sounded too fantastic to be real. She decided to keep the note and the story and the red freckle to herself, at least for the immediate future. Her mother was already grieving. Hope would only disrupt that, and Riley had no way of knowing if Quinn would ever return.

Riley slept in her mother's bed that night nestled under Jane's arm. She smiled to herself when she heard her mother coo. They had spent so much of Riley's life looking toward the next doctor's appointment or surgical procedure that neither one of them had taken the time to get to know each other. Riley was seven years old. For anyone else, that might mean that she was too young to know much about who she was or what she valued. But Riley had a big sister who was honest even when she shouldn't have been. Riley was no ordinary first grader. She understood things that even her teacher couldn't grasp, like the way a loved one's hand grows lighter and more tender the closer you are to dying, not because they're afraid of hurting you, but because the body imagines a world without you. The lighter the touch, the closer those you love most are to letting you go.

That night, Riley clung to her mother, and her mother clung to her. Nothing in this world or any other could break their grasp.

CHAPTER FORTY-ONE

Quinn had spent the last two weeks learning what she could about the other realm, an arduous but necessary task. The most basic questions had been easy to answer: essentially, everyone in the other realm lived like they were camping. They had no real need for electricity since almost every living organism emitted light, and plumbing was a luxury that most of the missing hadn't been familiar with before coming to the other realm. As such, they developed a crude system of makeshift toilets in small crannies throughout the caves, always in areas where the waste would be immediately carried off by underground streams. The small community lived in relative harmony, playing to each other's strengths and using the collective experiences of hundreds of people who had lived over more than a thousand years to solve problems as they arose.

Quinn still missed her family immensely, but she had found solace in Meelie and the children. Betty was a welcome spirit, and she reminded Quinn of Riley on an almost-daily basis. The others would take more time to understand. Maurice, in particular, made Quinn uncomfortable; he was nice enough and remarkably poised, but his role as a surrogate father to his younger siblings forced Quinn to think about her own father, something she had made a point of suppressing for half of her life. Without her mother around, she no longer had a reason to pretend that her father had simply stopped existing, but she also didn't have any way to answer the many questions she had about his exit from their lives.

Today, though, Quinn was on a mission: she had been scouring the other realm since her return for the pool that Betty had heard about, and she had finally found what she was looking for. She had gathered the necessary provisions and set out across the desert on Toast, a remarkably docile white rhinoceros that Meelie had helped her train her first week in the other realm. Toast seemed to enjoy having a rider; he moved so deftly across the barren plains that Quinn often sat straight up, holding onto nothing but the butterfly net, which had become her security blanket of sorts. Now that she knew where the crop of heart flowers was, she didn't use the butterflies as a guide. Instead, she was slowly collecting each new butterfly she encountered for a rudimentary butterfly garden in one of the central cave's chambers. Aimee had helped weave a barrier to house the butterflies, and Martha had been gathering flowers from various parts of the cave to fill the space.

At the moment, Meelie was on her way to check on Riley. Quinn would be able to see her family in the magical pool, but she had asked Meelie to visit for a fuller look at Riley's health. Now that Meelie had overcome her fear of returning, she was happy to oblige. In a way, saving Riley seemed to have helped Meelie make peace with not returning to her own sister. Quinn would have gone herself, but Aimee's theory had been correct: since Quinn had died in the other realm, she would never again be able to pass through the portals and return home. The realization had been a hard one to accept, and Quinn had picked up several bruises diving into various pools of water, only to find the bottom of every one. As she and Toast approached the pool, her throat began to ache with the now familiar pain of swallowed sadness.

She jumped down from Toast's back and walked over to the pool, which had a jade tint unlike anything she had seen, on Earth or in the other realm. She had asked around, and several people had heard that the pool acted like a channel between life at home and life in the other realm. As such, Quinn would have to find a way to connect her and Riley. She sat by the water's edge and began to tell a story, one of the many she had written and left for Riley. The words caused the surface of the water to ripple, as though she were skipping rocks across the pool. The jade intensified until the entire pool looked like a brilliant gem. Quinn heard a low hum all around her, and the pool went black.

She slapped the surface instinctively, the way she would have smacked her television back home for cutting out. And then, she heard voices. She couldn't see anything in the water, but she was certain that the sound was emanating from the pool. The noise crescendoed to a roar. That's when Quinn realized she was listening to a school gathering. Amongst the voices, she could pick out a few she recognized from class. They were presenting their research. She must be tuning into the evening part of the project. But why? The pool was supposed to connect her directly to Riley, and Riley hadn't been a part of the class. Quinn couldn't understand what would compel her to attend the presentations.

Light rose from the water, forming a picture of the auditorium. Quinn scanned the room, which was lined with classmates gesturing toward trifold poster boards and responding to parent questions. She couldn't see Riley anywhere, but she did see Meelie standing to the right of the exit doors. Her eyes were fixed on something that Quinn couldn't see. She got up and circled the pool, but the image didn't shift. Whatever, or whoever, Meelie saw was a mystery to Quinn. What she could see, though, were Meelie's eyes. They were bloodshot and waterlogged. Quinn hadn't known Meelie long, yet she had come to accept that her new friend kept most of her emotions to herself. The image in front of her was in stark contrast to the staunchly guarded woman in her mind.

"Good evening, and thank you for giving me a space to speak."

The voice was amplified by a microphone, but still plagued by a sort of smallness. Nevertheless, the milling crowd of parents and students stopped talking and turned in the direction that Meelie had been staring.

"You all know my sister Quinn disappeared two weeks ago. Or maybe you don't. I don't know. I guess Quinn didn't have many friends because of me."

Quinn felt a hard lump forming in her throat.

"The police say that she drowned, because they found some of her things in the river. You know, she was researching a woman named Amelia Earhart for tonight, and Earhart went missing over water, too. Her body was never found. Neither was my sister's. When I was in the hospital the last time, we read about some others: a girl from France and some kids whose house burned up; they disappeared, too. No bodies. I was thinking about that day and going through Quinn's backpack. I didn't really know what to say today, but I found some notes she left:

"When I look around this room, I see the people we read about in our books talking to parents, telling stories about their lives. We say that people die when they leave us, but if that's true, then what do we name the memories that still make us feel? What do we name the impersonations here tonight? Ghosts? No. Amelia Earhart is not a ghost. When we love someone, we aren't haunted by their absence. We are, some of us, more hollow. More empty. But we aren't haunted. Ghosts are a nuisance. An unwanted presence.

"I want nothing more than to feel Quinn beside me every day. She is not my ghost. But I am haunted. My ghost is the heart inside me. You see, I was supposed to die a few weeks ago. I have been dying since the day I was born. Now I have no sister, and the doctors tell me I am healed. That I will live a long life. Quinn is gone, and I am here. That is my ghost. That is my truth, the one that won't die.

"I don't even really know what I'm trying to say. I guess I just need you to know that Quinn, like the people you're studying right now, lives in us all. She lives in the stories we tell. So tell her story. Tell everyone."

Riley stopped speaking abruptly. Quinn saw Meelie's eyes get wide, and then her friend darted out of the auditorium. Quinn stared into the pool, willing the scene to shift so that she could see Riley's face. Quinn's cheeks were wet with tears, and her throat throbbed. She put a hand against the surface of the water, careful not to ripple the image. The air around her began to hum. Startled, she jerked her hand back. The hum stopped. Quinn tested the water, this time with both hands. Again, the air hummed. The sky on either side blurred, and then she was standing at the back of the auditorium. Riley looked right at her, but didn't react. Quinn stepped closer. Riley looked down, thumbing something in her hand. Quinn watched as she held a small brass kaleidoscope out to the crowd, the one with two wheels and stained glass. Quinn put a hand around the teleidoscope at her chest, the one Martha had given her when she came back to the other realm.

Riley looked past her, eyes still locked on the spot where Meelie had been. "Tell everyone that I don't blame my sister for leaving, that I know she's okay. Wherever she is, I know she has a good reason for not coming home."

Quinn walked right up to Riley and put a hand to her sister's chest. "*You* are my home, sis. You always were."

Riley blinked back the swelling in her eyes.

"Goodbye, Riley." Quinn lifted her hands from the water.

"Goodbye, sis," Quinn heard her sister say. "I'll see you soon."

The pool went dark, and the desert was thick with absence. Quinn stepped toward Toast, leaning into the rhinoceros's shoulder. Instinctively, Toast wrapped his neck around Quinn's body and lowered his head. They stood like that until the moons began to peek through the clouds. Then Quinn climbed onto Toast's back, gripped her butterfly net, and set out for the caves. If she made good time, she would arrive just ahead of Meelie, and the two certainly had plenty to talk about.

RONNIE K. STEPHENS is a full-time educator and father of five, with a strong interest in poetry, fiction, and activism. He recently completed an MA in creative writing and an MFA in fiction at Wilkes University. During his time at Wilkes, he was awarded two scholarships and won the Etruscan Prize. Stephens has published two full-length poetry collections, *Universe in the Key of Matryoshka* and *They Rewrote Themselves Legendary,* with Timber Mouse Publishing out of Austin. *The Kaleidoscope Sisters* is his first novel.